INTO THE STORM

"Gunslinger! You're awake," Tom said jovially. He untied Sherman's hands and moved away, out of arm's reach. "Remove your gloves, your jacket, anything keeping you warm."

"Why?"

"You're taking a little walk." Tom indicated the white prairie beyond. Up ahead in the distance, a storm was rolling in, a thick wall of white obscuring everything in its path. "Fine day for a stroll, isn't it?"

"You can't be serious," Sherman said, shivering. Already the cold air was working its way in through his clothes.

"Serious as I've ever been," Tom said. "You're gonna walk until you drop, and I'll be right there to see it happen. In fact, I'll be there to see your last ragged breath freeze in the wind."

He bound Sherman's hands tight again and climbed back up into his saddle, keeping one end of the rope in his hand, like a leash for a dog. Sherman looked at the storm blowing in and knew he would never reach the end of the prairie.

"Why are you doin' this? Why don't you just shoot me, like you did those innocent folk back there?"

Tom laughed. "What'd be the fun in that?" He pulled at the rope binding Sherman's hands, yanking him forward. Forcing him to move. "I want this to last. You betrayed me. There's a price to pay."

Slowly, one foot in front of the other, Sherman began to trudge across the prairie as the snowstorm rushed in and enveloped them both.

RALPH COMPTON

BLOOD ON THE PRAIRIE

A Ralph Compton Western by

TONY HEALEY

BERKLEY
New York

BERKLEY
An imprint of Penguin Random House LLC
penguinrandomhouse.com

Copyright © 2021 by The Estate of Ralph Compton
Penguin Random House supports copyright. Copyright fuels creativity, encourages
diverse voices, promotes free speech, and creates a vibrant culture. Thank you for buying
an authorized edition of this book and for complying with copyright laws by not
reproducing, scanning, or distributing any part of it in any form without permission.
You are supporting writers and allowing Penguin Random House to continue to
publish books for every reader.

BERKLEY and the BERKLEY & B colophon are registered trademarks of
Penguin Random House LLC.

ISBN: 9780593333891

First Edition: September 2021

Printed in the United States of America
1   3   5   7   9   10   8   6   4   2

Book design by George Towne

For my nephew, Charlie

THE IMMORTAL COWBOY

This is respectfully dedicated to the "American Cowboy." His was the saga sparked by the turmoil that followed the Civil War, and the passing of more than a century has by no means diminished the flame.

———◆———

True, the old days and the old ways are but treasured memories, and the old trails have grown dim with the ravages of time, but the spirit of the cowboy lives on.

———◆———

In my travels—to Texas, Oklahoma, Kansas, Nebraska, Colorado, Wyoming, New Mexico, and Arizona—I always find something that reminds me of the Old West. While I am walking these plains and mountains for the first time, there is this feeling that a part of me is eternal, that I have known these old trails before. I believe it is the undying spirit of the frontier calling me, through the mind's eye, to step back into time. What is the appeal of the Old West of the American frontier?

———◆———

It has been epitomized by some as the dark and bloody period in American history. Its heroes—Crockett, Bowie, Hickok, Earp—have been reviled and criticized. Yet the Old West lives on, larger than life.

———◆———

It has become a symbol of freedom, when there was always another mountain to climb and another river to cross; when a dispute between two men was settled not with expensive lawyers, but with fists, knives, or guns. Barbaric? Maybe. But some things never change. When the cowboy rode into the pages of American history, he left behind a legacy that lives within the hearts of us all.

—*Ralph Compton*

PROLOGUE

Fifteen Years Earlier

S URE THEY WERE due to come by this way?" Tom
Preston asked, grimacing miserably against the
biting cold, his breath freezing the second it hit the
frigid air.

Sherman Knowles sat with both hands on the horn
of his saddle, characteristically unmoved, watching the
road for sign of the coach. "I have it on good authority.
Believe me, I wouldn't have us out here freezing our
keisters off if I didn't trust my sources."

"You're the man in the know," Tom said, shivering.

The snow fell thick and fast around them. Sherman
looked at Tom. "Not really. In case you forgot, this
kinda job ain't exactly my forte."

"Jesus . . . ," Tom said, shaking his head.

"What is it?"

"Nothing."

"What?" Sherman demanded.

"This ain't your forte? Let me tell you something. Don't be a snob when there's good money on the line. I know this may seem like low work for you. I get it. But this is my livin'. This is how I get by. I've seen hard times all over, and let me tell you, a man's gotta make some coin somehow."

I'm no snob, Sherman thought, but he didn't bother to correct Preston. Their partnership was temporary. He did not care for Preston and he knew that the man had no love for *him,* either. Their partnership was born out of necessity and that was about as far as it went.

They didn't have to like each other—just get along well enough to complete the job.

"I don't look down my nose at this line of work," Sherman told him. "I was merely pointing out I don't ordinarily hold up coaches at gunpoint and rob the passengers. I make my living tracking people down, and shooting them when the situation calls for it. Sometimes when it don't, either."

"I have no doubt about that," Tom said. "It's just we've been sat here a long time. The cold is getting to me. The snow is getting to me. Gotta admit, I am beginning to doubt this coach is ever going to show. Likewise, I am beginning to doubt the person who gave you the information."

"I told you—they're good for their word," Sherman said firmly. "We just gotta hold our nerve, that's all."

"If you say so. But how long do we wait, huh?"

Sherman did not have an answer.

"I don't know," Tom said, shaking his head. He removed his gloves and blew into his hands. "The law sure is makin' this line of work harder and harder every damn year. Ain't like the old days."

Sherman watched what Tom was doing, thinking to himself, *If you just kept your damned gloves on, your hands might not get so cold.*

They were positioned up on a rise, the bare skeletons of trees at their backs, the road below winding its way like a river through the frozen landscape. It was dark already, the blanketed snow on the ground pearlescent in the moonlight. Sherman watched as Tom rolled a cigarette with trembling hands and lit it. He smoked to stave off the cold and to take the edge off his boredom. That was the difference between them; Sherman did not get bored. He was observant. He was a watcher and a listener. Silence was not his enemy, as it was for so many. It did not drive him mad—to the contrary, it brought him solace.

Preston had located Sherman in a small town called Lyman, catching up with him late one evening in the town's only saloon. At first, Sherman had assumed Tom was there to settle a rivalry that had existed between the two men for the better part of a decade, but he'd relaxed once Tom explained his presence. Over whiskey, Tom had spoken animatedly of a senator and his wife traveling up through Wyoming the following month. It seemed to be a big deal. "They got one escort with them. Can you believe that? They reckon it'll make 'em less . . . What's the word?"

"Conspicuous?"

Tom slapped his knee. "That's it! Less *conspicuous*."

"Why should I care about a politician and his wife?" Sherman said dismissively, reaching for the bottle to refill his glass.

Tom's hand fell to Sherman's wrist, stopping him. He leaned in, voice lowered. "Because they're traveling with a case of gold ingots." He let go but Sherman remained how he was, one hand still planted on the whiskey bottle, eyes fixed on Tom's.

Sherman said, "Go on."

"Worth a fortune," Tom continued. "Each ingot is worth at least a thousand dollars."

Sherman now took the whiskey unhindered and filled his glass. "How do you figure?"

"A kilo a bar. Thirty dollars an ounce. It's just over a thousand dollars for the kilo."

Sherman laughed a little. He sipped his whiskey. "And how many ingots in the case? One?"

Tom looked around. The saloon was busy and noisy, but there wasn't anyone standing nearby to overhear their conversation. "Twenty."

Sherman nearly spat out his whiskey. *"What?"*

Tom sneered at him. "Got your interest now, gunslinger?"

"Mayhap you do."

Tom grinned. "Thought I might."

"Damn." Sherman set his glass down. He looked off to the side, mental cogs grinding away. "Ten grand apiece . . ."

"Compared with whatever you make running down outlaws," Tom said dismissively.

"Outlaws like you, you mean?"

Tom shrugged.

At numerous points over the years, Sherman had wondered if Tom Preston's name would come up, but to his surprise, it never had. Of course, the bounties Sherman hunted were not the folks the law wanted you to collect. They were the undesirables the underworld wanted to be rid of.

Sherman eyed him suspiciously. "Why me?"

"Huh?"

"I said, why me?"

"I don't follow."

"You could've buddied up with anybody for this job, and yet you sought me out," Sherman said. "Probably rode all the way out here just to ask in person. Why?"

"Because you're the best damned gunslinger around

and I need an experienced hand who is also a crack shot, that's why."

"Right."

"And, well, you're the trustworthy kind. You stick to your word. That's well-known and accepted in our circles," Tom said. "I need someone I can really trust if I'm to pull this off."

Sherman drank. He set his glass back down slowly. "That can't be all, though, can it?"

"You're a shrewd dude, aren't you, Sherman Knowles?" Tom said, laughing with his signature high-pitched cackle. "Okay. I'll give it up. I need you to reach out to one of your contacts."

"I don't know what contact you mean, but whatever you're thinking, you're mistaken," Sherman told him.

"Only, I don't think I am," Tom said.

"Really?"

Tom nodded. "We both know you got a friend in high office, lets you in on all kinds of things. I heard you let this individual off in exchange for helping you out from time to time. Am I right?"

"Even if I do have a contact like that—and I don't, so don't get excited—what exactly do you want me to ask them?"

"The route the senator is gonna take. Dates and times. That's it."

"I don't know . . . ," Sherman said, running his hand over his beard as he thought about the proposition. "This fella may not like giving out that kind of information."

Tom said, "We can cross that bridge when we come to it. So, what d'you say? You're either in or you're out. Gonna rob a coach with me or not?" Tom offered Sherman his hand.

Sherman thought about his funds—or lack thereof.

He weighed up how hard it had been to find what work he had against the immediate but risky proposition of a quick ten thousand dollars that would see him through for quite a while. It was a healthy sum for such little work. And he had decided that he would quit anyway. This could be his final job.

"If I agreed to this, I'd want a promise out of you."

Tom eyed him warily. "What promise?"

"That we ain't gonna be spilling any blood that don't need spilling."

"Say no more. It's a deal," Tom said, and the two men shook on it.

T HE SNOWFLAKES SETTLED in Sherman's beard and he thought back to the month before, in the warm saloon, drinking whiskey. Times were strange indeed. Your fortunes could change like the wind. "You're not from these parts, are you?" Sherman asked, his mind back on the present.

"No."

"Didn't think so."

"That obvious, huh?"

Sherman said, "You don't sit right with the cold. People from around here, they're used to it."

Tom Preston glowered at the country before him. "I hate working in the winter. But no choice."

Sherman shrugged. "It's a hard time of year for folk, but I've always enjoyed the winter. For one thing, it sure makes you appreciate a fire."

"Well, I can tell you, I'd appreciate a fire right about now. . . ."

Sherman chuckled at that. He looked away down the road as it swung in and out of view behind inclines, running out on the flat. There down below he could just make out the front lamps of a coach led by four dark brown horses. In front of the coach by about twenty yards, a lone rider led on horseback. He looked through a set of old field glasses he produced from his saddlebag. "Looks like the show is about to begin," Sherman said, handing the field glasses to Tom.

"Just the driver and one dude on horseback riding in front of them," he said, looking through the glasses. "Two people in the back. Must be the senator and his wife."

He handed the field glasses back.

"How do you reckon we do this, then?" Sherman asked, tucking the glasses away, then fixing a length of navy blue material around the bottom portion of his face.

Tom did the same, leaving just the bridge of his nose and eyes visible above the top of the face covering. "I don't know. What do you reckon? You're the hired gun, after all."

"I think we should ride up alongside. One of us takes the driver. The other takes the lookout. Nice and relaxed."

Tom considered this. "Sound plan. By the time they realize we're there, it'll be over with anyway. I got me a lasso I can throw over the dude in front."

"Any good with it?" Sherman asked.

"The lasso? Sure am," Tom said, producing the coil of thin rope. "Probably the best there is."

"Okay, let's do it."

T HEY EASED THEIR horses down the hill, the beasts skidding in the snow a little as they picked up momentum on the downward slope. They traversed its steep angle without incident and were presently heading for the road. The coach lay ahead. Both men knew it would be best to approach from either side, pincer the driver and the escort. They would not expect an attack to come from the rear.

Sherman elected to take the driver, so he headed over the road to the other side. He snapped the reins and dug his heels into the sides of his horse, the noble beast surging ahead, closing the distance to the coach. He glanced to the right and noted that Tom had followed suit. Through the falling snow, he could just make out the lasso coiled around Tom's forearm as he spurred his own horse forward. He sure hoped the bandit was as good with it as he claimed to be. Whether they trusted each other, or even liked each other, was a moot point. Each man would have to play his part and do what he'd promised to do in order to pull the job off without a hitch.

Sherman rode past the windows of the coach, ignoring the man and woman within as they gasped at the sight of him charging past. He drew the pistol from his right-hand holster, sped up until he was keeping pace with the coach and aimed the weapon at the driver.

The man looked at Sherman, startled, eyes wide.

"Stop the coach!" he yelled at the driver.

Up ahead, the escort spun about in his saddle to look back, only to be met with Tom Preston's rope. It landed over his shoulders in one fluid movement, as if the lasso were an extension of him. The escort tried to shrug himself free, but it was too late. Tom pulled tight, the rope snagging around the man. He fell hard from his horse and hit the snow with an "Oomph!" and was then dragged away to the side by Tom and deposited on the verge. The escort's horse cantered away, snorting hot exhalation into the frigid air.

"I said, stop!" Sherman shouted.

The driver made to pull his own sidearm, but Sherman let off a round directly over the man's hat. The driver ducked.

"That was a warning shot. Don't make me have to do it for real!"

Evidently realizing that he would not be able to lose Sherman, the coach driver pulled back hard on the reins and brought the horses to a standstill. Sherman was sure to order him down from his bench, and as the man did so, Sherman climbed down from his horse and bound the driver's wrists behind his back.

"Don't do this. It's not worth the trouble, believe me," the driver said.

"Keep your opinion to yourself," Sherman warned him. "The less you say, the better it'll be for ya."

Meanwhile, Tom hauled the escort to his feet and forced him to stand at the side of the road. He liberated the man's guns from their holsters.

"I don't rightly want to," Tom was explaining, "but if you leave me no choice, I'll plug you full of lead, and believe me, I will not lose a night's sleep over it. Plenty of men killed by my hand and there's likely to be plenty more. Do as you're told and us two won't have a problem. Understood?"

"Yes."

"Good man," Tom said, binding the escort's wrists before removing the lasso. He shoved the man toward the driver. "Just stand there and keep quiet."

Sherman and Tom sized up the carriage and its occupants.

"You're a pretty good aim with that lasso," Sherman said.

Tom drew close, coiling the lasso back up as he spoke. "Did you doubt my abilities, gunslinger?"

"Not at all. Now, let's get this gold."

"Amen."

The senator held his wife in his arms and they trembled inside the relative safety of their coach. Sherman was wary of either being in possession of a firearm, no matter how small and novel it may have been. So he remained outside at first and proceeded to rap on the door to the coach carriage with his knuckles.

"Hello in there."

"Go away, you scoundrels!" the senator's wife screeched in a high-pitched, whiny voice.

Sherman smiled. "If either of you has got a gun of some kind, I suggest you lay it on the floor of the carriage. Pull something on us, you're liable to get yourself shot and killed. Do you understand?"

"We will not be giving anything to the likes of you!" the senator's wife shouted back.

"To hell with this," Tom said, yanking the door open and pulling the wife out first, casting her down on the snow with little regard. Then he hauled the senator himself out into the cold. The senator stumbled but did not fall, and immediately set about helping his wife up off the ground. She brushed herself off, mortified that she'd been treated that way. "Keep 'em there. I'll check the carriage."

"As you like," Sherman said.

Tom returned five or so minutes later from the confines of the carriage, dragging a wooden chest. He could barely move it. "Here, gimme a hand," he groaned, dragging it across the boards of the carriage.

"Sure," Sherman said. When he felt the weight of the chest, he looked at Tom. "Feels heavier than I expected."

"I thought so, too."

"You villains! You blaggards!" the senator's wife screamed at the sight of them hauling the chest from the coach carriage. "Dick, you've gotta stop them boys!"

Tom dropped the chest. "Can it, woman."

"Is that how you talk to a lady?" the senator's wife demanded. She looked Tom up and down. "You're nothing but a lowlife."

"No different from a politician, then," Tom said.

Sherman whispered, "Don't answer her. We're not here to converse with the marks. Let's concentrate on moving this thing along."

"Sure."

But the politician's wife was undeterred. "We did not come out here to be robbed by the likes of you!"

Both Sherman and Tom were grunting with effort, trying to move the chest. Tom shook his head. "Everyone's gotta get by, lady. One man's nest egg is another man's windfall."

"Man?" she spat. "*Man?* Not much of a man, are you? Hardly a prime example . . ."

The senator tried to shush her. "Please, Margaret. Calm yourself."

"Don't respond. Let's just get this done," Sherman said.

But Tom was not listening to reason. "Not much of a man?" he asked.

"That's what I said."

"Not much of a man . . . ," Tom repeated, shaking his head.

"That's right! A pathetic, small-brained weasel."

"Weasel?" Tom asked. "Weasel?"

Tom strode forward. He pulled his gun, aimed it at the woman's face and pulled the trigger. The shot echoed out around them. "How's that, huh? How's *that*!" he screamed into the ruin of her face.

Sherman dropped the chest, the promise of the gold within immediately forgotten. What he'd dreaded about this job had come true. The senator dropped to his knees, bawling after his wife. The contents of her skull were strewn across the white snow, and the blood kept coming and coming, forming an icy red reservoir beneath them.

"What're you doing?" Sherman demanded, his

hand on Tom's wrist, forcing his gun down. "Are you crazy?"

"She had it comin'," Tom said.

Sherman was furious. "I can't believe you. When word gets back that you killed the wife of a senator, you'll never get out from under the price on your head."

The senator looked up at them, eyes red. "What kind of monsters are you?" he asked in a distraught pitch. His despair soon turned to anger. "I'll see you both hanged!" he growled, visibly enraged by the injustice of his wife's abrupt death.

Wordlessly, Tom pushed Sherman's hand away, aimed his gun at the senator and, as he had the man's wife, blew the senator away. The crack of the gunshot rang out like a lightning strike. The senator flew backward, blood spurting from the top of his head, and fell against his wife's dead body.

"Damn it, I said no!" Sherman knocked the gun clean out of Tom Preston's hand, then punched him square on the jaw. The pistol landed in the snow somewhere nearby. Tom fell to the ground, temporarily immobilized. The driver and the escort took the moment to try sneaking off, but Sherman was already on them. He pivoted, aiming his pistol in their direction, and demanded that they stay where they were. "Nobody else needs to die tonight."

The gaze of the escort shifted to focus on something behind Sherman. He turned back around, frowning.

"Grrraaahhh!" Tom lunged at Sherman, rugby-tackling him and using the full strength of his legs to push him back. He held Sherman's gun hand up as he pushed him, his grip hard and biting, preventing Sherman from using it.

"We agreed no bloodshed!" Sherman boomed. He

beat at Tom with his left fist, but the bandit continued to force him back, the hits barely registering. His fists thudded against Tom's wiry frame.

Both men snarled and grunted like wild animals as they struggled against each other, Sherman's feet finally losing purchase in the snow. He felt himself slipping as Tom delivered the final almighty shove. Sherman fell back, the snow cushioning his fall. For a brief second, he could not move. But then he pushed himself up to a sitting position and raised his gun.

Immediately, Tom stepped up and kicked the pistol clear out of his hand.

Grimacing from the pain, Sherman clutched at his hand. Tom stalked off, retrieved his own gun and aimed it at Sherman's chest. "Stay down. Or so help me, I will punch a hole clean through ya."

"We made a deal."

Tom looked at him blankly for a moment. "I'm changing the terms," he said.

As Sherman looked on, Tom stalked back over to the driver and the escort. Both men turned on their heels to run in blind panic. Tom stopped, took aim and fired one shot apiece into their backs, right between the shoulder blades. They were flung forward onto the road and struck the hard surface with a wet sound like meat being slapped onto a butcher's block that made Sherman flinch.

He got up.

Tom turned on him. "Don't you even think about retrieving that pistol. Or the other one on your hip. You might be a gunslinger but even you can't outdraw a man already got his own weapon trained on you. Now, why don't you do us both a favor, take that pistol out with the tips of your fingers and toss it aside? Nice and slow."

Sherman did as he had been instructed. As much as he thought he might manage to shoot Tom Preston before he let off a decent shot, he could not be certain. And the uncertainty was what made him do as he had been told, dropping the second pistol into the snow.

"Good," Tom said. He rubbed his jaw. "I'll tell ya, that's one helluva right hook you got."

Sherman ignored him. He looked at the corpses of the senator and his wife. "There was no need for them to die, Tom."

"I say there was."

Sherman spat on the ground. "Damn you, Tom Preston, you know that's a lie."

"To hell with it! They would've blabbed their damned mouths eventually. I just saved them all the trouble. Especially the woman. Least now she's quiet and ain't squawking!"

Sherman's hands bunched into fists at his sides. "I must've been crazy agreeing to ride with you. I knew this was gonna end up a mistake."

"As did I. Now, back up over there. That's it. Right there. Don't you move," Tom said. He squatted down in front of the wooden chest and used a knife to jimmy the lock. He gaped in awe at the contents. "Well . . . look at that. I ain't ever seen that much gold in all my life."

Sherman was no longer interested in the wooden chest or the contents. He looked at the bodies around him and felt only shame. It was meant to be a clean robbery. Stop the coach, hold them up, then everyone be on their way without so much as a drop of blood being spilled. But that was not to be. He realized that Tom had never intended on things going that way. It was never going to be clean and free of murder.

He'd been so wrong. And now people were dead because he had helped Tom Preston kill them. Sherman had made it possible. "He was right, you know," Sherman said.

Tom looked up. "Huh?"

"The senator. He was right when he called you a monster."

Tom closed the lid on the chest. He stood up. "Let me tell you somethin' may not surprise you. I'm the worst there is," he said. "I've done things you wouldn't believe. Things nobody knows nothin' about. That's how bad I am."

"I was foolish to trust you."

"Naw," Tom said, approaching him with a look of intent in his eyes. "I was a fool to think you'd follow my lead. I thought you was like me, the genuine article. But you ain't. You're soft. You can kill, but it bothers you in a way it ain't ever bothered me. That's the difference between us. I look at these people I just killed, and I don't feel nothin' at all."

"Why you—" Sherman lunged forward, ready to kill him with his bare hands if he had to.

Tom bounced back a step, swung his arm up and over and brought the stock of his pistol down on Sherman's head. It cracked him in the skull, sharp and hard, knocking him clean out.

Sherman thudded to the frozen ground.

Tom stood over him, clucking his tongue. "What'll I do with you?"

WHEN SHERMAN WOKE, he was back on his horse. His hands were tied to the horn of his saddle. His boots had been pushed into the stirrups, and that way he'd remained upright.

He blinked. They were leaving a thicket of trees, his horse following Tom's at the end of a rope. Once out of the trees, they found themselves before a pale expanse.

Up ahead in the distance, a storm was rolling in, a thick wall of white obscuring everything in its path. A blizzard. Soon it would be on top of them and they would be in the thick of it, unless they were able to find shelter fast.

Tom looked back at him. "Gunslinger! You're awake," he said jovially. He stopped his horse and climbed down from the saddle. He untied Sherman's hands and moved away, out of arm's reach. At gunpoint, Tom instructed Sherman to climb down now that his hands were free of their bonds. "Remove your gloves, your jacket, anything keeping you warm."

Sherman looked at him. "Why?"

"You're taking a little walk. I don't want you to get too hot," Tom told him.

"A walk?"

Tom indicated the white prairie beyond. "Fine day for a stroll, isn't it?"

"You can't be serious," Sherman said, shivering. Already the cold air was working its way in through his clothes.

"Serious as I've ever been about *anything*," Tom said. "You're gonna walk until you drop, and I'll be right there to see it happen. In fact, I'll be there to see your last ragged breath freeze in the wind."

He instructed Sherman to hold his hands together and raise them. Tom then bound them tight again and climbed back up into his saddle, keeping one end of the rope in his hand, like a leash for a dog. Sherman looked at the storm blowing in. He knew what it meant. He would never reach the end of the prairie—that was for certain.

"Why are you doin' this? Why don't you just shoot me, like you did those innocent folk back there?"

Tom Preston laughed. "What'd be the fun in that?" He pulled at the rope binding Sherman's hands, yanking him forward. Forcing him to move. "I want this to last. You betrayed me. There's a price to pay."

Slowly, one foot in front of the other, Sherman began to trudge across the prairie as the snowstorm rushed in and enveloped them both.

PART ONE

◇

PHANTOM DIGITS

CHAPTER ONE

O N HIS LAST visit to Broken Bow, Sherman's brother,
Jed, had been in full health. Tall, broad shoul-
dered and lean from years of working the land, Jed
possessed the kind of wiry strength only a man who
worked with his hands possessed.

In his travels, Sherman had encountered all kinds.
Men who looked dumber than an ox but were gifted
with a genius intellect; women whose features were
hardened by tough lives and tough conditions but
could sing with such sweetness as to make even the
most hard-hearted son of a gun weep with sorrow.

His brother, Jed, was just so deceptive. The man
possessed not an ounce of fat on his entire body; he
was all bone, muscle and sinew. The last time Sherman
had seen him, Jed's hair had been beginning to thin at
the crown, but that was the only thing that aged him.
He looked far younger than his years.

That was not the case now.

The sickness had drained him. It had aged him, hollowing out his cheeks, darkening his once bright eyes. His hair had turned gray and all but fallen out. His once strong and sturdy frame had become little more than a withered husk. Jed was all paper-thin, dry skin stretched tight over bone. His hands, which had once been big and viselike, were elongated claws that could barely grip a spoon with which to eat—and Jed had stopped doing that three days ago. Sherman looked at his own hand, and his prosthetic appendage. The hook where his right hand had once been. *Our hands tell our story*, he thought.

Sherman peeked in at Jed through the open doorway. His brother lay on a cot, sleeping soundly, hands clasped on the chasm of his stomach. He'd grown so thin that his top row of teeth jutted out, pronounced in a way that Sherman had never seen before.

Hattie took his hat and jacket from him. "He's been that way a few days now. Just sleeping."

"Will he know I'm here?" Sherman asked.

"Oh, sure. He'll wake up and talk to you," Hattie assured him. "Just don't expect too much. As you can imagine . . . he tires ever so easily now."

Sherman watched her busy herself. "I want to say something—"

"No need to say it, Sherman. I know, and I appreciate it."

But he felt the need to explain himself. To let her know, whether she wished to hear it or not, that he appreciated her caring for Jed. He appreciated the dignity she'd afforded him as the sickness took hold and reduced him to his present state. "Hattie . . ."

"Please, don't."

Sherman pressed on, undeterred. The whole ride from Elam Hollow, he'd been thinking about what he'd say to his sister-in-law. How to express his gratitude to her. "Hattie, I just want to say, what you've done for

Jed these past couple of months, you've gone above and beyond, you really have—"

Hattie shook her head. "No, no, no. Not here, not now. There will be a time, but that time is not now. I can't do this now."

"Okay," Sherman said softly.

Hattie looked through the open doorway to the angular shape of her husband flat out on the cot, breathing shallowly as he slept. "Whatever I did, it wasn't enough to stop him dying, was it? So I'm not sure I can stand any gratitude or platitudes just yet. Because we all failed him, even God. Ain't nobody was able to stop it happening, just as there isn't anything in heaven or earth gonna stop what's coming, either."

"I know." Sherman bowed his head. He glanced back at his brother. Sherman hadn't yet crossed the threshold of the door and stepped foot in the room. A part of him didn't want to, either. "It almost seems cruel to wake him."

"It does. But you will not get another chance. The doctor told me as much this morning."

"Really?"

Hattie folded her arms and sighed. "Really."

"Did he say how long?"

Jed's wife sighed. "Maybe by the morning."

The prediction made Sherman's blood run cold. How many people had Jed's doctor seen die before he had been able to make such a prediction? Before he had gotten a feel for how long patients had left before they met their Maker?

Sherman changed tack. "How is Annie getting on?"

"Like a young woman who is watching her father die," Hattie told him.

The brutality of her words, the sharpness of her tongue, made Sherman flinch. He had always admired and respected Hattie. And he'd always feared her, too.

But she had done everything she possibly could for Jed. His brother couldn't have asked for a better wife. And for all her hard edges, Hattie was a warm, loving woman. When Jed finally passed, Hattie would be inconsolable, Sherman knew.

Hattie looked at him. "Are you going to go in there and talk to your brother or not?"

"Yes."

"What're you waiting for, then? Time is wasting away."

Sherman considered this. He didn't seem able to step over the threshold. Perhaps because once he did, there was no going back. He could smell the unmistakable stink of death coming from within the room and the reality of what was about to happen to his brother sank in with awful finality. It took every ounce of strength and determination he possessed to enter the room and stand at his brother's bedside.

"Jed?"

His brother barely stirred. Sherman leaned in, placed his hand over Jed's.

"Brother, I'm here."

Jed stirred, cleared his throat. His eyes opened lazily and it took him several seconds to recognize Sherman. Then he attempted to sit up, but Sherman insisted he stay as he was.

"Don't get up."

"Brother?" Jed croaked, eyes widening, the whites turned nicotine yellow. He lay back against the pillow, visibly exhausted. "What're you doing here?"

"Came to see you, Jed."

Jedediah Knowles looked up at the ceiling. "Because I'm dying."

Sherman thought how to soften the impact of what he had to say, how to make it easier on Jed. But there was no way of breaking it to him that would have been any less cruel than the harsh reality of his diagnosis. The ticking clock that now existed between both men. Counting down every second of time that was already spent.

"Jed, I don't think there's long."

His brother swallowed. "I know."

"When I heard you were sick, I got to thinking of the old times," Sherman said. "You know, when we were young. How we grew up. How we went our separate ways."

"I seem to recall one of us choosing a direction and the other deciding to fly wherever the wind took him."

Sherman said, "Sure sounds familiar. But we always got on, didn't we?"

Jed smiled weakly. "Have you come to clear your conscience, Sherman?"

"Not at all."

"All right, yes, we got on. We had our ups and downs, like everyone. But I am mighty proud of the way you turned things around in the end. The way you saw sense. It just took you a while, is all."

"Sure did," Sherman said.

Jed continued. "Nobody knows how to live, Sherman. You just have to pick a road. I picked mine and was lucky to have what I have. Others weren't so lucky, which I guess is just a case of the odds stacked against them. Like whatever this is that's killing me. Ain't nobody or nothing to blame, it was just my time, brother. It was just my time."

Silence fell between them, both men reflecting on their words, on their own paths and how they had converged. One about to carry on, the other about to pass.

Sherman had to ask the inevitable question, and he had to look away from Jed in order to do so. "You scared?"

His big brother thought on that question for a long

moment. Finally he said, "I don't know if I'm scared of dying. I guess I'm scared of not knowing what'll happen to Hattie and Annie."

Sherman took his brother's hand. "I'll be there for them, as you were there for me. When I needed direction, you and Hattie were there to show me the way. You were my compass."

"You'll do that for me?"

"No harm will come to either of them while there is breath in my lungs. I swear it."

Jed squeezed Sherman's hand tight. Sherman realized, much later, when Jed had already passed, that it must have taken all his strength to do so. Almost as if Jed wanted Sherman to know he still had some fight in him.

The sun broke through the clouds outside, the thin, watery light filling the room.

"I don't want you to go," Sherman admitted, his voice cracking.

Jed smiled. "And I regret having to leave, brother."

That night, Jedediah fell asleep with Sherman, Hattie and Annie sitting around him. They were there as his eyes closed and his breathing slowed to an irregular rhythm. Just before midnight, he stopped breathing altogether and lay perfectly still, his passing gentle as rain on a spring night. Sherman watched as Annie rose from her chair and pulled the sheet up over her father's face. "Good night, Pa," she said in her soft voice, and not for the first time in his life, Sherman felt something inside of him break in a way it never had before.

J EDEDIAH HAD LEFT home and pursued a life working the land. First, he was the hired help, and then, when he'd squirreled away enough money, he had the means by which to purchase his own farm in Broken

Bow. Every year he invested in buying more land and expanding his property. Jed made a deal with free grazers, giving them permission to drive their cattle through his property in exchange for a modest fee. This combined with what he made from the crops kept him above water. He was earning enough to build a house, and a barn, and a cattle shed. He hired people, all year-round, to keep up with the workload. There were bad years. There were bad crops. But he pushed through, and he made a living, and he provided. They'd wanted more children, and they tried for them, but they never came.

Hattie had had Annie and never fallen pregnant again. That was how it was sometimes, Jed guessed. The Knowles of Broken Bow were happy with their lot, regardless. They had a life, a home, a family. They had security and were principled, respected members of their community.

The trouble was Sherman. The trouble had *always* been Sherman.

When Jed had left home to go learn his trade and apply himself, Sherman chose another path. He rode with the wrong crowd. He discovered he was a natural with a pistol—even better with two. He could shoot a glass bottle off a fence post at an impossible distance and do so in a manner that made it look easy. While Jed was up to his knees in mud, plowing a field for little pay, Sherman was a great distance away, running a man down in the town of Godwinson. He shot that man and stood over him as he drew his last breath. And what Sherman came to realize was that he had no issue with taking a life. He could render himself judge, jury and executioner with the pull of a trigger. One shot and a life was extinguished at his whim. It filled him with terror and awe to be so powerful.

When Jed was purchasing his first stretch of land,

Sherman was working bounties. He took a second horse with him at all times. Either for the living, breathing bounty to sit upon—or to carry their cadaver. The outcomes were generally determined by how the bounties conducted themselves, and when all was said and done, it mattered little. Whether they died at his hand, or by a noose around the neck, every man with a price on his head knew the eventual outcome as surely as Sherman did. The reaper took them all in the end.

Jed had never understood Sherman's reasons for shrugging off the trappings of a settled existence. Because to Jed, they were not trappings at all. They were the bounty of life. A roof over his head; the warmth of the fire after a day's work in the cold; Hattie's body lying next to his after they'd made love; Annie growing up, more beautiful with each passing year—they were truly life's treasures.

For his part, Sherman could not fathom why Jed would have chosen such a rooted, stagnant existence. Hunting people down and collecting on their bounties had afforded Sherman the opportunity to see every corner of the country. From sea to sea he had ridden, from north to south and back again. He'd interacted with all walks of life and felt all the more enlightened for it. His brother was happy farming the ground and digging in roots ever farther with each passing year. Sherman found the idea smothering. Who would have preferred that to riding with the wind into the sunset?

After he lost his hand, and things changed for good, Sherman dropped by frequently. Despite his previous misgivings about Jed's lack of worldliness, he found the Knowles farm a safe haven. A place to return to where he could be nurtured and cared for. Where he could feel the warmth of his brother's love, and what became a genuine friendship between the two men.

For all the time they'd been so different, so distant, in time maturity had brought them back together.

Sherman and Jedediah found they had more in common than what divided them.

T HEY HELD A quiet service in Broken Bow Ceme- tery, and when the priest had finished his oratory, Sherman was invited to stand over the chasm into which his brother's coffin had been lowered and say a few words. He had nothing prepared, so he fumbled for a moment for something to say something about Jedediah that would bring solace to his widow and child. Sherman looked down at Jed's casket, and to his surprise, the words found him. They rose from the grave, as it were. He thought on a day they'd spent fish- ing the Mountain Fork, talking for hours. How Jed had described seeing Hattie and loving her the moment their eyes met. Sherman had never felt that feeling and doubted he ever would. He envied Jed for experiencing something so pure in such a harsh, volatile world as theirs. Tell the truth, he envied him still.

"Jedediah was one helluva brother," Sherman said. "If anyone deserved to reach a ripe old age, it was Jed. He was a patient and thoughtful man. We never had cross words, but he never shied away from tellin' me where my faults lie. Not that he was perfect. Difference between Jed and most other fellas is he took every- thing on the chin. He accepted his faults, and that made him a better man. If I'm being honest, he was the kind of man most aspire to be."

He looked at Hattie dabbing at the tracks of the tears coursing down her cheeks. Annie hugged her mother to her, trying to comfort her. How she'd grown—how tall, and strong, and reminiscent of Jed she was. Sherman thought of Annie covering Jed with the sheet, and he pushed the image away. It was too painful.

It was too soon.

Wearily, he peered down at the coffin. Was this the ultimate price for taking a life? That you got to live while those you cared about died before you?

"Jedediah set down roots here in Broken Bow and established himself as a gifted, principled member of the community. I know that many of you will mourn my brother, not least his wife, Hattie, and daughter, Annie. But I will perhaps mourn him the most. Right now I stand before you, half the man I was prior to his death. I woke up this morning, knowing what we would be doing today, and the world seemed impossible to me. I regret that death didn't see fit to take me first. . . ."

Tears filled his eyes. Annie stepped forward, took Sherman by the arm and led him away from the graveside. "Come on, Uncle Sherman," she said.

Sherman wiped at his eyes. He hadn't cried in years. Maybe decades. "Sorry I made a fool of myself," he whispered.

"You did not. We are both immensely proud of you."

"Really?"

Annie smiled weakly at him. "Really."

The minister spoke his last words, blessing Jed into heaven, then gave the nod to the diggers to begin shoveling the dirt in on Jed's coffin. Sherman stood a short while watching the men work, then decided he could not stand to be there any longer listening to the dry tumble of the dirt striking the casket lid. He caught up with Hattie and Annie, and together they headed home.

T HE NEXT DAY, Sherman rose before dawn and saddled his horse to leave.

"I made coffee," Hattie said, stepping down off the front porch and handing Sherman a hot mug of the strong black brew.

"You should not have troubled yourself," Sherman said, accepting the coffee. He blew across its surface and took several sips. It was good. "But I am glad that you did."

"Can't be setting out without a good cup of coffee inside you," Hattie said.

Sherman tipped the brim of his hat. "Much obliged, as always."

"Will it take you long?"

"Not too long. Couple of days," Sherman said, shrugging it off.

Hattie stuck her hands into the front pocket of her pinny. "I'm surprised you didn't get the train out here."

"Well, you know I'm not all too fond of locomotives, Hattie," Sherman said. "A horse I can understand."

"Were you never worried you might miss seeing Jed before he passed? You know, if you didn't get here in time."

The question stunned him. Sherman rolled his answer around in his head while he sipped some more coffee. "No."

"Why not?"

"Because I'm a coward."

"You are not," Hattie said, looking completely baffled. "What do you mean?"

Sherman lowered his eyes. "A part of me hoped that when I got here Jed would be gone already. I can't stop thinking about that, and I can't stop feeling guilty over it, either."

Hattie touched his arm. "Sherman, there's nothing to feel guilty about. It's not straightforward. There ain't no wrong or right. There were times I wished Jed would just up and breathe his last to put an end to his misery. Release the burden on me. It's natural to feel that way. You didn't mean no wrong by it."

Annie appeared in the front doorway, rubbing at her eyes. "Are you leaving already, Uncle Sherman?"

"Afraid so, Annie," Sherman said. "Got a long ride ahead of me."

Hattie said, "Won't you have breakfast, at least?"

"Thank you kindly, but I really do have to get started. I'll swing by here in a couple of months, though. Take you up on that offer of breakfast if it's still going."

"You know it will," Hattie said. "Well, we're sad to see you go. You could always stay."

Sherman looked at the house and felt the mourning rise, his heart leaden in his breast. He swallowed it down with the coffee and hoped he could keep the sadness subdued until he got home at least. "I'm afraid Titus will be missing me. And I'm sure by now he'll have driven the Lynch family crazy."

"He is a bundle of energy, that dog," Hattie said. She drew Sherman into a hug and clung on to him a second or so longer than was customary. "You take care on the road."

"Yes, ma'am."

Annie walked down, followed suit. She hugged her uncle, and he grinned from ear to ear at her affection. "Tough leavin' you."

"Stay."

"You know I can't," Sherman said. "Now, if you need anything, either of you, just write me. Okay? Anything at all."

Annie let go. "We will."

"Okay."

"Thanks for spending time with us," Annie said.

"Neither of you have to thank me. A cavalry couldn't have kept me away," Sherman said. He handed

Hattie his empty cup, climbed up onto his horse and regarded them both from the vantage point of his saddle. "He truly did love you both."

Hattie dabbed at her eyes with the bottom of her pinny. "You're making me cry."

"Story of my life," Sherman said, smiling.

Both Hattie and Annie broke out in laughter. Sherman waved them off, then spurred his horse into a steady trot. He did not look back to see if Jed's wife and daughter were watching him leave, because he knew all too well that they would be.

CHAPTER TWO

SHERMAN STOPPED BY the Lynch farm to collect Titus, and no sooner had he begun to cross their main field than he saw the dog coming. Titus was a big boy, a mixed breed with paws big as saucers. He was so long legged, he sometimes resembled a foal the way he galloped around. The dog was graceful and elegant when he ran at speed . . . and clumsy as all hell when he didn't. He lumbered about, too boisterous and curious, knocking things over and getting into mischief. But Sherman loved him regardless. From the way Titus launched himself at Sherman, straddling him with both front paws, giant pink tongue lolling from the side of his mouth, Sherman knew his affection was reciprocated.

"Good to see you, boy," Sherman said, patting and scratching and generally making a fuss over the dog.

Dougray Lynch ambled over to the fence and bade Sherman a good day. "Fair ride back?"

"Aye, I'd say so. Free of incident, if that's what you mean."

"Never know, crossing the prairie by yourself these days. Lot of strange folk about," Lynch said.

Sherman patted Titus. "I can't recall seeing a single soul on this occasion."

As a young man starting out, it had scared him, being so alone for hours, sometimes days, at a time. How could the world be so big that you could ride into the wilderness and not encounter another human being for hundreds of miles? But what he'd come to learn was that the world *was* that big. Whether compacted into cities, or spread out in the wilds, men and women were just ants in a jar when it came down to it. He had grown to feel at ease in the loneliness, to embrace it. When he did that, any fears he had melted away, never to return.

"Was he well-behaved?" Sherman asked.

Lynch rolled his eyes. "Titus was Titus, if you get my meaning," he said, and broke into laughter. "That dog has had devilment on his mind since the day he was born."

"Yeah, I know," Sherman said. On cue, Titus cocked his head and looked at his master, as if attempting to understand what was being said. "Ain't that right, boy?"

He thanked Dougray for watching after Titus for him and promised to swing by in a couple of days. Sherman said he'd get Mary Lynch something nice for putting up with Titus, and though Dougray told him there was no need, Sherman insisted. He rode for town with Titus trotting alongside his horse, keeping pace and occasionally glancing obediently up at his master.

THE GENERAL STORE was still open, and Sherman took the opportunity to purchase what he'd run low on. He bought canned and dried goods, tobacco, and indulged in his craving for bitter chocolate. Like smoking a pipe in the evening or taking a nip of something medicinal when he could feel the cold in his bones, Sherman couldn't shake his taste for chocolate. The contrast of sweet and savory made his mouth water. He didn't understand it. But Mac, who ran the store, made sure to stock it for him and Sherman rarely ever failed to buy himself some.

But this time he spotted a new kind of chocolate. "Say, Mac, what's that up there on the shelf behind you?"

Mac got a bar down and handed it over. "From Belgium. Came in last week."

"Belgium, huh?" Sherman said, turning the bar over in his one and only hand. "Where the hell is Belgium? California?"

"It's a country in its own right," Mac said. "I think it's between France and Germany."

"Is that so?"

Mac told Sherman to wait, went out back for a moment and returned with a foldout atlas of the world. He showed Sherman where Belgium lay. "Right there."

"I'll be," Sherman said, impressed. "So this little bar came all the way from there?"

"Yes."

"How?"

Mac folded the map back up. He said, "I don't rightly know, tell the truth. I guess by boat."

Sherman was amazed that he could hold in his hand something that had come halfway across the world. Over land and sea. All so it could land on a shelf in Mac's general store in Elam Hollow, and end up in his possession. And after all that, it would end up between his teeth.

"I'll take two," Sherman told him.

"Sure? That chocolate is pretty darn expensive, Sherman."

"That's why I'll take two instead of three," Sherman said with a lopsided grin.

He heard the unmistakable sound of Titus barking outside. Titus had several ways of communicating. He would howl to tell Sherman where he'd gotten to if he was lost. Other times, Titus would use short, sharp barks to let Sherman know he was following a scent trail. But when there was some kind of danger, or something to be wary of, Titus used long, loud barks—as he was doing now.

Mac said, "Hey, now, what's all that racket?"

Sherman didn't hesitate in dropping what he was doing and moving through the store to the front entrance. He opened the door and saw the cause for Titus's barking straightaway.

Three men were harassing a young drunk in front of the saloon. They pushed the young man and he fell on his face, at which point they each kicked him in the ribs, then stepped back to see what would happen. Sherman quieted Titus down and watched as the town drunk got to his feet—only to be knocked back down again. The three men laughed cruelly, the folk of Elam Hollow gathering around to see, but failing to intervene on the young man's behalf.

"I don't like this one bit," Sherman mumbled to Titus. He stepped down off the porch of the general store and crossed the street.

The three men were in their late twenties. One had black hair slicked back and a half mustache. He was tall and gangly. Another had brown hair to his shoulders and was shorter and squatter in frame than the other. The third man hardly had any hair at all. He was the one doing a lot of the shoving and seemed to be heavily inebriated himself.

As for the town drunk, he'd rolled into town a couple of months before. He was barely in his twenties, without a cent to his name. His clothes were threadbare, and he looked as though he hadn't eaten a good meal in a good long time. The townsfolk took pity on him now and then, buying the kid drinks from the saloon and offering him what they could to eat—hunks of old bread and leftover stew.

On the few occasions Sherman had crossed the young man's path, he'd thought, *Come winter, you'll freeze to death on this street, carrying on the way you are.*

Sherman cleared his throat to holler. "Hey! Leave the kid alone!"

The squat bald one looked up, saw Sherman coming and bellowed drunken laughter. "Look, boys, run for your lives. It's an old . . . codger . . . with a *hook!*"

The kid stood, swaying side to side. The man with long brown hair punched him in the face, which sent him flying backward. He landed in the dirt, arms and legs splayed apart, out cold.

Sherman got down on one knee, checked the young man's pulse. It was strong and steady. He would be okay. The kid looked worse up close, though. Smelled bad, too. Sherman glared up at the three men and felt the old rage rising in him. His blood felt hot after so many years, and when he stood back up, Sherman was certain of his next course of action. He knew what he would do and he knew how he would do it. He pointed at each of them in turn. "You'll all three clear the hell outta here if you know what's good for ya."

"Stick to fishing, old man," the man with brown hair said. "Put that hook to use somewhere else."

All three of them broke into hysterical laughter. "You're killin' me," the man with the half mustache said, bent double with his hands braced on his knees from laughing too hard. "Lemme catch my breath, boys. . . ."

Sherman made a quick assessment of the three men. Only the one with the slick black hair and half mustache had a gun belt. The other two were unarmed. It was clear to him which of the three he needed to eliminate first.

While they were still laughing, Sherman moved in close to the man with the half mustache and punched him straight in the throat. It was amazing just how quickly the laughing stopped. The man clutched at his neck with both hands, gurgling, gasping for breath. With satisfaction, Sherman watched him drop to his knees in the dirt, trying to suck in air. Not one to waste any time, or the grace granted him by surprise alone, Sherman hit the man again—his eyes fluttered and rolled up into his head, and he collapsed on his side. As Sherman turned to face the other two, the man with long brown hair was already advancing on him, the shock of the moment gone.

Sherman backed up a step, pressed the first two fingers of his left hand into his mouth and whistled loud and sharp. As the man with the long brown hair was about to dive on him and unleash a pounding, Titus leapt on him. Growling like a feral beast, Titus soon had the man with long brown hair pinned to the ground, curled up in a ball, as the dog tore the clothing from his body.

The squat bald man grabbed a length of timber from a nearby cart and held it at the ready. Sherman tentatively closed in, fist and hook raised.

"Come on, old man!"

Sherman ducked back as the bald brute lunged at him with the length of timber; then he leapt back in. When the other man attempted once again to skewer him with the length of timber, Sherman did little more than grab hold of it with his hand and pull on it. It sent the bald man stumbling forward toward him. Sherman stuck him with his hook, which caught the soft flesh of his flabby stomach and ripped it open. Sherman pulled the hook free and his opponent staggered away, holding his stomach and wailing in agony.

Sherman flicked the blood from his hook and turned slowly in a circle, looking for more trouble, but none came. The crowd looked on in horror as Titus made short work of the brown-haired man's garments. "Titus, heel," Sherman ordered. Immediately the dog withdrew and waited by his feet.

"What in the hell is going on here?" a voice thundered. Sherman looked to see Freehan push his way through the crowd. He took in the scene—the town drunk out cold in the street, the three abusers in various states of defeat and Sherman catching his breath, blood glistening on the curve of his prosthesis. The sheriff blinked.

"He stabbed me!" the bald man cried, pointing at Sherman. "Ripped my guts open!"

"I can see that, you dolt," Freehan said. "But Sherman Knowles don't go around town stabbing people with his hook, not unless they're doing something real bad, that is."

Sherman nodded over at the kid. "They were beating on him, Sheriff. I couldn't stand by while three men took on one. Just ain't fair."

"Is this true?" Freehan demanded of the three men.

The man with the half mustache got woozily to his feet. He was still holding his throat, and when he spoke, his voice was raspy and with a distinct whistle to it. "He punched me in the throat."

"I can hear that," Sheriff Freehan said. He looked at the man with the long brown hair and at his state of dishevelment. "As for you, I'm guessin' the hound got to you, didn't he?"

He nodded. Shamefaced and beaten.

The sheriff sighed, bent down, petted Titus fondly. He drew himself up and addressed Sherman next, arms folded. "As for you, did you really have to let 'em have such a bad whoopin'?"

"When they're beating three on one, yeah, I did," Sherman said.

Both men looked at the town drunk.

"It was bound to happen, making a pest of himself the way he's been doing," Freehan said with a sigh. He turned to the three louts. "Now, you three. I've never seen a one of you before. I want you to drag your sorry keisters inside that saloon, fetch your belongings or whatever you got in there and then get the hell out of my town."

The three of them hurried inside the saloon and, moments later, were hobbling down the street.

Sheriff Freehan turned to the crowd of townsfolk. "Show's over. All of you, go back to whatever it was you were doing before. Go on now."

On the ground, the town drunk stirred.

Freehan removed his hat and ran his fingers through his hair. "Damn . . . what am I gonna do with him, huh?"

Sherman looked at Titus.

Titus looked at him.

Sherman said, "I'll take him."

"You?" Freehan asked, stunned. He looked at Sherman. "Are you feeling all right? Did you take a knock to the head or anything? Come to think of it, did *any* of those idiots land a hit?"

"Not one," Sherman said. "I'm old but I'm not out."

Freehan slipped his hat back on. "Clearly. So explain to me, because I'm confused . . . exactly where will you take this young man?"

"To mine."

"What the devil for?"

Sherman shifted on his feet. He couldn't just leave the kid to fend for himself. He had defended him and now what? Was he supposed to just wash his hands of him? "I'll get him clean and sober. Set him right," he said.

"That's a mighty big undertaking," Freehan said doubtfully. "How—"

"Leave the how to me. All I need is a small wagon so I can pile him in the back. I don't want him falling off the back of my horse. Wagon's for the best. Gotta get him to mine somehow."

Freehan looked at the kid again. He rubbed at the stubble on his jawline as he pondered the problem. He looked up. Saw Mac at the threshold to the general store. The sheriff pointed to him. "Hey, Mac, you still got that wagon of yours?"

"Of course," Mac said nervously. "We use it for deliveries and the like."

"It'll be perfect." Sheriff Freehan turned to Sherman.

"He'll never let me use it," Sherman said.

The sheriff pulled a face. "Where there's a will . . ."

M AC PULLED THE bolts across at the back of the wagon and lowered the rear flap. He sounded flustered and annoyed that he'd been coerced into helping Sherman. But since the sheriff had ridden with them also, his tongue was tied. It did not, however, prevent Mac from glaring at Freehan with contempt when he wasn't looking.

"These are not the deliveries I am used to making," Mac said, grimacing from the smell of the kid as he and Sherman pulled him out of the wagon. Mac had him under the armpits, Sherman had his feet, and between the two of them, they managed to get him out. The stench was a mixture of stale sweat, old booze and dried urine. They carried him into the house, where Sherman instructed Mac to back himself into the bedroom.

"I'll give him my bed for a couple of nights," Sherman said.

"You're a braver man than I," Mac said, helping deposit the kid onto the bed. "What with that stink . . ."

"Believe me, Mac, it ain't out of the goodness of my heart," Sherman said, ushering him from the room. "There are no windows, and I can fit a bolt to the outside of the door."

Mac looked at him in shock. "You . . . you . . . can't be serious."

"What?"

"You're going to imprison him here?"

Sherman shrugged. "Only way this is gonna work. Kid's gotta be contained and put through it. Gotta be a—what d'you call it?—an intersection."

"I think you mean an intervention."

"That's the one."

Sheriff Freehan stood in the entrance to Sherman's cabin, thumbs hooked in his belt, listening to the whole exchange. "Cold turkey will be just the ticket."

"You both should know, cold turkey can kill a man," Mac warned them.

Sherman looked at the kid, asleep where he'd been laid on the bed. Out for the count following his beating in town. "Either he'll make it, or he won't. I guess we'll know for sure in a couple of days."

S HERMAN AND SHERIFF Freehan watched Mac head off in his wagon. The sheriff offered Sherman his bag of tobacco and the two men sat on the porch a moment having a smoke. Titus nosed about around the sheriff's chair and he leaned down to scratch the dog between the ears.

"Mac's the jittery type, ain't he?" Sherman ob-

served, nodding in the direction the store owner had
headed off in.

"True, but he's a good man. You don't oftentimes
find good, brave men, in my experience. Mostly good
cowards and brave fools."

"I reckon you're right."

Sheriff Freehan drew on his pipe. "Brave man with
bad intentions is a dangerous man indeed. Wouldn't
you agree?"

Sherman kept his mouth shut. It wasn't that he
didn't have an opinion about what the sheriff had just
said—it was that sharing his opinion would not have
done him any favors. Not where the sheriff was concerned, at least.

Freehan continued. "That sure was something, the
way you handled those men from the saloon. Single-
handedly, too. Literally *and* figuratively."

"I've been in my fair share of scraps."

"I don't doubt it," the sheriff said, chuckling. "Me,
too. But I've never seen a man stabbed with a hook
before. Just goes to show, there's a first time for everything."

Sherman had to admit there was a funny side. He
couldn't help but laugh, too. "Don't think those three
idiots are gonna forget Elam Hollow in a hurry."

"Amen to that."

Sherman shook his head in disgust. "Settin' on that
kid, three on one like that . . . I couldn't let it stand."

Freehan said, "Y'know, I gotta say, Mac's right
about one thing. Cold turkey can kill a fella. Wonder if
the kid's strong enough to make it to the other side."

"I know he's right. But either the kid dies here on a
bed, or he dies on a street. This is the only chance he's
got, the way I see it."

"I fear you're right," Freehan said. "I didn't want to
kick the kid out of town. But didn't know how to get

him off the street, either. Maybe I should've put him in a cell and let him sweat it out. I don't know. I should've seen it."

"People gotta fix their own problems, Sheriff," Sherman said. "Ain't nobody gonna hold your hand in this world. Not out here in the sticks, livin' this kinda life."

Freehan drew on his pipe and blew a couple of smoke rings. "Time will tell, then."

CHAPTER THREE

H E WAITED FOR the kid to come around, and as the young man looked about in bewilderment, Sherman told him not to panic and explained where he was. "You're in my cabin. I brought you here so you can rest. You know, get on the mend."

"I hurt all over," the kid said, wincing as he tried to sit up.

"Lift your shirt up. Let's get a look at those ribs."

The kid pulled his shirt up, moaning from the pain involved in lifting his arms. Sherman made a quick examination of the boy's ribs. He was black-and-blue all over. Those three brutes had given him a good kicking—that was for sure.

"You'll want to strap those. Want me to do it?"

The kid nodded but was in too much discomfort to speak. Sherman bound the boy's ribs tightly, the only way he knew. He'd picked up a few things over the years: how to set a broken leg, a broken arm; how to stitch up a wound; how to retrieve a bullet when it was embedded in flesh or bone. None of which compared to his most gruesome skill from time spent on the trail: pulling teeth. That one was always guaranteed to separate the men from the boys.

He told his guest to lie back down.

"Thanks for that."

"Don't mention it. You got a name, kid?"

The kid swallowed. "Bobby."

"Just Bobby?"

"Bobby Woodward."

"Good to meet you, Bobby Woodward. I'm Sherman Knowles."

Bobby said, "What am I doing here?"

"You're here to get better," Sherman said. He left the room and returned with an empty bucket, two skins of water and some food.

"What's that for?"

"That's to see you through," Sherman said. "Fresh drinking water. A bucket to puke in, or go to toilet in, whatever the case may be. Some food there to build your strength. There's plenty of wood there to feed the burner. You'll be warm."

Bobby frowned at him. "I . . . I don't understand."

"All of that will last you a couple of days, at least. I'll be back in here after that to check in on you. I'm only the other side of the door."

Bobby tried to get up but couldn't. He was too sore. Too beaten. "Please, I don't understand what's happening here."

Sherman was already backing out of the room. "You're gettin' clean, Bobby Woodward. Won't feel like it for a few days. In fact, it'll probably feel like you're dying. But don't fret. Just get through it. I'm going to save your life."

Before Bobby could stall him with a slew of questions, Sherman left the room and shut the door behind him. He hammered it shut with a couple of nails and fixed a bolt in place. He slid it across, to hold it for certain. Sherman had seen men go cold turkey and it was not a pretty sight. The addicted became unstable. They cracked. The best thing for Bobby was to keep him contained and pray he didn't succumb to his addiction.

Titus scratched at the door, whining. "Settle down now," Sherman told the dog, ushering him away from the bedroom door. He led Titus outside for a walk. They were no more than a hundred yards from the cabin when the shouting started.

B OBBY MUST HAVE fallen asleep because Sherman had been back inside the cabin a couple of hours, preparing a stew, before he heard movement from the bedroom. He could hear the kid pacing back and forth in there.

Titus had been dozing a couple of feet away from the fire. Now he sat up, listening. The dog looked at his master uncertainly. Sherman resumed stirring his stew. "I know, boy. It pains me, too. But it's for the best."

Bobby smacked his hands against the other side of the door. He yelled, but it was indiscernible noise, muffled by the thick timber. Sherman sat listening, fighting every urge to call the whole thing off and just cut the kid loose. But how would that be helping him? Sherman knew that if somebody—it didn't even need to be him; it could have been anyone—if somebody didn't intervene and put a stop to what Bobby was doing, he'd drink himself to death. That or he would upset a couple of guys at the saloon, and this time there wouldn't be a Sherman Knowles around to save him. They'd kick him until he died and leave him to rot in the street.

Sherman had seen men go cold turkey. He'd helped them through it. It was like an exorcism. Running the devil out and seeing to it he didn't make a return. It was hard to become addicted to something, then have the thing you're hooked on taken away with nothing to replace it. But getting to the other side made you stronger, made you better. He wanted that for Bobby Woodward. Bobby was somebody's son. . . .

Since coming to Elam Hollow, Sherman had given a lot of thought to paying penance for past sins and misdeeds. Righting the wrongs, best he could. The local priest, a Danish immigrant called Hulegaard, had explained to Sherman the concept of atonement, and ever since that conversation one Sunday, it had been all that Sherman could think about. On the ride out to see his brother one last time, Sherman had thought about ways he could repair a little of the damage he'd done. What atonement might mean for a man who'd shot and killed people.

Sometimes he caught himself slipping into his older, selfish ways. In those moments it was all he could do to change his course and get himself back on track. He'd killed many people in the past, most of them bad . . . some not. Bounty hunters acted under the sanction of the law. They were not viewed as monsters but enforcers performing a service. He had not been so different, even if his own services were on the outside of the law. The difference was, he could remember *willing* his quarry to run just so he could shoot them as they fled. And did he relish the act of killing?

Sherman was ashamed to admit that he had.

Bobby beat against the door, yelling at the top of his lungs. He seemed to have sobered up some, because there was an edge to his anger that had not been there before. Sherman stopped stirring his stew. He set the ladle aside and got up. Standing next to the door, he could see the wood resounding with every hit. A bigger man than Bobby might've got the door jumping against its hinges and lock, but Bobby's hits registered more like tremors through the timbers. His voice was louder now, though. More certain of itself.

This time Sherman could make out what the kid was saying, though he did have to strain to hear it all. The kid threatened to go to the sheriff, to have Sherman arrested for imprisonment and so on.

Sherman looked at Titus. "Little does this calf realize the sheriff's just as damned guilty as I am," he said, shaking his head and chuckling to himself.

The kid said that when he got out, he was going to kill Sherman himself. He was stronger than he looked, apparently, and Sherman would regret treating him the way he was.

"I've heard enough," Sherman groaned, returning to his stew. He picked up the ladle again and stirred it. "I'd rather watch these carrots soften than listen to that dross."

The kid pounded his fists against the door.

Titus laid his head on his front paws, closed his eyes and fell asleep listening to their guest's protestations.

O N THE THIRD day, no sound came from the bedroom. Sherman was hesitant to just unlock the door and open it, lest the kid try to bolt. But he found himself with a conundrum. The kid was due fresh water now. Food, too. He'd probably need his bucket emptied, while Sherman was at it. But Sherman envisioned all kinds of scenarios to account for the newfound silence. The kid could've passed out, could've committed suicide for all he knew. He could also be waiting with a bucketful of his own urine and feces, waiting for the door to open so he could throw the disgusting contents over Sherman. Whatever the case, Sherman knew he could not leave the kid alone any longer. He had to open the door, see what was what.

The kid was lying on his stomach, face to one side with a steady dribble down his cheek as he slept. He was ghostly white, with heavy bags under his eyes. The room stank from what Bobby had left in the bucket. Sherman made sure to dispose of that first and returned the empty bucket to the room. Next, he replenished the water and the food—not that Bobby had eaten much. Just scraps, really. A bite of this, a bite of that. Sherman tossed the rest into Titus's bowl, where it was devoured happily.

Added to the smell of human waste was the stench of Bobby himself. The sweat and booze and staleness. As if he'd gotten wet, dried in the sun, gotten wet again, dried . . . and on and on. As Sherman looked on, Bobby stirred. He cracked an eye open, looked directly at Sherman. He did not attempt to speak, as if he didn't possess the energy, but he followed Sherman as he moved about the room.

"Look like you're good again. I'm going to check on you every couple of hours now. I've seen men go through this before. You fight it. Then you get ill," Sherman said. "Next you'll likely get a fever. That's when it'll make or break you, Bobby."

He left the room and bolted the door shut again.

A T THE BREAK of the next day, Sherman unbolted the door to the bedroom and walked in to find Bobby shivering on the cot. The kid was curled up, hugging himself. Sherman placed his palm to Bobby's forehead, found him dripping wet with perspiration. He was red-hot to the touch, too.

Bobby was hallucinating. Staring up at the ceiling,

eyes wide and fearful, obviously glimpsing something
up there in the shadows and the cobwebs. Something
nightmarish.

"What you're seein', it ain't real," Sherman told
him. But he couldn't be sure that Bobby heard him
at all.

Sherman took one of the skins and forced Bobby to
drink. Then he wet a rag with water and dabbed at
Bobby's forehead.

The kid raised a hand, pointed at the recess over his
head. "He's coming!" he exclaimed through clenched
teeth. "He's coming to do to me what he did to them. . . ."

"Who?"

No answer.

The men Sherman had watched go cold turkey to
beat the demon in the bottle had all gone the same
way. Imagined monstrous things. Remembered old
torments and sins. Saw faces of men and women long
gone, consigned to the dust.

Bobby covered his eyes. "I can't let him see me.
He's the devil."

"Who's the devil, kid?" Sherman asked.

But Bobby had begun to weep and all Sherman
could do was try to keep him cool and hydrated. When
Bobby settled again, Sherman left the room, but this
time he did not shut and bolt the door. Titus padded in
and out of the room, checking on Bobby himself. Sherman checked on him all through the night, and by the
morning, to Sherman's relief, the fever had passed.

The next day, Bobby rose from the cot and wandered into the main room, the fur off the bed around
his shoulders. He looked at Sherman and frowned.
"Who are you?"

"Sherman Knowles. We're already acquainted."

"Are we?"

Sherman nodded.

"Where am I?"

"My home."

"Why?"

Sherman got up, steered the kid to the table and forced him to sit. "First things first. I'm making coffee."

"Coffee?"

"Yeah, you know . . ." Sherman searched for some way of giving further meaning and found himself wanting. He shrugged and said, "Hell, it's coffee. What is there to say? Are you having some or not?"

Bobby nodded. He looked thin and wasted. He looked cold.

"Where did you say I am again?"

Sherman set the coffee going. "My cabin."

As they waited for the coffee, Sherman told Bobby about the beating he had received in the street. He told him how the sheriff and Mac, the owner of the general store, had helped bring Bobby to his cabin.

"Why would you help me?"

Sherman didn't have an answer straightaway. He poured them both coffee and set Bobby's down in front of him. "I don't really know."

Bobby sipped the coffee. He winced, it was so hot. "Was I in a bad way?"

Sherman smiled. "Have you seen yourself right now? You're *in* a bad way, kid, no doubt about it. But you were about to go drink yourself to death or, worse, get yourself in more strife and wind up dead that way."

"Why didn't I go to the doctor's?"

Sherman set about filling his pipe. "Doc Walker wouldn't go easy on you. He'd likely have thrown you out and told you just to sober up. Trouble is, I've been around a long time, and I know that approach don't work. You have to have it all taken out of your hands.

Once the bottle's got a hold on you, there's only one thing for it."

"What's that?"

"Cold turkey. Make a clean break from it. Only thing you can do."

Bobby sipped at his coffee. "I don't get what's in it for you."

That stunned Sherman. He stopped stuffing the tobacco into his pipe. "What do you mean?"

"I don't see what you have to gain."

"Nothing."

"Then why help?" Bobby asked.

Sherman put the pipe down for a moment. "I was once a very different kind of man. I haven't done a lot of good. Let's put it that way. But I'm trying to fix that. I figure, helping folk out of a jam, that's one way of repenting. It helps me rest easy, knowing I've paid something back."

Bobby sipped more of the coffee, then turned a sickly shade of green. The blood drained from his face and he looked as though he were about to hurl. Sherman helped him get outside, seconds before Bobby spewed uncontrollably over the side of the porch, clutching the rail as the contents of his stomach burst from his mouth. Sherman had to look away. Bobby was throwing up bile now, bright yellow and toxic in appearance.

"Damn, kid. You got anything left?"

"I don't know," Bobby moaned, clutching the porch rail. He was shaking even though it was almost warm out.

"You done?"

"I think so. . . ."

Sherman helped him back to the bedroom and told him to lie back down. "Get yourself some more shuteye. In a couple of hours, try some food."

Bobby lay back down. "The men you said went cold turkey . . . how did they fare?"

"Like you, I guess," Sherman said. "Like they'd been put through hell."

Bobby asked, "Did they ever touch booze again?"

"Hard to say. Every man is different."

"Think I will?"

Sherman said, "Only you can answer that one."

He left the room, pulled the door to and looked around for Titus, but the dog was not in the cabin. Sherman went outside, found Titus down by the side of the porch, licking Bobby's vomit off the grass. Sherman yelled at the dog, waving his arms up and down. "Damn you, Titus! Get away from that! Ain't there anythin' you *won't* eat?"

I T WAS DARK before Bobby rose again. Sherman gave the kid bread that was past its best and tea with honey in it. He instructed Bobby to eat just a little at a time. While Bobby ate, Sherman heated a pot of water over the fire. Next he filled a big basin with it.

"What's that for?"

Sherman folded his arms. "Well, you're gonna strip down to what God equipped you with, and you're gonna wash the stink from your body. I got hot water. I got soap. I got some clothes you can wear, though they may not fit too good. But, you know, it is what it is."

"Do I smell that bad?"

"Afraid so," Sherman said.

Bobby lifted his arm and winced when he sniffed himself.

Sherman said, "See what I mean? Not much difference between you and a skunk's behind right about now."

* * *

THE CLOTHES BARELY fit—Bobby was far too skinny—but they were better than the rotted rags he'd been wearing. And by the time he finished washing himself, Bobby looked positively reformed to Sherman's eyes.

"Couldn't get you any boots," Sherman said. "Unfortunately I don't have spares. So you'll have to either wear what you had or go barefoot. It's up to you."

"Guess I'll just wear my own for now."

Sherman nodded. "Good. How you feeling?"

"Not too bad," Bobby said. He hunkered down next to Titus, paying the dog some attention for the first time since he'd come around. "Hello."

"That there's Titus."

"He's a big old boy, isn't he?" Bobby remarked, Titus lifting his head so that Bobby could scratch under his chin.

Sherman said, "Same as his pa was. He was a working dog, too."

"A working dog?"

"I'm a houndsman. That's what I do for a living," Sherman explained. "Titus and me, we go out, track and kill mountain lions. Track wolves. Go trapping. It's a way of life that ain't to everybody's taste, I guess, but it suits us."

"So you live here on your own."

"When I'm not helping fellas out and takin' 'em off the streets."

Bobby looked away, visibly ashamed. "This isn't what I come from. It's not what I'm meant to be."

"But it's what you are, and you gotta accept that. Can't paint a rosy picture of something when what's needed is for you to take a good hard look at it on its own terms."

"Are you always this philosophical?"

"Not usually, no," Sherman said. "Tell the truth, I don't get any visitors out here. Don't hold that many conversations, ordinarily. Except with Titus, and he ain't got a lot to say for himself."

"I can imagine . . . ," Bobby said, stroking the dog.

The kid seemed to be on the mend, but Sherman knew it would not be so easy or so simple. You did not pass through the worst of the withdrawal and be completely rid of it. The craving, the thirst, it came on you when you least expected it. Later, Bobby would want a drink. No, he would *need* a drink. His body would cry out for it. His blood would burn in his veins and his brain would feel like it was roasting in his skull. A fire only booze could ever extinguish.

S URE ENOUGH, AS the afternoon transitioned to evening, Bobby began to shake all over. Sherman told him to go sit as close to the fire as he could bear. But it became clear that there was more than a chill making Bobby tremble head to toe.

He looked on as Bobby clutched his stomach, the cramps kicking in. "You all right there, kid?"

"Wh-what's happening t-to me?" Bobby gasped, curling up in a ball in front of the fire as it crackled in the grate.

"Your body wants booze because that's all you've been giving it. It's got used to the taste and the effect. It knows that you'll do whatever you can to stop the shakes, stop the pain," Sherman told him. "You gotta realize, you're not fightin' the booze. You're fightin' your body."

Bobby grimaced from the discomfort and hugged himself so hard, his knuckles turned white. Teeth bared, gnashed tight together, Bobby rode each wave of pain as it came and passed through him. All Sherman could do was watch and wait for the inevitable question, the one he knew the kid would ask—the same question he'd heard from other men facing down the demon. To his surprise, it came sooner than expected.

Bobby looked at him with a pained expression. "Do you have anything?"

"Like what?"

"Whiskey? Beer? Anything to take the edge off," Bobby said, wiping at his drool. "Just a little."

"Oh, you're asking if I'm gonna be weaning you off with small amounts?"

"Yes." Bobby closed his eyes. His legs twitched, jerking up and down sporadically as the cravings came and went. "Please . . ."

Sherman almost wanted to get the kid some booze, just so he wouldn't be in any further discomfort. But he knew it would be the worst thing he could do. So he got Bobby up, helped him to the cot. "Push through it. You'll be on the other side sooner than you think."

Bobby lay back on the cot, shivering. "Just . . . one . . . drink . . ."

"Listen to me," Sherman said, speaking loud and clear. "You ain't gettin' booze from me. That's not what I did this for. I'd sooner put a bullet in your head than give you a drink. In fact, take that as a promise. I *will* put a bullet in you before feeding your habit."

Bobby began to cry like a child.

Sherman left the room and bolted the door shut. Sure enough, it wasn't long before Bobby was slamming himself against the door to get loose. Yelling for a drink (*Just the one!*) and promising to make it his last.

Sherman had heard it all before.

Titus went to the door and began barking furiously. Sherman called him over and sat holding the dog's head in his hands. "Stay here," he said in a soothing manner. He looked into Titus's eyes and did not see what he saw in the eyes of men. Things were simpler with dogs. They were black-and-white.

"Why can't people be like you, eh, boy?" he asked him.

The dog looked up at him with his large magnanimous eyes, so filled with wisdom that Sherman sometimes wondered if he actually did understand man's language. But if Titus had an answer to Sherman's query, he kept it firmly to himself.

CHAPTER FOUR

I T CAME AND went, but after nearly a week, there
were no more fits of rage. No more fevers. No more
aching cramps or crushing headaches. As Sherman
looked on, Bobby's appetite grew stronger, as did
Bobby himself. He ate like a man: roasted rabbit,
hearty bowls of stew, scoffing down plates of eggs and
bacon cooked in a skillet.

"I think you're through the worst," Sherman told
Bobby one morning.

Bobby rubbed at his stomach. "Feels like it," he
said.

"Fancy helping me fish?"

"Today?"

Sherman nodded.

"Sure," Bobby said without hesitation. "You takin'
Titus along?"

"He'd tag along even if I didn't *want* him to," Sherman told him. They set out after breakfast and headed
for the stream that cut through a meadow two fields

over. Sherman led Bobby through tall grass, elbow high. It was the farthest Bobby had been since he'd come to the cabin.

It was quiet save for the distant trickle of the stream and the dry sounds of crickets in the grass rubbing the edges of their forewings together. The azure firmament seemed to have no limits, the perfect blue marred only by a thin ridge of white cloud on the horizon.

"Thanks for everything you've done," Bobby said. "Y'know, savin' me and all."

Sherman glanced at him. "I didn't save you. I just locked you up, kid."

"Well, you know what I mean."

Neither man said anything further until they reached the stream and Bobby remarked that it was more like a river than a stream. He'd expected something narrower and not so deep.

"It's wide, but it's shallow all the way. This whole section, all of it, shallow as hell," Sherman said. He took his rod and line and walked out into the middle of the current to demonstrate. The water barely reached his knees. "See? No good for fishing. Not really. But we're not after fish."

"We're not?"

Sherman shook his head. "We are not."

"What're we after, then?"

"Eels," Sherman said with a grin.

Bobby pulled a face. *"Eels?"*

"You bet. Some good eating, they are," Sherman said, casting a line into the water.

Titus bounded out into the water and attempted to swim up into the current, paddling energetically with his head held high above the roiling surface. The dog was past his prime now, not that anyone would've been able to tell. He still had the energy and strength of a pup.

Sherman let the float drift with the current along

the bank, and when it'd gotten too far, he reeled it in and repeated the process. After several attempts, both men just watching the water, Sherman got a bite. He took care in reeling it in, and sure enough, there was an eel writhing at the end, coiling itself around the hook to climb the line and escape. "Here we go."

Sherman carried the eel over to where Bobby was standing. Once on dry land, he proceeded to take hold of the eel and cut it free. It slithered around his hand, encircling itself around his wrist. "That bucket I told you to bring along, go fill it halfway with water."

"Sure," Bobby said. He fetched the bucket, filled it with water from the stream and watched as Sherman deposited the eel in it. "You're not gonna kill it first?"

"No need. Just cover the top with something, prevent it from escaping."

"It can do that?"

Sherman shrugged. "It's basically a snake. It can get out of that bucket with ease if it wants to. That's why you only ever fill it halfway and make sure somethin' is covering the top."

Titus hopped through the shallows of the stream, and on the near bank, the dog stood on the muddy silt and shook all over, droplets of water flying everywhere.

Sherman returned to fishing the edges of the stream, playing the float and lure through the fine, silky vegetation just below the water's surface. Sure enough, before too long, Sherman had another bite. Within an hour, there were half a dozen eels in the bucket, all writhing around and attempting to break free.

"You fish this stream much?" Bobby asked as they gathered their gear to head back to the cabin.

"On and off. A few times I've pulled a pike out of here. They're good eating, I can tell you. Tough to beach, though. And they've got a set of jaws on 'em."

"They bite?"

"If you let 'em."

Bobby looked at Sherman's hook. "Is that how you lost your hand?"

To his surprise, the houndsman busted out laughing at the suggestion. He laughed so hard, so loud, he had to catch his breath. "No, kid, no," Sherman said, still chuckling to himself. "They got a bite but they ain't no alligator."

They walked back toward the cabin, Bobby carrying the bucket of eels. He could feel them moving around. "Have you always lived in Nebraska?"

"Just the last decade or so," Sherman said. "Maybe a bit longer than that. The years blur for me sometimes. You won't understand this, kid, but the longer you live, it all kind of blends together."

"So where are you from, then?" Bobby asked.

"Wyoming."

"Ever been back there?"

Sherman's face hardened. "A few times."

"I don't think I'll ever go back."

"Where do you hail from, kid?"

Bobby said, "Hellhole called Amity Creek."

"Your folks there?"

"Sorta," Bobby said. "Mom died when I was a kid. Pop brought me up after that."

Sherman nodded. "No siblings, huh?"

Bobby told him there'd just been him. "Pop was a cattle rancher. We had a big say in that town. Could pretty much do whatever, to be honest."

"Sounds like a powerful man."

"Yeah."

"You talk as if he's died," Sherman said. "Has he?"

Bobby moved the heavy bucket from one hand to the other. "I don't know. I hope so."

Sherman did not remark on the kid's statement, just took it for what it was. "My parents passed a long time ago now. Had a brother. Jedediah. He passed only recently."

"Did he? I'm sorry," Bobby said.

"I was on my way home from the funeral when I saw those three fellas beating you up in the street, and the townsfolk just standing there watching."

"Cowards," Bobby spat.

Sherman frowned at him. "Kid, you can't blame 'em for not getting involved. They didn't know you from Adam. And to tell the truth, to their eyes, you weren't worth the trouble. Way you was at the time, can't say I blame them."

"That bad, huh?"

"Yeah. That bad."

"How did your brother pass?" Bobby asked, steering the conversation away from that fateful afternoon in town—of which he had no recollection at all.

"A sickness. He died with us at his side. Just kind of slipped away in the end, which was best for him," Sherman said. "I've seen men die. I've seen 'em scream and scream. Of all the deaths I've witnessed, Jed's was the most humane, by far."

"I feel kind of bad you're grieving your brother and you've got stuck with me," Bobby admitted.

Sherman said, "Actually, I think you helped."

"How d'you reckon that?"

"I didn't mope about in grief over Jed. There wasn't time. You gave me something to do."

"I think I understand that."

They reached the cabin. Titus heard something in the grasses behind, and he dashed into them, disappearing completely in the tall, thin green stems.

"Ain't you worried he might get lost?"

Sherman waved a hand. "That dog? No. He'll be back. Hopefully, he catches something worth cooking. . . ."

* * *

THEY STOOD ON the porch as Sherman showed Bobby how to prepare eels. First thing he did was take an eel from the bucket of water, hold it to the porch floorboards and stave it in its head with a hammer. "Some use a mallet. Some like to use one of those truncheons. You know, like a baton. I've always used this hammer." It was the small kind, attached to a handle no more than an inch thick, useful for knocking in pins but not much more. "It's light enough and gets the job done without any fuss."

Sherman gave the eel one quick, sharp blow to the head. It was killed instantly and fell limp in his hand. He immediately cut the head off and the tail, then set the body to one side. One by one, he did the same to all the eels in the bucket, save one.

"What's happening to that one?"

Sherman handed him the hammer. It was slick with slime and blood, the end smothered in gelatinous crushed eel brain. "That one's for you, kid."

"Okay," Bobby said, gingerly removing the eel from the bucket. It writhed and slithered in his grip, attempting to break loose.

"Hold it to the boards." Bobby did so and Sherman watched over his shoulder. "That's it. Pin it down so you get a clear shot at its head. One good clean kill is what you want. It's the only way to end an animal's life—so it don't know what's happened."

"I've killed an animal before," Bobby said.

Sherman said, "Then you should have no trouble with this one."

Bobby lifted the hammer and brought it down on the eel's head in one sharp movement.

The eel ceased writhing.

Sherman took the hammer. "Good. Here you go. Off with the head and tail, just like I did."

Bobby accepted the knife from him and immediately severed the eel's head and tail. He put the eel's body alongside the rest.

"Okay. Now we need a smaller knife for this next part," Sherman said, swapping the bigger knife he'd given Bobby for a smaller, more delicate knife. "Slice it up the belly, from one end to the other. Then peel it open with your fingers so you can see the guts."

Bobby did as he was told, not relishing in the slightest the warm, moist innards of the eel against his fingertips.

Sherman nodded along. "Good job. Push those guts to one side and slice along the membrane. That's it. Cut it away from the backbone."

Bobby ran the sharp edge of the small knife along the backbone, separating the membrane from the bone.

"Move the guts to the other side and do the same thing. Cut the membrane away. The guts should then just fall out and pull away."

With that done, Sherman instructed Bobby to run the knife along the backbone from the outside, easing the flesh from the spine.

"There we go. We've got eel fillets," Sherman said, patting him on the back. "Just a few more and you're done."

When Bobby had done them all, he was left with a pile of eel fillets, and a pile of eel guts and bones. The boards were covered in blood and slime. Titus padded over and began to lick at it.

"Right. Go fetch some fresh water. We gotta wash these. Then we can cook 'em."

When the fillets were rinsed clean, they took them inside and Sherman demonstrated how to fry them, turning the fillets frequently in the hot fat so they didn't blacken and burn. "Eel is a sweet, delicate meat. It don't take a lot of cooking. But if you don't cook it through, that's when you get sick on it. Been there, done that a few times."

Sherman fried the eel and they ate a couple of fillets each with their fingers, hot from the pan, saving the rest for later.

"How is it?" Sherman asked.

"Well, my fingers stink of eel, but you're right. That sure is sweet meat. I'm pretty impressed."

Sherman winked. "Told you."

S HERMAN KEPT AN old mule in the barn next to the cabin and would often take her along when he went trapping. She'd carry the supplies and whatever he caught, while his own horse bore the burden of carrying him wherever they were headed. He wasn't a heavy man, but he wasn't light, either. However Bobby was small enough for the mule to manage, so they rode that way into town early the next morning. Sherman told Titus to stay behind, and when the dog attempted to leave the porch and follow along, Sherman pointed a finger in his direction. "Stay, I said."

Titus whined in disapproval.

"Good dog," Sherman said.

"Ain't looking forward to this," Bobby said, glancing back at Titus. The dog lay down on the porch boards and watched them leave. "Ain't looking forward to this one bit."

"I know it knocks your pride, returning to town," Sherman said, "particularly because you're sober now. But it's gotta be done. You need the doc to have a look at you, give you the once-over."

"I feel fine."

Sherman rolled his eyes. "There I was thinking we'd already settled this. . . ."

"If I feel fine, and I'm off the booze, what's there to check?"

"A lot," Sherman said. "Damn, kid. You're going and that's it."

Bobby looked at him. "No disrespect, Sherman, but you're not my pop. I'm a full-grown man. I can decide for myself if I need to see the doctor or not."

"Well, will you look at that? Ain't that a thing?"

"What's that?"

Sherman's face was stern, his voice more so. "You couldn't have told me any of that a week ago when you were curled up in a ball on the floor, crying in pain because you needed a drink, eh? Or am I wrong?"

Bobby mumbled something under his breath.

"What was that? I didn't hear you."

Bobby spoke up. "I said, fine, I'll see the doctor. Are you happy now?"

Sherman spurred his horse forward.

T HEY APPROACHED TOWN and Sherman took the opportunity to fill his pipe. He'd not been back since the fight and wondered if there'd be any uncomfortable interactions with the townsfolk upon his return, but there were none. They just gave him a wide berth, which didn't bother him in the slightest. He'd grown accustomed to people keeping out of his way and he much preferred that to having them in his face.

Bobby kept his head down, but it didn't stop folk from looking in his direction and talking among themselves in hushed voices or gossiping from behind covered mouths.

"Pay them no mind," Sherman told him as they

hitched the horse and mule to a nearby post. "Some of these people got nothin' better to do with their time."

"I don't care," Bobby lied, when he clearly did. The kid had no poker face—all his emotions on display for the world to see and interpret.

Sherman walked with him to the doctor's office and told him he'd wait outside until he'd been seen. Half an hour later, Bobby emerged from the office, followed by Dr. Walker.

"Can I see you for a sec, Sherman?"

"Sure thing, Doc," Sherman said. "Won't be a minute, kid."

Bobby didn't say anything.

Sherman followed Walker inside to his office. "What's this about?"

"Are you crazy?"

"Not that I know of."

Walker sat on the edge of his desk and crossed his arms. "You hit your head recently? Anything like that?"

Sherman knocked against his temple with his knuckles. "Nope. Still as hollow as ever."

"It's not funny."

"Sorry."

"You know you could've killed that boy? It's one of the most reckless things I've ever heard of," Walker said.

Sherman raised his hands. "Doc, I don't wanna step on your toes here. But I've seen men go cold turkey before. Men I knew very well. I know what I'm doing."

"Only you *don't*. It was a reckless thing to do, and I wanted you to know that."

Sherman nodded as if accepting the criticism. "Fair enough. I'll take that."

"Good. Glad we understand each other."

"Hold on, I'm not done," Sherman said. "I'll accept there's a chance going cold turkey could've killed the boy. But I'm the only one in this godforsaken town was willing to do anything to help him. That's gotta count for something."

Doc Walker sighed. "Is the young man your ward now, Sherman?"

"I don't know. Hadn't really thought about it. Why d'you ask?"

"Because he's gonna need a watchful eye looking out for him," Walker said. "If you've the experience you claim to have had, you'll know that he could slip into his old habits anytime."

Sherman rolled his eyes. "Can't tell an old dog what he already knows, Doc," he said. "I know what to watch for."

"So long as you do."

"Has anyone ever told you that you're the baddest man in all of Elam Hollow?"

Walker gestured to the door. "Get the hell out of my office, Sherman."

B OBBY WATCHED SHERMAN leave the doctor's office and push his hat down onto his head.

"What was that about?"

Sherman frowned at him. "Curious about other's affairs, ain't you, kid?"

"I'm just asking."

"What was said in there is between doctor and patient," Sherman said.

Bobby looked away. "Keep your secrets, then."

"I intend to," Sherman said with a chuckle.

They crossed the main street and walked down a ways, past the saloon and the inviting air of frivolity and jovial comradeship spilling out from within. He saw Bobby wet his lips at the tang of the spilled beer wafting from the other side of the swing doors.

Sherman said, "That's right. You keep walkin', Bobby. You're a better man for it."

Bobby wiped at his mouth with the sleeve of his shirt. The smell of the beer had caused his mouth to water. They continued walking until they were outside the sheriff's.

"What're we doing here?" Bobby asked, attempting to peer through the windows. "I'm not a fan of these places."

"Why's that? You been in trouble, kid?"

"Years ago. I spent a night in a cell after I caused some trouble. Didn't like it much," Bobby said. "Guess that's the idea, it being a deterrent as much as a punishment."

"True."

"Worked like a charm—that's for sure. I never wanted to go back," Bobby said.

Sherman thought of his own disdain for the law prior to his arrival in Elam Hollow. How he'd conditioned himself to see lawgivers as the natural-born enemy of bandits and criminals. When you got down to it, you came to realize those who enforced the law were just the same as those who actively broke it. It was just a case of different sides of the same street. Crooks one side, people like Sheriff Freehan the other.

The sheriff opened the door to his office. "Howdy."

"This here is the kid," Sherman said. "Bobby, this is Sheriff Freehan."

The two men shook hands.

"Good to see you looking so well, Bobby. You two coming inside for some coffee?"

Sherman shook his head. "Afraid not this time, Sheriff. We're a bit pressed for time."

"A shame, for sure. So what can I do for you boys?"

"Any news on those three men who beat down on Bobby?" Sherman asked.

"What kind of news?"

"Well, word on 'em coming back around here," Sherman said.

The sheriff pulled a face. "Not a whisper. Like I said to you before, I doubt we'll ever seen them again."

"True."

"If anything turns up, I'll tell you two," Freehan told them. "But unless that happens, just relax."

Dr. Walker's comment about Bobby being Sherman's ward now played on his mind. Was that what he'd done? Taken a broken wreck of a person and fixed him up, for the purpose of taking him into his stewardship? That hadn't been his motivation for helping Bobby . . . but the more Sherman rolled it around in his head, the more it seemed true. Bobby *was* his ward now, whether Sherman liked it or not. So he needed to give the kid a reason to stick around.

"See you, Sheriff," Sherman said.

They left the sheriff's and headed for the tailor shop.

"What on earth are we doing here?" Bobby asked.

Sherman showed him inside, the little bell over the door ringing as they stepped through. "Picking out clothes."

"With what? I don't have any money, last I checked," Bobby said.

"You just pick what you need, have it put on my tab," Sherman told him, giving Charlie Hunsicker the nod. "That all right by you, Charlie?"

"Your credit's good here, Sherman," Charlie said, coming out from behind the counter. He was an older man with a thick white beard, small round glasses and a bald head. "You know that. I got no problem with a man who pays his bill in full and on time."

"Appreciate it. Get the kid whatever he wants,"

Sherman said. He surveyed the hats on display, picked one off its peg and tried it on. "I'll take this, too. About time I was in line for a new one."

"Right you are, Sherman," Charlie said, making note of the hat's price.

Bobby drew near, voice lowered. "I don't get how this is gonna work. I can't afford this stuff."

"I know that."

"Then what's going on?"

"What's going on is, you're gonna get new clothes, which you're gonna need when the colder weather hits. Which it does sooner than later here."

"How am I supposed to pay you back?"

Sherman shrugged. "Maybe you can work with me. Pay it off that way."

"Really?"

"I could do with another set of hands if I'm honest. It'd be to my advantage. Consider this the same as having your wages in advance."

Bobby chewed it over a second. Then he said, "Okay, sure, that sounds pretty good to me."

Sherman placed a hand on the kid's shoulder. "I'm tellin' you now, though. Just to clarify things. I'm having my cot back. We can build you something in the other room. But I gotta say, I've missed my bed. My old back has, too."

WHERE BEFORE BOBBY had looked dejected and downtrodden, the new clothes, boots, hat and jacket seemed to lift his spirits. He walked with a spring in his step now, as if he were a new man. In some ways, Sherman supposed that he was. They weren't the finest clothes. They were rough and crudely made, but they were better than the rags he'd been wearing.

Before they left, he'd been sure to have Charlie throw in a pair of hard-wearing work gloves. He knew all too well the importance of keeping your hands protected from winter's cold, merciless bite.

"What're these for?" Bobby asked, looking at the gloves in his hand.

"For when you're working with me. Those you won't have to pay off with work. They're a gift."

Bobby looked at him. "Thanks."

"Don't get all emotional on me. It's just a pair of gloves," Sherman said dismissively. He produced his pipe. "Hang back a minute. Just want to fix a quick smoke before we head back."

Bobby leaned against the post and looked out at the town. "D'you know, months I was here and I never really got a good look at the place."

"That happens when you're perpetually drunk."

The kid looked ashamed. "I guess you're right." He cleared his throat. "Sherman? I wanted to say something."

"I said, don't get emotional, didn't I?"

"I know. I just—"

Sherman held up a finger in warning. "Save it," he said. "There's no need for that. Just remember you owe me now, so you'd better work for it. That's all I ask. Keep off the booze and work hard."

Bobby seemed to accept this. "Okay."

"I'm not being cold with you. But like you said earlier, I ain't your father. I ain't your blood. You're a grown man, and we got to work alongside each other as men. That's the understanding we gotta have. That's how it's gotta work, understand? The work I do is tough, and it can be miserable when things go wrong. Family don't come into it. Friends don't come into it. When we're out there, we're just two men."

"Understood," Bobby said. "Just two men."

Sherman's eyes narrowed as he looked ahead of them. "What the—"

Bobby matched his gaze.

Shouting broke out farther down the street. There seemed to be a commotion developing outside the sheriff's office. A lot of shouting and hollering in anger. Sherman looked at Bobby. "On the back of that wagon. Those boys look familiar to you, kid?"

Bobby peered down the street. At first his expression was blank. Then he walked down a couple of feet to get a better look. The three men who'd beaten Bobby and nearly killed him were in the back of a wagon. An older man, with dark gray hair and a dark gray mustache, was shouting and arguing with the sheriff from the front of the wagon.

"My memory was hazy before. But I remember them now!"

His smoke forgotten for the moment, Sherman said, "Walk with me, but hang back."

"Sure."

Together they headed back toward the sheriff's office, Sherman in the lead. As they got closer, Sherman's left hand went to his gun belt, unclipping the holster of the gun on that side. He kept his hand there, hovering over the weapon.

"You any good with that thing?" Bobby whispered.

"Used to be," Sherman said.

Sheriff Freehan was attempting to reason with the man in the wagon, trying to calm the situation down. But Sherman could see Freehan's patience wearing thin. He was decidedly flustered in the face and the sheriff was not a man who got flustered easily.

"You're unarmed, kid, so keep your distance. If anything starts, you have my blessing to make a run for it. Either that or let 'em use you for target practice. There's no such thing as yella when the bullets start flying."

Bobby didn't say anything. He just nodded once and veered away from Sherman a bit. Ready to make a break for it if needed.

Freehan was saying, "You boys were told last time to leave and I'm gonna say it again. There's no arguing over what happened. Just accept the whoopin' you got and be on your way."

"It ain't right!" the squat one was saying, lifting his shirt so that Freehan could see his wound. "Lookit them stitches!"

The three men were in various states of dishevelment from their beating in the street the week before. And when they laid eyes on Sherman and Bobby and saw them approaching, their presence seemed to tip the scale in favor of escalating their grievance.

"Speak of the devils and they appear," the man with brown hair said, leaning over the side of the wagon and spitting on the ground.

The older man at the front pointed at Sherman and Bobby. "This 'em?"

The man with slicked-back black hair looked at them with what seemed a mixture of hatred and curiosity. "That's them all right."

Freehan said, "Now listen, Mr. Strickland. Your boys were breaking the law doing what they did. That young fella there, he had all three beating on him. Can't tell me that's right, sir."

"No, I cannot," Strickland said. "But the fact remains they were set upon, and my oldest there got stabbed."

"I did it." Sherman lifted his hook. "With this."

Strickland said, "Sheriff, you hear him confessing?"

"I do."

"Well, ain't you gonna do somethin' about it?"

Sheriff Freehan remained impassive. "Don't believe I will. Your three boys don't belong here. I'll wager they cause trouble wherever they go, too. Best thing for all y'all is to turn around, head back the way you came."

Spencer Strickland stood, then got down from his wagon. Before Freehan could react in time, Strickland senior took hold of the sheriff by the lapels and threw him to the ground. Freehan hit the dirt.

"Hey!" Bobby yelled. "You can't do that!"

The Strickland boy with slicked-back black hair rose up at the rear of the wagon, pistol in hand.

Spencer Strickland gave the sheriff a short kick. "Stay put, lawman," he growled. He pointed at Sherman. "Goes for you too, old-timer. No one takes advantage of my boys when they're drunk. How's about you try it now with 'em sober, huh?"

The short, squat son with the bald head stood shoulder to shoulder with his weasel-faced brother. "Yeah, you *and* the runt!"

Sherman addressed them directly. "You boys should've learned your lesson."

They howled at that. All four Strickland men. Sheriff Freehan on the ground, his hand slowly moving toward his holster . . .

"What you gonna do with that old hook of yours? Gonna try 'n' gut me again, old man?" the short, squat brother leered.

Slick-back grinned. "I say we don't give him the chance," he said, thumbing back the hammer on his pistol.

Before he could so much as take aim, let alone let off a single round, Sherman pulled his own pistol and in one fluid movement, shot the gun from the man's hand. Slick-back screamed and bent forward clutching his hand as blood poured from it. His bald brother dove for cover.

The horses at the front of the wagon reared up on their hind legs, startled into action by the explosive

power of Sherman's pistol. He aimed his gun up away
from the wagon and let off two more shots. The bullets
ripped through the air over the boys' heads. Frightened out of their wits, the horses burst forward, sending all three Strickland brothers flying to the bed of
the wagon. The aimless wagon turned a half circle and
set off at a gallop in the other direction, out of town.
The Strickland clan was in the back of the wagon, in a
tangled heap, being thrown every which way and yelling for the horses to stop.

In the commotion, Sheriff Freehan got to his feet.
Distracted by the rapidly escaping wagon, Strickland
Senior turned back around and Freehan hit him square
on the jaw. He staggered back, dazed by the hit. Freehan freed his pistol and held the man at gunpoint, jab-
bing the muzzle into the middle of his chest. He
pressed the man back with shoves of his hand. "I
should hang you for attacking an officer of the law.
Now, you have got approximately sixty seconds to get
the hell out of here. Or your son won't be the only
Strickland with a hole shot through him today."

Without further argument or protestation, Spencer
Strickland left town on foot, hoping to catch up with
his sons at some point distant.

Sherman holstered his piece. "You all right there,
Sheriff?"

"Fine. Only thing bruised is my dignity from getting
shoved over," Freehan said. "Must be getting old."

"Aren't we all?" Sherman remarked.

Freehan spotted slick-back's pistol on the ground.
He bent down, picked it up and examined it. He
rubbed off the dirt with his sleeve. "Not a bad shooter.
Either of you two want it?"

"I can only manage the one," Sherman said.
"Sorry."

"I'll take it," Bobby spoke up.

"Know how to shoot it?"

"Yes, sir."

The sheriff handed it over. "Then it's yours. Those idiots won't be back to claim it—that's for sure."

They all looked down at the blood trail the three men left in their wake and Sherman was reminded of an elk he had shot one time. His aim had been thrown by a strong breeze that sent his shot wide. It was catastrophic to miss by a hair and have the animal suffer. He'd tracked the elk and found it, on its knees, panting in the snow. As if it were waiting for him to kill it. Blood ran down its side, gathering beneath it. Sherman lined up his shot but hesitated when the beast looked back at him, eyes still bright. Finally the gunshot had echoed throughout the forest. For Sherman it echoed still.

"When was the last time you fired that thing?" the sheriff asked.

"Ten years."

"Really?"

"I'm telling you the truth."

Freehan nodded. "What made you fire it now?"

Sherman holstered his pistol and looked at Bobby. He shrugged. "I don't know. Ain't a lot of thought comes into it. Sometimes you just do what you gotta do. It's no more complicated than that, really. You do what you gotta do."

CHAPTER FIVE

"An eventful day, huh, kid?" Sherman asked when they were halfway to the cabin.

Bobby drew up alongside him on the mule. Now that he wore proper clothes and a hat, he looked ridiculous riding along on the short, stubby creature, though, for its part, the mule was contented enough.

Bobby whistled through his teeth. "Could say that, yeah. Didn't think I'd ever see those guys again."

"I did."

"Really?"

Sherman spat off to the side, into the bushes. "Yep."

"How come?"

"Because I've seen that kind before. Hell, I've *been* that kind before. Sometimes men just can't let something go. Pride gets the better of people, makes them do things they'll regret because they got their ego hurt."

"Why didn't you fire your gun for ten years?"

"Didn't need to."

"Ever use it for practice?"

Sherman shook his head.

Bobby asked, "How come?"

He looked at the kid. "Didn't need to," he said again. "I spent a very long time relying on the pistols at my hip. When I came here to the Hollow, I learned I didn't need 'em all the time. Living this life as a houndsman, my pistols were mostly useless to me. And to tell the truth, I was happy for it to be like that."

"What was it you done before?"

Sherman mulled that question over. He wasn't sure how much he wanted to tell the kid. One question could easily lead to an endless succession of them that he'd struggle to answer definitively. But he had to tell him something. After all, he'd left enough bread crumbs.

"I suppose you could say I was a gunslinger. A kind of . . . hired gun."

"I met someone in that profession once. Back home in Amity Creek. He rode into town and that's when all hell broke loose," Bobby said.

Sherman looked at him. "Catch his name?"

"Ethan Harper," Bobby said.

"I know him. Well, not too well. But I rode with him once to do a job. There was a pair of brothers causing havoc, up in some town in the hills, and I needed a partner," Sherman said. "One of the best gunslingers out there, though he never got into some of the kinds of jobs I did. He was more . . . straitlaced, I guess you could say. Only taking on jobs to get by. That kinda fella."

"He weren't too kind to me. . . ."

Sherman said, "Maybe at the time you deserved it."

"Maybe," Bobby admitted.

"I did some bounty hunting. You know, tracking people down. Bringing them in. But that line of work is dangerous, and sometimes there's a lot to it for the pay. Gotta go after the small fry to get the big fish. Does that make sense?"

"I think so."

"Anyway, I did a few robberies in the early days, didn't much care for it. Offered my services as a gunslinger, got paid to take care of a few men here and there."

Bobby didn't attempt to mask his shock. "Take care of them? You mean, shoot them, right?"

"Yes."

"I can't picture it," Bobby said. "You don't seem the kind."

"Come across a lot of stone-cold killers in your short life, have you, kid?"

"Well, no . . ."

"Thought not," Sherman said. "Most dangerous people you cross paths with look like they couldn't hurt a fly. That's the truth. I picked up a job this one time. We were sitting in a saloon. I'm talking to this guy about what he wanted and how he wanted it done. You know, the nitty-gritty of the job. And he says, 'I could've had Selt but I didn't want to deal with him,' and I says, 'Who the hell's Selt?' The man nods in the direction of an unassuming nobody sat in the corner of the saloon nursing a beer, one eye covered with a patch. Looked like he wouldn't be a threat to a hen, let alone a man. I laughed and said, 'Come on, stop joking around,' but he was deadly serious. Adamant that this dude Reuben Selt was deadly as they came. He says, 'I heard he's killed so many people, he's lost count.' If you can imagine such a thing."

"Wonder if it was true," Bobby said.

"Funnily enough, a year or so later, I heard a man called Selt killed a mayor in his sleep. Snuck into the house in the dead of night, stabbed him in the heart. On his way out, he got shot at, but they never caught up with him. There were enough eyewitnesses to say it was him, though—Selt, the same man I'd seen in the saloon. Eye patch and all."

Bobby said, "I can see why you left all that behind."

Not out of choice, Sherman thought. He could've made himself look real good by making out to the kid that it had been part of some big plan of his. That he'd left that life behind through sheer wanting to. Instead, through luck, or destiny, or divine intervention, he'd come to the life he lived now. He'd been saved, and then he'd hidden himself away in the prairie land where the landscape was so big, so wide, a man could get lost in all that expanse. And that was just what he'd gone and done. Got himself lost. Remade himself as a different man.

The only thing he'd decided all those years before was that he was going to stop killing. He'd do something else. But before he'd figured out just what that might be, his fate was writ for him by another's hand.

"You did all that stuff . . . Were you never wanted by the law?" Bobby asked.

"Of course."

"How did you get around that with the sheriff?"

"You mean, when I came here to Elam Hollow?"

Bobby nodded.

Sherman ducked under an overhanging branch. "I came clean to Freehan. Told him who I was, what I'd done. I told him I'd come to Elam Hollow to see if I could better myself."

"And he didn't arrest you or report you."

Sherman busted out laughing. "Well, kid, turns out Freehan was a wanted man himself before he came here."

"Wanted? What for?"

"Cheating at cards, I think. Something like that. Anyway, you could say he understood where I was coming from. We're two crooks together, not that his past is comparable with mine of course. But he was wanted all the same."

"Quite a story," Bobby said. They rounded a bend in the road, the cabin now in sight. "How did he tell you about himself? Surely he didn't just offer that up."

"I said I recognized him from somewhere. Then I told him about a wanted poster I'd seen down in Broken Bow, when I was visiting my brother and his wife. We had an unwritten agreement from then on, really," Sherman said. "We wouldn't turn each other in, and we agreed not to say any more of the past."

"Sure seems fair enough."

Titus bounded up the road, tongue lolling from the side of the dog's mouth as he ran.

"There you are, boy! Miss us?"

Titus barked, circling the horse and the mule excitedly. He escorted them to the cabin that way, tail swishing from side to side with excitement.

Sherman got down from the saddle and petted Titus, patting his flank, rubbing him under the neck just the way he liked it. "Good boy, good boy . . ."

Bobby hopped down from the mule. "After seeing you shoot that fella's hand, I can imagine you bein' a gunslinger."

"Well, I don't recognize the man who came to Elam Hollow years ago. But I know the man you see before you now. I know him very well."

"Ever think about going back to it?"

Sherman didn't have to think about his answer. "No."

"Why?"

"Because I'm not foolish, that's why."

Bobby licked his lips. "Listen, I know you don't want thanks. But I'm gonna give it anyway. I got to. You could've just left me on the street. That's what everyone else would've done."

"Yeah, well, I ain't everybody else."

"I just wanna say, I appreciate all you've done for me."

"Good to hear," Sherman said brusquely. But when the kid's back was turned, he couldn't help but smile a little.

LATER, THEY ATE leftover stew, and when the meal was done, Sherman sat by the fire, Titus snoozing by his feet. Bobby watched as Sherman stuffed his pipe with tobacco and proceeded to smoke. He sat holding his own hands, trying to control them, to still the jitters running from his wrists and down into his fingers.

Sherman looked over. "They shaking, kid?"

"Like I'm cold, but I'm not."

"It's just your body wanting a drink, is all," Sherman said. "It'll pass."

Pipe dangling from his mouth, Sherman detached his hook from his wrist and set it aside. He winced as he massaged the stump, working at the twisted scar tissue with the thumb of his only hand. One time it had thoroughly repulsed him to even look at the stump. If familiarity bred contempt, then his own familiarity with that scarred part of himself had bred acceptance. He'd gotten used to it, hideous as it was to look at. And every couple of days, it felt good to remove the prosthetic altogether and massage the end of his wrist.

"Do you ever get used to it?" Bobby asked.

"Used to what?" Sherman looked up. He raised his stump so that Bobby could get a good look at it. "This?"

Bobby nodded.

"I'm not sure you could ever get used to it, to be honest."

"Do you ever forget you don't have a hand that side?"

Sherman smiled thinly. "I did in the beginning.

Dropped a fair few things before I began to remember. You don't realize just how much you use your hands instinctively until you lose one. It's the strangest darned thing."

"I don't think I could deal with it."

"You could. Nobody knows what they can or cannot deal with until they find themselves havin' to. Truth is, sometimes I feel like the hand is still there. Like I can open my hand and flex the fingers. In the cold it feels like my knuckles are stiff—even though I know there ain't no knuckles."

"There's a name for that, isn't there?" Bobby said.

"Phantom digits," Sherman told him.

"That's it!" Bobby said. "I heard about it before. So how long have you had the hook?"

Sherman said, "Well over ten years ago now. Had a man make it for me. There were all kinds of things I could've had on the end of my arm, but a hook seemed right. Comes in useful sometimes."

"I guess you gotta make the best of a bad situation."

"Any situation you ain't got no control over tends to be a bad one, in my experience."

Bobby quit clasping his hands and held them out before him. They still trembled and shook, but the involuntary movements were lessening. Bobby couldn't help but look embarrassed at his weakness, his vulnerability. "You say I'm getting these because of the drink. Weird thing is, I don't even want one."

"You do. You just don't know it. That's what happens. I've seen it get men before. They think they're over it. But they ain't. They never are. It has a way of coming up on you. I've seen it."

"I guess," Bobby said, watching his hands as if expecting them to resume shaking any second.

Sherman decided a change of conversation was in order. "Let's see that shooter the sheriff let you keep."

Bobby fetched it, handed the pistol over. Sherman examined the weapon—it was nice. "You're a lucky fella, Bobby Woodward," he said, handing it back over. "New duds and a pistol in one day. I should be so lucky."

"That fella's hand sure was busted up good. Still, better than getting shot in the face, I guess," Bobby said, attempting to make a joke that Sherman did not see the funny side of. He merely looked at Bobby, his expression blank. "Anyway . . . ," he said, searching for something more to say.

Sherman sighed. "You feel the need to fill the silence, don't you, kid?"

"What do you mean?"

"Talking on the way you do," Sherman said, making a rolling gesture with his hand. "I know what it's like. I was like that myself way back when. Being out there on your own soon remedies that, I found. The silence becomes your friend."

Bobby frowned. "How come? Don't it get lonely?"

"You embrace silence because when it's quiet, and there's nothing moving, it means there's nothing comin' to get you. Do you follow my meaning? It means you're alone but you're safe."

"Better than being in company you can't trust, I guess."

Sherman nodded, smiling. "You're getting it, kid. Now, I was thinking, how's about tomorrow we start teaching you how to make a living around here? How to work with Titus. How to hunt and set traps for fur."

"Sounds good to me. Not like I've got anyplace else to be, and besides, I gotta debt to pay off, haven't I?"

"Sure have."

"How did you get started doing all this?" Bobby asked. "You know, how did you go from shooting people to skinning animals and hunting for a living?"

"It's a long story," Sherman said, trying to evade the subject.

"It'd be interesting to hear it," Bobby said. "'Cause right now, it don't make much sense, to tell the truth. They're so different, I can't understand how you went from doing one to doing the other."

Sherman finished with his pipe. "I didn't realize I was such an enigma. You're a bit of an enigma yourself."

"How so?"

"Well, you come from a rich family, from what you were saying. Why would you leave wealth and property behind to drink yourself to death on the street?"

"If you knew my whole story, you'd understand. If I had the chance to walk away again, I would do it."

Sherman said, "Level with me, kid. How did you get yourself in the state you were in?"

Bobby got up and paced back and forth as he attempted to put it into words. "I had to run. The things my pop did . . . no way could I have stuck around in Amity Creek and ever got past that. So I left, and I hit the road. And as the months went on, I hit the bottle. One town after another, until what money I had ran out. I took a job here, a job there, just to get enough together for more booze. I don't know why. I guess just to drown the past. Wash it away. To tell the truth, there wasn't a whole lot of thinking behind a lot of it. It just happened that way. And before I knew it, I was a prisoner. I couldn't stop myself. I drank until I ran out of money. Then I sold everything I owned, just drinking and keeping myself numb to everything. Eventually I had nothing left. When the thirst hit me, I begged people to buy me a drink. That's how it was."

Sherman recognized himself in the kid—in the way he felt there wasn't a place for him in the world. Not to belong to any place, it was something that had bothered Sherman for a long while, until he came to settle in Elam Hollow. Here he felt able to finally rid himself of the past, to start again and live simply, and feel at home.

"For what it's worth, I know where you're comin' from, kid," Sherman said.

"So how did you lose the hand?" Bobby asked quietly, a little tentatively.

Sherman rubbed at the stump, feeling the phantom movement of his lost fingers.

"I've never told anyone the story," Sherman said. "Never thought I would, either."

"Care to tell me?"

Sherman tipped his head. "As you like." He leaned back in his chair. Gathered his thoughts. The only place to begin was the beginning. "There was this senator in Wyoming. . . ."

PART TWO

— ◇ —

FIFTEEN YEARS AGO

CHAPTER SIX

ALREADY THE COLD air had worked its way in through his clothes.

Tom Preston instructed Sherman to hold his hands together and raise them. He then bound them tight. Tom kept one end of the rope in his hand, using it as a leash. Sherman looked at the storm blowing in and knew what it meant. He would never reach the end of the prairie—that was for certain. Tom tugged on the rope binding Sherman's hands, yanking him forward. Forcing him to move in the way that he'd instructed. Slowly, painfully, one foot in front of the other, Sherman began to walk across the prairie.

Tom looked down at him from atop his horse. "Didn't have to come to this. Shouldn't have turned."

Sherman didn't say anything.

"Don't matter anyhow. You're gonna freeze to death in this cold. Nice and slow."

"Should've killed you when I had the chance," Sherman growled.

"There he is," Tom said, delighted he'd finally elicited a response from Sherman. "Knew there was a red-blooded male in there somewhere."

"Your plan was probably to kill me all along," Sherman said, glaring up at him as they walked. "No way you were gonna split it. Should've seen that before."

The wind whipped through them, howling in the empty spaces, a thousand mournful voices in the vast amphitheater of the world. Sherman shrank within himself, wincing at every biting part of that wind, feeling it lash his skin and penetrate his flesh to freeze the marrow of his bones. He faltered and Tom snapped the rope, pulling him forward.

"Don't dally," he said. "Snake."

"If I could get my hands on you right now, I'd wring your damn neck," Sherman said, and he meant it. He'd killed people before. But he'd never felt a truly murderous rage come over him as it had now. There was something professional about shooting a man who chose to run—because your quarry had made a conscious choice to do so, knowing you were left with no option but to stop him dead in his tracks.

But to grab a man around the neck and squeeze the life out of him, and enjoy it, that was something else. That was straight-up murder. And far as Tom Preston was concerned, Sherman would've happily indulged in some carnal murder.

"You call me snake," Sherman told him. "I call you dog."

Tom pressed a hand to his chest. "Damn, Sherman. If I had a heart, that would've hurt!"

That served to make Sherman only all the madder. His face stung from the biting wind, his beard gathering ice crystals that formed into thick white clusters. His ears burned from exposure. He'd never felt so cold in his entire life.

Whatever energy he had bled out of him as if he'd been cut.

It did not take long for him to start dragging his feet. Slowing down as they walked into the wind. The muscles in his legs getting stiff and sluggish. Tom pulled on the rope, but Sherman could no longer respond by picking up the pace again. His limbs simply wouldn't move faster. They were too cold. Sherman could feel them seizing up on him.

"Get!" Tom yelled. He yanked on the rope and Sherman stumbled forward, falling face-first in the snow. "No time to lie down, snake. No time to rest, you lowest of the low! We got progress to make."

Now Tom dragged him along, not affording Sherman the chance to get back to his feet. Dragging him through the snow, his legs striking obstacles hidden beneath it, the impacts barely registering because his legs were so numb.

I bet they end up black-and-blue, he thought. *Not that it'll matter. I'll be dead soon. It won't matter how beat up I am.*

Sherman couldn't be sure just how long he got dragged along. Could've been seconds. Could've been minutes. He did not know. Time seemed to slow to treacle around him—the way it did for a man who was staring death down and knew what was coming his way. But at some point, whether seconds, minutes, or who knew how long had passed, Tom stopped dragging Sherman along.

He heard Tom get down from his horse and walk around to where he lay. He had just enough feeling left in his wrists to know that Tom was loosening the bindings to remove them.

Sherman lifted his head. Tom grinned down at him.

"Y-y-you s-s-son of-f-f a b-b-bitch," Sherman said through chattering teeth. "I'll k-k-kill you."

Tom laughed to himself. He coiled the rope around his hand, then stuffed it into his saddlebag. Tom stood over Sherman, huddled up in his layers against the cold. "Looks like this is the end of the road, snake. Funny that you're gonna die from cold just the same as a reptile would."

Tom retrieved something from the saddlebag on the other side of his horse. As Tom came back around to stand before him, Sherman saw that he was holding his twin pistols.

"That reminds me. You're gonna need these if you plan on killing me. I hear you give the famous Ashford Sinclair a run for his money when it comes to gunslinging. Or used to. What a waste of talent."

He dropped the pistols in front of Sherman within reach. Then he climbed back up onto his horse and turned her around. Tom rode slowly away and Sherman scrambled to grab his guns.

To his distress, his hands would not work. His fingers were frozen stiff, and there was no way to will them to operate again. He batted uselessly at the guns in the snow while Tom gradually receded.

Snarling in frustration, Sherman lunged forward, his hand smacking against one of the pistols. "Damn you!" he cried, his hand momentarily opening, his fingers painfully closing around the gun. He pulled it toward him, rolled onto his back and peered through the snow at the departing silhouette of Tom Preston atop his horse.

Sherman tried to work his finger to pull the trigger, but he couldn't do it. There was nothing there. Grimacing, teeth clenched together so hard they threatened to shatter, Sherman forced both hands to work together, aimed and fired.

The shot went too high. The silhouette of Tom Preston on the back of his horse faded away, lost to the storm. Having expended his energy in trying to shoot Tom Preston, Sherman collapsed forward on the snow. The thick, frozen carpet of white had never seemed so inviting. It did not freeze his skin, because his skin was frozen already. It did not hurt, because he could no longer feel pain.

He felt nothing.

The snow was soft and that was all that mattered. The softest thing he'd ever felt. Sherman sank into it and closed his eyes.

S HERMAN WAS MOVING. Gliding along on thin air, above the ground, above the snow, above the thick white clouds. He was rising and rising, into the cloud banks and then through them. Up there the sky was bright blue, and Sherman could feel the sun's kiss on his skin. It began to thaw his body, pushing the cold away, thawing him as he basked in its radiance.

He saw things. Moments and memories. His brother, Jed, talking with him outside their childhood home. It was the day their father was buried, and Jed had implored Sherman to give up his way of life and change direction. Try to be a good man, whatever that was.

Sherman saw his father teaching him and Jed how to fish. Showing them where best to situate the lure. How to bring in whatever took the bait. The three of them stood up to their knees in a local tributary, the water flowing like time around them.

In his travels, Sherman had rarely thought about his mother and father. Hadn't given them much thought at all. But in the end, when they were sick, he had returned home and reconnected with them. For that, he was grateful. Kicked himself that he hadn't done so sooner, but glad in the end that he'd gotten the chance.

He saw all the places he'd been. All the mountains

and valleys. He saw the ocean—could hear the thunder of the waves and taste the salt on the air. The young lady he'd met there on the coast, and the brief, passing romance they'd had before he up and left.

Then he was gliding down over a sea of white. Down and down, until he saw himself lying outstretched in the snow. So close to death as to be hardly living at all. He saw his eyes no longer closed but wide open, and the snowflakes drifting down from the turbulent sky. They settled on his eyeballs until his eyes were completely coated in icy cataracts like frozen cobwebs. . . .

T HE MAN PROBED and prodded Sherman's neck, feeling for a pulse. He checked Sherman's wrist to be sure, feeling for a pulse and eventually finding one. The thread of life was weakening, but very much present. Grunting with effort, the man lifted Sherman under the armpits and dragged him away to a wagon led by two mares. With some difficulty and considerable effort, he managed to single-handedly lift Sherman into the wagon. He laid him in the back and covered him with blankets. They were old and coarse, but they trapped the heat beneath them and that was what Sherman needed.

"You stay put," the man said. "We'll be in the presence of a good fire within the hour."

The wagon jostled this side and that, ferrying Sherman away with the promise of heat.

"Don't worry none about your guns, mister. I picked 'em up for you. Saw 'em there in the snow. They're some fine pistols you got there. Too good to leave behind."

Sherman tried to speak but could not.

"Save your energy. My cabin isn't all that far from here."

The man raised the back flap of the wagon, secured

it into place, then walked around to the front. He climbed up, took hold of the reins and shook them out. "Come on, girls!" The mares surged forward and he shook the reins again. "That's it. Good girls, good girls."

Sherman couldn't tell if the journey was an hour or not. Time held no meaning as he slipped in and out of consciousness. He would open his eyes, see the sky. Open them again, see the tops of trees as the wagon passed beneath them. What he did know was that every time they went over something and the wagon jolted without warning, it hurt him all over. Every inch of his body responded to every dip and rut they encountered. Beneath all those blankets, it got hot. His face remained cold and numb, but beneath the blankets some of the feeling returned to his limbs and his digits—and that was not a good thing. He hurt. The cold had burned him, and as he thawed, the numbness that had taken hold of him gave way to searing pain. It made him want to cry out. It made him wish the man who'd plucked him out of the snow would just put a bullet in his head and end his misery.

But eventually, the wagon stopped and the man was pulling him out from beneath the blankets. He pulled the last blanket away and helped Sherman up to a sitting position.

"Hello there."

Sherman cleared his throat. His voice sounded scratched and roughened, as if his voice box had been dragged over hot coals. "Hello."

"I've got a fire going. Should help."

"Thanks," Sherman managed.

The wind picked up, and both men shrank inside their clothes.

The man continued. "Can you stand? I'll help you inside."

He assisted Sherman to the end of the wagon, and

Sherman nearly collapsed when his feet hit the ground. Luckily the man was there to catch him, hold him up, keep him upright. He assisted Sherman toward the cabin and helped him inside. There was a fire burning, and beside it was a chair with big furs draped over it.

"There you go. Sit right there."

Sherman sat. A dog bounded over. Sherman hadn't noticed it when they'd arrived, but things were blurring. In truth, he couldn't be altogether sure he wasn't imagining his savior rescuing him from the snow—for all he knew he was still out in it, freezing to death on the prairie, caught at the precipice of death itself. The surface of reality seemed very thin in that moment, and Sherman knew that if he looked down long enough, he'd see the ice begin to fracture under his feet. He looked at the man who'd saved him. "Who are you?"

"My name is Elmore."

"I'm Sherman."

"Good to meet you, Sherman."

The fire was hot. His body was hot. His mind was on fire. "I don't feel too good. . . ."

Elmore touched Sherman's forehead with a big coarse hand. "You're runnin' a fever. I'll get you something. Try to keep your eyes open, you hear? Don't close 'em."

Sherman nodded slowly, but his eyes were already sliding shut. He tried—he really did—but it was useless.

When he opened them next, he was no longer in the chair but lying flat. He determined that he'd been moved to the floor. The fire still burned, but he was farther away from it.

Sherman looked up, and a big dog stared back down at him. Its black eyes seemed to see all and know all. He wanted to reach up and touch the dog, feel its fur beneath his fingers. For some reason he wanted that more than he'd ever wanted anything else. As he looked, a thin globule of drool formed at the corner of the dog's mouth and hung there suspended for a long moment before gradually falling toward him. Then he was asleep again.

Time stretched and contracted around him. He once more saw the dead. Heard their voices and felt sorrow that they were no longer a part of the world. Sherman felt his mother's hand cover his own, her skin hardened from work, wrinkled and scored like the skin of a chicken foot. She recited words from the play he'd seen, *Titus Andronicus*.

"'Vengeance is in my heart, death in my hand,'" she said, the voice speaking the words not belonging to her, but to him. Hearing himself say it. "'Blood and revenge are hammering in my head.'"

Sherman felt the deepest sorrow for those who'd died by his own hand. Fred Nilson drifted up out of the ether, and Sherman did not want to see him, wanted it all to stop, but Fred came for him regardless. He took Sherman by the shoulders, demanding to know why Sherman had shot him. "I surrendered! You shot me anyways!"

The truth was, Fred Nilson had committed such heinous acts of barbarity that when Sherman took the bounty on, he'd already decided he would not bring Nilson in alive. He wanted to deal out justice by his own hand, see it done himself. On this occasion he had spoken to the victims himself and had heard the pain in their voices. More important, he'd seen it in their eyes. It left an impression on him. Sherman had cornered Fred Nilson in a cave, and the man surrendered easily enough. Held up his hands. "I guess you've come to take me in, eh?"

Sherman saw it all again: Sherman raising his gun. Telling Nilson all he needed to know.

"Please, mister. I surrender. Can't you see? Don't shoot me."

Sherman hadn't said a word. Just pulled the trigger and watched the bullet rip through Fred Nilson's throat, above the Adam's apple. Nilson clamped his hands there as blood pumped through the cracks in his fingers. Gasping for air the way he had, he'd looked like a fish sucking up oxygen it couldn't use.

Sherman could have shot him square in the forehead. Made it quick and clean. But Fred Nilson had kidnapped young women, violated them, then tortured them to death. Their loved ones were irreversibly broken by what he had done. By the human wreckage he'd left in his wake as he plowed through people's lives. He deserved to die and to *know* that he was dying. So Sherman had stood there the whole time and watched Nilson expire. It took over a minute for his blood to pool around him, till he passed out, then breathed his last on the floor of the cave.

Sherman hadn't thought about Fred Nilson in a long while. But now he was with him, deploring the injustice of his death. Sherman looked down. He had a gun in his hand. He lifted it, pointed it at Fred Nilson and pulled the trigger. When the bullet hit him, Fred Nilson was blown apart like a cloud of smoke shred to ribbons by a sudden gust of air ripping through it.

He opened his eyes and saw Elmore next to him, sawing away at a length of wood. He could hear the metal grating against the hard wood. Elmore seemed to have berry juice on his hands. Startled to see Sherman awake, he looked directly at him but did not stop what he was doing.

"Probably for the best if you close your eyes," the big man said.

But Sherman looked on, wanting to know what Elmore could be making. The strange thing was, the wood seemed to be growing out of Sherman.

Am I wood now? Do I grow?

"I said, shut your eyes."

Sherman did as he was told. The sawing continued. At some point he opened his eyes and saw Elmore wrestling with flame. He was using fire to scorch the end of the wood. The dancing light made Elmore look satanic.

What are you doing? Sherman wondered. He wanted to ask this aloud, but his mouth wouldn't work. His voice had left him. Like a whistle that no longer produced a tune. *What are you burning?*

Elmore could hear his thoughts. He now had the face of the devil himself.

"It ain't growin' back," Elmore growled.

Sherman felt frightened. Fearful of what Elmore was doing—what he'd become. But everything subsided. It fell away and he was left with just the darkness washing over him again, and rolling into its embrace.

T HE NEXT TIME he woke, things made more sense. He was on the floor, on a large fur that had been laid out for him. He was sweaty and hot still, but no longer feverish. Whatever he'd gone through, he knew himself to be through the worst of it. *Must've had a fever,* he thought.

Elmore sat across from him, at a small table, cleaning a pipe. He was a stout man, with a mop of wiry brown hair, small beady eyes like chips of black coal set within folds of wrinkles and crow's-feet. Elmore looked up, sensing that Sherman had woken.

"Good to see you back." His voice was slightly high-pitched, nasal almost—it felt out of place in a man visibly capable of looking after himself. Not the baritone of the devil in Sherman's hallucination.

Sherman attempted to sit but could not. He flopped back against the fur, exhausted. "How long was I out?"

"Days."

"Really?"

Elmore nodded. "Afraid so," he said. "You drifted in and out. If I'm bein' honest with you, fella, I thought you were gonna die on me at one point. I don't know how you didn't perish out there in that storm, honest to God. Must be lucky, is all I can say. Any other man would've died in minutes."

"I don't know how I survived it either."

"Now, there were some complications," Elmore said, getting to his feet, the pipe momentarily forgotten. "I had to take care of a few things."

"Take care of a few things?"

Sherman's feet throbbed. His right arm throbbed also, like a dull ache coursing up his forearm, through the bone. The more he woke up, the more it pulsated— and the more he wanted to jam his arm into a snow pile just to cool it off.

"This won't be easy for you to hear," Elmore continued.

"What is it?"

"I had no choice, you understand. . . ."

Sherman vented his frustration at Elmore's evasiveness. "Damn it, just say what you gotta say!"

"All right, then. Your hand. I had to saw it off as it was dead with frostbite. Same for a few of your toes. They'd turned black by the time I got to them. Nothing I could do."

It didn't register. Sherman thought he was joking. He even laughed. "Come on . . ."

He lifted his right arm and stopped in his tracks. There was nothing there at the end of it. Just a stump.

A dead end where his hand had been attached to his wrist. Sherman had to look at it a long while for it to make sense.

Then it became all too real.

"Wha . . . wha . . . what have you done!?" Sherman cried, horrified by what he was seeing. *"What have you done?"*

"Try to stay calm," Elmore implored him.

Sherman wept. "No, no, no . . ."

"I'm sorry," Elmore said, his hand on Sherman's shoulder. "I had no choice."

Sherman swallowed. "I don't understand."

"I tried what I could to save it, but it was no good. I've seen it before. The cold gets to a man's extremities, and the exposure kills the flesh off. Once the blood stops flowing somewhere on the body, it's pretty much a given it ain't ever gonna flow there again," Elmore said. He showed Sherman the nub of the pinkie on his own left hand. "Look. You're not the only one. A couple of years back, had to cut that one off myself."

"I've got only one hand now," Sherman said, his own voice hollow to his ears.

"Afraid so."

"I've got only one hand now," Sherman repeated. He hadn't cried since childhood and yet here he was, tears coursing down his cheeks from the corners of his eyes. Hot and salty and full of hurt.

"You were in one hell of a fever for days. Luckily, I was able to do most of the work while you were out of it," Elmore explained. "Cauterized the wound, too."

"I woke up. I saw you burning something. I thought you were burning wood."

Elmore shook his head. "Definitely not wood. I'm sorry."

Sherman lay back. Closed his eyes. Elmore was still talking, but he didn't hear any of it. He tried to flex his hand, but it wasn't there. And yet he could still feel it, at least in his mind. As if his hand were now made entirely of air. It was maddening. It was unbelievable. He wondered if he'd fall asleep, then wake to find it was all just another delusion of a fever dream. But hours later, the hand was still gone. The pain was very much real. So, too, was the concoction Elmore was lifting to Sherman's lips. It smelled of pine, and roots, and something rancid.

"Drink. It'll help," Elmore told him.

To Sherman's surprise, it did.

CHAPTER SEVEN

THREE MONTHS AFTER pulling him from the snow and saving his life, Elmore had begun to show Sherman the ropes. The dog was called Sid and it was unlike any dog Sherman had ever known.

"So what d'you call your line of work anyway?" Sherman asked.

Elmore squatted down with a piece of fur in his hands. He held it for Sid to sniff, encouraging the dog to get right in there and fill his nose with its scent. "Go on boy! Find 'em! Go on!" he said excitedly. Sid's tail immediately swished from side to side, and he set off, charging up the hill. Elmore stood. "Thattaboy."

"What stops him from just takin' off?" Sherman asked.

Elmore looked at him. "That big old dog is scared of the dark. He never strays too far, not this close to sunset."

"Right."

"I call myself a houndsman. That's what people

know me as. That's what the fella was called who taught me everything when I was starting out," Elmore explained. "He's long since gone in the ground now. He was a houndsman, just like his daddy was before him."

"Okay. So what does it take?" Sherman asked.

Elmore squinted up the incline, watching as Sid mounted the top of the hill and disappeared out of sight. They'd traveled out to a valley, not far from Elmore's cabin, where there'd been a sighting of a mountain lion. It had killed three sheep so far, picking the weakest of the flock and isolating them in the middle of the night before going in for the kill. Jonny Maberry, a local farmer, discovered their eviscerated carcasses in his fields come first light, and after the third he finally declared he'd had enough. Something had to be done.

"This particular job, I gotta hunt this lion down before it kills any more of Maberry's flock. Every time he loses a beast, he's losing money. Don't forget, everything gets sold. Fleece. Meat. Bones. You name it. Hell, even the eyes!"

"Sheep's eyes?" Sherman asked doubtfully.

Elmore grinned. Gnashed his teeth together theatrically. "Crunchy."

Sherman winced. "Sounds . . . enticing."

"Don't it?"

"So Sid sniffs that fur and goes and finds the lion?"

Elmore shook his head. "No. He'll get so far, lose the scent, get distracted by something. I'll have to catch up to him, get him enticed by the scent again . . . et cetera. Back and forth it goes until he's zeroed in on the beast. There's only so far it can run and hide."

"And when he finds it, then what?"

"Well, then it's down to me to kill it," Elmore said, producing his bow and arrow. "The cleanest way of doing so is with this. Keeps the fur in good condition, too. Which helps later on, when it's ready to be sold. Killing the creature . . . that's one thing. Getting the fur off in one piece, intact, now that's the trick. That's where the money is."

Sherman lifted his stump. "I don't think I'm going to be much use with a bow and arrow."

"Unfortunately not. But we can cross that bridge when we come to it," Elmore said. He regarded Sherman then. Sizing him up. "You really wanna learn this stuff?"

"I do," Sherman told him. "Time for a change, I think."

"Okay, then. Let's start by tracking this damn dog down. No doubt he's got himself into some mischief or other. Maybe today we'll snag ourselves a lion before night falls. Like I said, Sid's scared of the dark. He'll be about as much use as a skillet with a hole in the middle come nightfall. Just you watch."

THEY FOUND SID as dusk was falling. The dog was barking at a gnarly silver-barked tree that seemed to be no longer alive. Up in its twisted branches was a mountain lion. As they'd pursued Sid through the rugged countryside on foot, Elmore had told Sherman that ordinarily a big cat would take on two or three hounds, and almost always leave them worse off. But Sid was big, and he didn't rush in snout first like most dogs. He had a way of scaring cats off, and either chasing them into a tree, as he had done now, or getting them cornered in a tight spot like a cave. Elmore produced his bow and arrow. "The name of the game here is quick and clean. One shot, if I can. But sometimes they dart around the place, looking for a means to get the jump on you."

He lined up his shot. Pulled the arrow back, the

strings of the bow going taut from the tension. Elmore adjusted his aim just the once. The lion hissed, showing its sharp white fangs.

Elmore took the shot.

The arrow drove into the mountain lion's skull from beneath, through its chin. The beast fell off the tree and onto the ground in a heap of fur and claws. It writhed for a moment, blood oozing from its nostrils as it fought off a death that it could not avoid. Then it fell still, its chest ceasing to rise or fall. Sid went straight to it, tail wagging, and Elmore was quick to pull him back. He glanced at Sherman. "Just because it looks dead don't mean it *is*."

"I've experienced that before," Sherman said.

"Oh?"

"Shot a fella once. Went down. Thought he was dead," Sherman explained. "Walked over to him there on the ground, you know, to take his gun belt, then realized he weren't dead when he snatched my wrist and pulled me down on top of him. Had a bullet hole in his chest, too."

"How'd it end up?"

Sherman shrugged. "Managed to get free enough to pull his own pistol on him. Blow his brains out. I was close, though. Real close."

"Know the feeling," Elmore said. He showed Sherman the lines of scars up the side of his neck. "Got these hauling a mountain lion I thought was dead to my horse. Came alive on me and scratched me near to death. It was back in the early days when I didn't know no better. Should've known that even after pulling it to my horse, I'd have never got it stowed up on the horse's back."

As Sherman looked on, Elmore prodded at the creature with the end of an arrow. He was conscious of the fact the mountain lion might prove itself very much alive any second and take its pound of flesh. But when it did not stir, he knew his arrow strike had been true.

"Is it?"

Elmore nodded. "Yessir. Dead as a dormouse."

"What do we do now?" Sherman asked.

Elmore put the bow and arrow away. He looked up at the sky. "Get back to the cabin. Then I'm gonna show you how to butcher and skin one of these. It's a whole lot more complicated than you're likely thinkin' it is. But give it some time, you'll get the hang of it. I mean, I did. And if a dolt like me can learn how to do something and do it well, anyone can."

"How're we gonna move this? It's at least six feet long. Must weigh a hundred pounds or more."

"I'd say that's pretty accurate," Elmore said. "Well, what with you havin' only the one hand, I'm gonna have to improvise. I mean, I'm strong, but I can't haul a creature like this on my own."

Sherman watched as Elmore tied a configuration of ropes around the lion's front half, something akin to a harness. The ropes ran around the lion's neck, under its forelegs and around its torso. It resulted in a long hoop at the front—something that could be managed with just the one hand.

"There you go. It'll be heavy, but it's manageable. I'll take the back end."

Elmore was right—the lion was heavy. And heading back to where their rides were hitched proved to be hard going, particularly for Sherman; not being able to change hands was one gripe of his. By the time they reached the horse and the mule, Sherman's palm was rubbed red raw from the weight of the animal and the chafing of the rope against his skin.

But between them they had succeeded in their task.

And the two men managed to lift the lion up onto the back of Elmore's horse.

"Tonight I'll show you how to get the fur off in one piece," Elmore said. He slapped the hide of the dead mountain lion. "The fur of this deadly feline is gonna fetch a pretty penny in town, as will the teeth and claws."

"What about the rest of it? The meat and the like."

Elmore slapped him on the shoulder. "We feast."

OVER THE COURSE of the next six months, Sherman Knowles took to the peculiar life of houndsman, fur trapper and hunter with gusto. Elmore taught him what he could, and for his part, Sherman was eager to listen and absorb the man's knowledge. Elmore could've left Sherman to die, but he hadn't. He could've turned Sherman out the moment he was out of danger, but he hadn't. He'd given him shelter and fed him. Most important of all, he'd shown Sherman that disappearing into the wilderness and giving the rest of the world time to forget him was something that could be achieved if he just stayed the course. If he lived off the land and ate what Mother Nature provided.

The world would move on.

But as much as Sherman embraced the challenge of his new life, he knew that someday trouble might come to find him. In a short period of time, he had made a lot of enemies. He was a wanted man here and there, which made it all the more important he step back from the limelight a while. Someone could figure out where he was staying—what he was doing—and decide that now was the time to hit back at him. Sherman could not blame them if they did but that didn't mean he shouldn't prepare himself.

* * *

SHERMAN PULLED THE trigger. The tin can remained on the tree stump, untouched by his wayward shot.

Elmore scratched his head. "I thought you carried two of these things?"

"I did."

"Just to be clear, you used to use both hands. One gun in your left, one gun in your right?"

Sherman looked at Elmore with disdain. "Where are you goin' with this?"

"I'm just wanting to be clear. You've shot with your left hand before."

"I have."

Elmore opened his arms. "Then what's the problem?"

"I don't know," Sherman said. He made to elaborate, then stopped himself.

Elmore saw it. "Go on."

"It's nothing."

Elmore sat on a stack of logs and set about stuffing his pipe with tobacco. "I could see you wanted to say somethin', so best get it off your chest, Sherman, before it eats you up from the inside."

"I don't want to use it."

"Your own gun?"

Sherman nodded.

"Well, that's a first."

"I don't plan on killing another soul," Sherman confessed.

Elmore considered this, then said, "Sometimes planning don't come into it. If you're ever in a bind and have to choose between your own life or someone else's, you need to know how to shoot that thing. Or you're good as dead already, Sherman. If I've learned anything out in these parts, it's that a man can't leave nothin' to chance. That kinda thinkin' will get you killed."

"Guess you make a good point," Sherman said.

Elmore slid the end of his pipe into his mouth. "It'll get you killed every damn time," he said. "Now I want you to do somethin' for me. Okay?"

"Yes."

"Imagine that can there on that tree stump is the dirty dog left you for dead in a snowstorm. Imagine that can is responsible for you losing your hand. Hell, blame it for your toes too while you're at it. Focus all your intent on that can and blow it clean off that stump."

Sherman weighed the gun in his hand.

"Do it. Don't hesitate!" Elmore snapped.

Sherman aimed, pulled the trigger. The can went flying. He looked at Elmore, astounded that it had worked.

The big man shrugged. "Very good. Now how's about you go collect that can and do it again? Make sure that hand of yours remembers what it's gotta do."

◇

PART THREE

LIKE HE GOT GLUED BACK TOGETHER

CHAPTER EIGHT

B Y THE TIME winter closed its fist around the town of Elam Hollow and the surrounding prairie land, Bobby had been Sherman's protégé for just over three months. He'd taught him how to hunt and how to trap, and was attempting to show Bobby how to skin an animal. Just as Elmore had instructed him all those years before. Unfortunately the kid's first couple of attempts at preparing the furs had been a disaster.

"Reckon we'll get much for those?" Bobby had asked.

Sherman lifted the torn fur up to the light to examine it. "Afraid not."

Ever the patient tutor, Sherman persevered with Bobby, because every man must have his legacy, and he truly felt that he was having an impact on the kid. He'd rescued him from a certain death with his head in the gutter. He'd gotten him off the booze and taught him how to live by his own hand, by his own agency. Any man who could go out into the wild and feed himself, water himself and return with something he could earn money from was a man fulfilling his potential as far as Sherman was concerned. There had to be a reason God had breathed life into you and sent you into the world. Had to be. Sherman had thought hard on it. Mostly on those long, lonely nights by himself out in his cabin, looking out over the dark prairie. Gazing up in awe at the wheel of stars turning through the dark, wondering how and why it had all come to be. He had no doubt that everyone, at some point, mused on such things. But that had been his time. *Surely God didn't put me here to shoot people for no real purpose other than to make money,* he thought. *Surely he gave me a skill for a reason.*

He'd looked at his stump and wondered what the purpose was behind him losing a hand, because there had to have been one—or all was chaos. And at his time in life, he needed to believe in something just to get him through the night. A world of chaos no longer appealed the same way that it had.

The first snowflakes had begun to fall when Sherman stepped out on the porch to smoke while the kid prepared dinner. Just a simple stew, but he'd gotten good at it. "Can't be feeding you all the time. Works both ways," Sherman had told him. "I ain't your mother, kid."

To Bobby's credit, he'd not grumbled. Like most things Sherman had thrown his way, Bobby took to the challenge with intent and a determination to try. Sherman couldn't fault the kid for that. He gave everything a go. And when he failed, he got right back up and tried again. It was an admirable quality in such a young man—it was a quality that would see him through the hard times when they came. Which they inevitably always did, of course.

Sherman lit his pipe and stood leaning against one of the posts, blowing white smoke into the frigid air, when he heard hooves approaching. Something in

Sherman always tensed when he heard someone riding up unannounced, because you never knew who it might be and what they might want with you.

Sherman felt a mixture of emotions when he saw that the rider was none other than Hattie, his brother's widow. He first felt relief that it was a friendly face and one that he knew well. Then he felt pleasure at the sight of her. They'd exchanged one letter since Jed's burial, and he'd wondered how she and Annie were getting along. So much so he'd considered taking Bobby along with him for a visit. But all of that gave way to another emotion when she got closer and he saw the hard expression she wore. The redness of her eyes and her pallid complexion. Sherman felt his relief melt away. In its place came dread.

He stepped down off the porch and took the horse's reins. He hitched the animal to the front porch and gave Hattie a helping hand getting down. Not that she needed the help.

"Hattie . . . ," Sherman said, studying her face. "What has happened?"

At first, she was unmoved. Hattie just looked at him with that same hard look to her, ears and nose flush from the cold. Then her face crumpled up in pain, and she collapsed against him, sobbing. "It's Annie. Oh, Sherman, it's Annie."

Sherman held her away from him at arm's length. "What's happened to Annie? Tell me, Hattie. Tell me right now."

"They took her. They *took her*, Sherman," Hattie cried. "You've gotta help me get her back!"

SHERIFF FREEHAN PRESSED the glass of brandy into Hattie's hands. She looked at it numbly, as if unsure what to do with it.

Shock has set in now, Sherman thought.

"You drink that, miss. It'll help," Freehan told her.

Hattie took a sip.

The sheriff sat opposite them. Sherman looked past him, through the window, at Bobby, who stood outside tending to the horses. He saw Bobby look at the saloon, then turn away.

Good job, kid. Don't let it call to you.

"Now, Mrs. Knowles, Sherman here tells me you're his sister-in-law. That you were married to his brother. Is that correct?"

"Yes."

"And Annie is your daughter."

Hattie nodded. "Yes."

"Explain to me what happened."

Sherman prompted her to drink more of the brandy. Hattie lifted the glass to her lips and took a long swallow. She told Freehan what she'd told Sherman before they'd ridden into town—Annie had bought a seat on a coach from Broken Bow to Elam Hollow. She'd learned of a position going in town with a local lawyer.

"That's right. Mr. Bergamot. He's openin' a practice here," Sheriff Freehan said. "Had your daughter inquired beforehand?"

"Yes, she had. It was almost guaranteed. She just needed time to find lodgings. I was hopin' Sherman would put her up for a while. Until she was settled."

"Of course I would have," Sherman said. "You know I'd do anything for you two."

The sheriff nodded. "Please, Mrs. Knowles, do continue."

Hattie said that the journey was a long one but would be worth it in the end. Annie was a smart girl, smart as they came, and she'd taken instruction, lessons of the secretarial kind. There weren't many opportunities in Broken Bow, not for a young girl like

Annie. But somewhere like Elam Hollow she could make her mark.

"I hadn't expected to hear from her for quite a while. It wasn't easy for me, not knowing where she might be or how she might be doin'. Let me tell you that. But I swallowed it because it was for Annie. And Jed would've wanted her to pursue a job like that. Workin' for a lawyer, it has a kind of prestige to it, don't you think?"

"Certainly does," the sheriff agreed.

Hattie said that she heard news of wagons being attacked by two bandits. They injured the men and took the women if they were young enough.

"When did you hear about this?"

"A few days after she left," Hattie said. The tears started back up as her emotions rolled in to claim her. "I tried not to brood on it, but then the wagon she'd left in returned and it was all I could think about. One man killed. Two injured. An older woman with a cut across her forehead where she'd been whipped in the face with the butt of a revolver. And the two young women taken. Annie . . ."

Freehan ran a hand over the white stubble covering his chin. "Damn." He went to the bottle of brandy and poured himself one, then topped up Hattie's glass.

Silence fell between them then as the sheriff drank and Hattie sipped at her glass, some color returning to her face now that the warmth of the liquor was working its way into her system.

The sheriff cleared his throat. "Do you recall at all the names of the two bandits responsible?"

Hattie shook her head. "Sorry. All I know is, the people on the wagon said Annie didn't go without a fight. But they took her and another girl anyway. Dragged them away, tied them up and gagged them. I can't . . . I can't even bear to think about it."

"I know," Sherman said, rubbing her shoulder. "I'm so sorry, Hattie."

She looked up at him. "When I think of how scared she must be, I die inside, Sherman. A part of me breaks."

"We'll get her back. Don't you worry. We'll find her."

Hattie squeezed his hand.

"I heard about a few attacks happening south of here," said Freehan. "Let me see what I got. Must have it written down here somewhere," he said, moving off to find it.

"Thank you," Hattie said.

"Listen, I'm gonna send the kid off on an errand. I'll be right back," Sherman said.

Hattie nodded.

Sherman stepped outside, closing the door behind him. It was bitterly cold. The snow had stopped for now, but there was a fine dusting of it everywhere. The roofs of the buildings along the main street were frosted white. A nearby trough, full of water for the horses, had a skin of ice on the top.

"Hey, kid, take this," he said, handing him a small pouch of money. "Go to the general store and tell Mac I want full supplies for a week on the road. Tobacco, too. Get some of that candy, too. The hard kind. He'll know what I'm talking about."

"You mean, the red-and-white one, tastes like peppermint?"

"That's it," Sherman said. "I'll meet you outside here in half an hour."

"Got it," Bobby said, already on the move.

Sherman returned inside to the warmth. Freehan looked up from his desk, where he was leafing through various papers. He was not organized in any way and cared little for paperwork duties, as was evidenced by the mess strewn across his desk. But he seemed to have found what he was looking for.

"Here we are. Wanted for kidnapping, murder—you name it, these two dudes have done it. One of these names goes way back. Tom Preston and Leroy Jenkins."

Sherman felt the air catch in his lungs. "Say that again?"

"Tom Preston and Leroy Jenkins. They're both wanted in just about every town from here to the Mexico border," Freehan said, whistling through his teeth. "Damn, these are two bad apples if ever there was one."

Hattie gave Sherman a worried look. "You know one of them, don't you? One of those names is familiar for some reason, but I can't think why."

"Tom Preston," Sherman said, glancing at his hook. He was lost in thought, in memory, in the past, and spoke as if roused from a dream. "We, uh, rode together the one time. He almost killed me. Well, he *wanted* to kill me, I should say. Would've succeeded, too, but I got lucky . . ."

"That the fella left you for dead, Sherman?" Freehan asked.

Sherman nodded. "I haven't heard that son of a bitch's name in a long while. Tell the truth, I could've happily never heard it again till the day I die."

"So that's why that name rings a bell," Hattie said. "Oh, Sherman . . ."

"Seems like Tom Preston and Leroy Jenkins most likely have your niece," Freehan said.

"What for?"

"Says here, 'This pair of bandits has been enslaving young women and selling them into forced prostitution. Preston and Jenkins started out in Oklahoma and have since targeted wagons and coaches all over Nebraska. They have so far eluded the law.' Seems a sure thing to me."

Sherman scowled. "Selling young women into prostitution," he said in disgust. "I didn't know it was possible to sink any lower, but clearly it is."

"Does that mean—," Hattie began to say.

Sherman nodded slowly. "If we don't get Annie back soon, she's gone for good."

Hattie gasped in shock and held a hand to her mouth.

Sherman felt cold all over and it wasn't from standing outside in the breeze. He had gone cold inside, his body reacting to the threat he now felt toward his loved ones. Getting ready to fight. He knew the feeling well, not that he savored it. Sherman walked over to a large map the sheriff had on the wall opposite. "Where are they targeting specifically?"

Freehan cast his eyes over the document again. Then he fetched some pins and mapped out where the known kidnappings had taken place. "Seems to be along known trails. These boys know where coaches and the like come and go."

"Well, any idiot can work out the common routes. It's just a case of spending a while observing the comings and goings, taking note of the patterns," Sherman said. "Coaches are pretty regular, wouldn't you agree?"

"Sure would," Freehan said. He turned to Hattie. "Mrs. Knowles, do you have any idea where your daughter's coach was attacked? Did they say?"

She got up, set her glass aside and took a pin from the sheriff's palm. "That's the one thing I *do* know, because I spoke with the driver myself. Well, it wasn't a two-way conversation. You see, they broke his jaw, so he couldn't speak. But he was able to show me on a map."

She stuck a pin in it and stepped back.

Freehan drew around the pin with a pencil. "That's forty miles from here, Sherman."

"You're sure?" Sherman asked Hattie.

She nodded. "Sure as I'll ever be."

"Come on. We've gotta ride out there now, see if we can pick up a trail before the snow sets in proper," Sherman said. "It'll take us a day and a half to cover it at least."

Freehan held up his hands. "Easy there, pardner. I can't get involved in this. It's out of my jurisdiction."

"You're kidding."

"Afraid not. Besides, if I go, who's here to watch the fort while I'm forty miles out? In case you haven't noticed, there ain't no deputy in Elam Hollow. Just me," Freehan said.

Sherman growled low in his throat. "Damn! Well, where do we stand on getting a marshal involved, then?"

"Chances are high," Freehan said. "But you'd be in for a long wait. A week or more. Last time I saw a marshal was three summers ago. We're not exactly on the map for them. Not on the way to anywhere, either."

"We don't have that kinda time," Sherman said. "As it is, we're gonna have to stop halfway to give the horses a breather."

Hattie looked at him, desperation in her gaze. "Please, Sherman. I want to see Annie again."

"You will," he promised.

Hattie picked up her glass of brandy and tossed the rest back in one go. She ground her teeth against the burn. "I'm going with you."

"Ordinarily I'd say no," Sherman said. "This is going to be dangerous and the going will be hard. But I know better than to argue with you, Hattie."

"What are you planning to do?" Sheriff Freehan asked.

"Ride out there. See what I can find. Might be a trail, some kind of marking I can follow. Put Titus to work."

"It'll be like finding a needle in a haystack, Sherman."

"I understand that, Sheriff, but I gotta try."

"I wish there was something I could do to help," said Freehan, looking guilty that he'd refused to ride with them.

Sherman looked at the two horses hitched up outside the sheriff's office. "You know, we could really do with another horse. I don't think the old mule Bobby's been using is gonna cut it. Not for this kind of work."

"Now *that* I can help you with," the sheriff said with satisfaction.

M AC STOOD WITH his hands on his hips. "I can't believe this, Sheriff. It's an outrage!"

"Calm yourself, Mac," Sheriff Freehan said as he helped Sherman to saddle one of Mac's horses. "It's just a temporary loan. Call it a short-term requisition on behalf of the sheriff's office of Elam Hollow, if you prefer."

"I don't like this one bit."

Sherman tightened the straps. "I'll get her back to you in one piece, Mac. You have my word."

"Well," Mac said, uncertainty leaking into his voice now. "I can't say you're not good for your word. I'd be a liar if I did."

"I promise. We'll take good care of her."

Mac tipped his chin. "You'd better."

Sherman shared a look with Sheriff Freehan, both men fighting the urge to smile. Mac was about as imposing and threatening as a plucked chicken but it had to be acknowledged the mare was his property, and Sherman would see to it that he had his horse returned in the same shape she'd been loaned.

Or *requisitioned*, as the sheriff had put it.

Freehan was a hustler if ever there was one. Once a crook, always a crook. No matter if you wore a tin star on your breast or not.

Bobby loaded the horses with the last of the supplies. "That's the lot."

"Good," Sherman said. "Now, we got one more stop to make. Hattie, you come along, too."

"I'll say fare thee well now, Sherman. Mrs. Knowles. Bobby," Freehan said, pulling on the front edge of his hat. "Best of luck to the three of you. Hope you find that girl of yours."

"Thanks for your help," Sherman told him.

"Don't mention it." Freehan waved them off and headed back to his office.

Sherman, Hattie and Bobby walked across the street to the gunsmith. Bo Farman had been the resident gunsmith for twenty years, not that Sherman had ever had that many dealings with the man—but he knew him to be polite and helpful. Bo looked up as the bell rang over his door, bushy white eyebrows peaking in surprise at the sight of them. "Well, hello there."

"Hey, Bo," Sherman said. "I got some business for you today."

"What can I do for y'all?"

"I'm gonna need ammo." Sherman nudged Bobby. "Show Mr. Farman your piece, kid."

Bobby removed it from the holster and passed it across, butt first.

Bo examined it. "Nice."

"You got a box of shells for that?"

"Sure do." The gunsmith handed Bobby's pistol back and ducked down behind the counter to retrieve a box of bullets. He slapped them down on the counter. "That be all?"

"Not quite." Sherman removed his own pistol. Then he produced something wrapped in oilcloth. He unfolded the cloth. It was an identical pistol to the one he had on his hip.

"Wow," Bobby said.

Hattie looked over at the two guns. "You still have them."

"Might've lost a hand, and with it my ability to shoot two guns at once . . . but I couldn't stand to let one of them go. I know it sounds corny. It's just, these two shooters have been good to me. They're reliable and powerful."

"You want shells for those, too?" Bo asked.

Sherman turned to Hattie. "I don't suppose you've got a gun belt, have you?"

"No. Why would I?"

"Because I'm giving you one of these pistols. Can't ride with us if you're not armed."

Hattie swallowed. "Okay."

"You can shoot, can't you, Hattie?"

She pulled a face. "I can shoot better than *you*, Sherman. Trust me."

"Now that's fightin' talk. We'll need plenty of that." Sherman smiled. "Bo, we'll take two boxes of shells and a gun belt for the lady."

"Coming right up."

"How're you gonna afford all this?" Hattie asked.

"I've got good credit," Sherman said with a shrug. "Who knows? Maybe I'll be lucky and get shot before I have to pay for any of this stuff."

"That's not even funny," Bobby said.

FEELS HEAVY," HATTIE said, adjusting the gun belt on her hips.

Sherman helped her up into the saddle of her horse.

"You'll get used to it, trust me. Now, you're sure you can shoot the thing?"

"Listen, Sherman. *You* taught Jed, am I right?"

Sherman nodded.

"Well, Jed taught *me*. Does that satisfy you?"

"I guess it'll have to do."

Bobby patted the neck of Mac's horse. "Feels good to be riding up high again."

"Don't get too used to it. He's gonna want that horse back," Sherman said. "By the way, whatever happened to the horse you rode in on?"

Bobby scratched the side of his head. "I think I sold it."

"Damn kid," Sherman grumbled, climbing up onto his own horse. "We gotta swing by the cabin. It's on the way anyhow. You both ready?"

They told him that they were, and all three set off together. Taking their horses at a gentle trot through the main street, then opening them up when they hit the road that led out of town. They headed that way until they reached the turnoff for Sherman's cabin.

There Sherman retrieved three large furs from his stocks. "I'm gonna be selling these when we get back, so don't muss 'em up, you hear? We'll need these to keep warm," he said, peering up at the white sky. "Snow is coming and it's gonna be heavy."

Titus nosed around by his boots.

"What about the dog?" Hattie asked.

Sherman rubbed Titus between the ears. "We'll need him if we're gonna pick up their trail."

"Will he keep up?"

"He'll have to. A hunting dog can cover twenty miles a day with ease," Sherman said. He beckoned them both down from their horses. "We got one more thing to take care of."

"I hope so," Hattie said. "My daughter is out there somewhere, Sherman."

"I hear you on that. But I gotta know the people I'm riding with can actually shoot what's on their hips."

He lined up a half dozen rusted old tins on the far fence and instructed Bobby to shoot the three on the right.

"Go ahead, knock 'em off the fence. One shot per can."

Bobby lined up his shot. "I'm not saying I'm the best."

"I never said you were. Just shoot, will you, kid?"

Bobby shot once. The tin at the very end went flying. He shot again, missing the tin in the middle. His last shot, he hit the third tin dead center and knocked it clear off the fence.

"Two out of three ain't bad," Sherman said, giving Bobby a pat on the back. "I'll take that. Hattie, you're up."

She weighed the gun in her hand. "Boy, this is heavier than I'm used to."

"Look, if you don't think you can shoot it, it's fine. I just gotta know, is all. If we're in a tight spot—"

Hattie didn't waste another second. She thumbed the hammer back, aimed, pulled the trigger once, then repeated the sequence twice more. The rusted old tins went flying as each shot found its mark. "Oh, sorry. I missed one. Don't worry, Bobby. I'll take care of yours for you," she said, using her free hand to push the hammer down and, in the same fluid motion, firing a fourth shot that obliterated the tin he'd missed.

Sherman nodded appreciatively. "Damn, Hattie. You're a better shot than I reckoned you to be."

"I told you, Jed taught me," Hattie said, holstering her pistol. "And he learned from the best."

That warmed Sherman's heart. "Okay, then. Let's get out of here. Time's workin' against us already."

Their furs stowed on the backs of their horses and Titus trotting along beside them, Sherman, Bobby and Hattie set off once again, this time cutting up into the countryside and leaving the road behind them. Where they were headed, there would be no roads, no clear markings or signposts. Sherman would have to guide them, with Titus's help. Where the white sky hit the distant hills, it had already begun to snow. In a day or so the prairie would be turned white as far as the eye could see. You couldn't predict the weather, but you sure could count on the weather to be predictable.

"Pick up the pace now on my lead," Sherman said, applying pressure to the sides of his horse with his heels. "If we're gonna find her, we've gotta reach the place they were taken before the snow comes in proper, else we ain't got a chance in hell."

"Don't have to tell me what's at stake here," Hattie said, her face set hard with determination.

"I know, Hattie. I know," Sherman said softly, thinking: *If only Jed could see you now, he'd have a new reason to admire you. I wish you were here, brother. I will get Annie back. On your grave, I swear it. . . .*

CHAPTER NINE

Tom Preston and Leroy Jenkins made camp in the heart of a wood, among the thin trunks of young cottonwoods. Leroy set about getting a fire going, bundling dry leaves on top of the smoking beginnings. Once the fire truly took hold, he built it up with kindling and soon enough they had a source of heat to warm their cold hands and faces.

"Get some of that rabbit cookin', Leroy," said Tom.

"I ain't no maid," Leroy snapped as Tom tossed him the four rabbits they'd caught earlier in the day. "I ain't no cook, either."

"Naw, but you sure do smoke a rabbit good," Tom said.

Derailed by the compliment, Leroy peered sidelong at his partner in crime, then set to skinning the rabbits. "Whatever," he grumbled as he got to work.

The two women from the coach were tied to a cottonwood. The men had given them furs to keep them warm—it wouldn't do to have them freeze to death before they could be sold, after all. But for the racket they'd been making, they'd had to be gagged.

For as dumb as Leroy tended to be most times, he had an awful temper and Tom lived in fear that one day Leroy would snap and kill the women they'd worked so hard to snag. Damn it, he wasn't about to have that hard work come to nothing because two women couldn't keep their mouths shut when they were told to.

"Now, if I take these gags off, you both promise me you're not gonna make a racket?" Tom asked them.

They nodded in unison.

"All right, then. I ain't untying your hands. But I will let you off these trees so you don't lose circulation. How does that sound?"

Again, the two women nodded at him. Eager to be rid of their gags, and eager to be freed from the trees they were tied to.

Tom waved the knife at them. "Don't make me regret this. I'm trusting you. Understood?"

He cut the gags from their mouths and removed the rope holding them to the tree trunks. Their hands remained bound in front of them, but they could move their arms and legs now that they were free from the trees. It was better than nothing.

All in all, Tom Preston thought he was downright humanitarian, being so nice to the prisoners. Keeping them warm. Feeding them. Trusting them to move around.

He flashed the knife again. "Either of you try something, I'll cut you. Now, it won't be nothin' that affects a sale. It'll be a toe or a pinkie. Or maybe I'll cut your tongues out. Won't be many men complaining they were sold a woman can't make no noise!"

Leroy bellowed loudly from beside the fire, skewering the skinned rabbits with fresh branches. He sounded like an excitable donkey, making a *hee-haw* sound as he laughed. "Damn, Tom, you get me every time!"

"I do, don't I?" Tom said, sneering at his partner. "A regular court jester, I am."

In moments like that, he always thought how easy it would be to use the knife on Leroy. Hold his forehead with one hand and, with the other, drive the knife into the base of Leroy's skull. He'd twitch and jitter for a moment (after all, most folk danced when they died), but then he'd be still. No one would miss him. Not one person in the entire world would miss Leroy Jenkins when he eventually met his Maker.

Nor, for that matter, would they miss Tom Preston. He knew that all too well.

In some way, it was what stopped him ending Leroy at every opportunity. That and the fact Leroy was made for robbing coaches and kidnapping folk. It was the man's calling, as if Leroy had been born to fulfill that one function. Tom had never seen anything like it.

Leroy, oblivious to Tom's musings over his potential murder, turned the rabbits. They sizzled over the dancing flames.

"Smells good," Tom said.

He put the knife away. Rolled a cigarette for Leroy and one for himself.

"Thank you," Leroy said, accepting the smoke. He lit it off the fire and sat smoking as the rabbits cooked.

Tom leaned down, lit his own cigarette. "Ain't this the life, Leroy?"

"Sure is. Nicer in the summer, I'll admit. But I'll take it any way it comes, I guess."

Tom nodded along but thought, *What the hell kind of answer is that? Damn fool.*

Leroy turned around, glanced at the two women they'd kidnapped. "Gotta say, Tom. They're both mighty pretty. I'm almost tempted not to let 'em go."

"What, and keep 'em?"

Leroy shrugged.

"Idiot. They're worth more because they're so dang pretty. Don't you get it? Once we've made our money, you can buy whatever kind of wife you want. Preferably one that ain't gonna run out on you first chance she gets. Slit your throat in your sleep or worse."

Leroy rubbed at his throat. "What d'you mean, *worse*?"

"Well, your neck might not be the only thing they'll wanna slice," Tom said, making a cutting gesture across his crotch.

Leroy recoiled in horror. "Oh, God. Hell no. Not *that*. No, sir."

"See what I mean? Minute we took these two, they was damaged goods, partner."

"My old mother used to say, 'Hell hath no fury like a woman scorned,'" Leroy said.

Tom nodded. He rolled up his phlegm and shot it into the fire. "Mother knows best, I'd say."

A NNIE KNOWLES WATCHED the two men talk beside the fire, laughing at their own jokes, at what they considered to be their own great intelligence when it came to the workings of the world. They'd not done a very good job of keeping their identities a mystery. The more cunning of the two men was called Tom. The dim-witted one, who seemed to have a particularly combustible temper, was called Leroy. From what she'd seen, Leroy respected Tom because he probably realized Tom was smarter. But she'd also observed that Tom was somewhat scared of Leroy. He pushed at the man but he didn't push too far. He always stopped short of getting the man to snap, and that was interesting.

The other girl was called Joan. They'd got to talking on the coach, and their familiarity helped them cope when they were taken. Tom and Leroy attacked their coach in the dead of night, and it'd been hard to grasp what, exactly, was going on. There were gunshots, raised voices, a thump here and there followed by a pained cry. The door to the coach was yanked open and she and Joan were dragged out into the frigid night air. They were ordered to wear their warmest clothes; then they were bound and gagged. But not before Annie tried to get a few licks in. She kicked out, caught Tom Preston in the shin. Leroy Jenkins bear-hugged her from behind to prevent her fighting even more. When Annie tried her hardest to stamp on his feet, Tom stepped in and took her legs. Seconds later, Annie had to stop because she wasn't getting anywhere.

Because they were on speaking terms, Annie and Joan had been able to give each other the strength to keep calm and carry on. Annie knew that it was only a matter of time before their kidnappers made a mistake. Then it would be down to her and Joan to make a run for it. Get as far as they could, quick as they could.

Joan spoke in whispers. Her voice rattled with nerves, eyes flitting from one thing to another. "How will we know when it's the right time?"

The shock's got to her already, Annie thought. Though their wrists were still bound, Annie was able to rest her hands on top of Joan's and give them a reassuring squeeze. "Once those two pigs start eating. We've got until then to get these ropes off."

"I'm scared," Joan admitted.

"I know you are," Annie whispered. "Me, too."

They scoured the woodland floor for something that might cut through the ropes binding their wrists, but there wasn't anything. "I don't see nothin' sharp," Joan said.

"Me neither. It's not the end of the world. We still got our legs. We can run, can't we?"

Joan licked her lips. Her frightened eyes watched the two men in front of the fire, and Annie saw their black silhouettes against the firelight reflected in Joan's eyes. "What's to stop them catching up with us?"

"Nothing. So we gotta make sure we split up."

"Split up? No, I don't think I can do that, Annie. I can't run off alone."

Annie squeezed Joan's hands again. "Joan, listen to me. *You can do this*. If we don't split, they've got more chance of catching us and bringing us back to camp. We split up, which means *they* have to split up."

Joan shook her head. "I don't like it."

"I don't like it, either," Annie told her. "But it's the way it's gotta be."

"I . . . I . . . I can't . . . ," Joan said, breaking down.

Annie gave her a stern look. "Hey!" she whispered, shaking Joan's hands. "You can do this because you're brave. Do you hear me? You're brave and you've got guts. We're tougher than those pigs think we are. We got grit, Joan. We both got grit the likes of which they ain't ever encountered before, trust me."

"I do trust you," Joan said uncertainly. "I'm just scared."

"I know. You said," Annie remarked. She watched the two men. They were oblivious to what their prisoners were doing. She stood and got Joan to her feet.

Tom turned around. Looked at them both with suspicion. "What're you two up to?"

"Just getting the blood moving in our feet," Annie told him.

"Good. Don't wanna have to chop 'em off. Can't walk on stumps, you know."

Leroy burst out laughing. The two men turned their attention back to the fire, and the skewered rabbits siz-

zling over it. Annie had to admit, it smelled good. Her
stomach growled from the warm aroma of the roasting
meat. It'd be hard running away from that. But if they
were going to do it, it had to be now.

"Quickly. You gotta run like you never have before," she told Joan.

"Annie—," Joan began to say.

"Go on now."

Joan shook her head. "Not without you."

"Just go!" Annie ordered. And as she gave Joan a
gentle nudge in the opposite direction, Annie, too, set
off, silently at first, then breaking into a run. Through
the trees. Down a slippery embankment. Through yet
more trees. On and on, her heart hammering in his
chest. She faltered for a second, leaning against a
young cottonwood while she caught her breath. But
then she heard one of the men yelling and knew they'd
be hot on her trail. She pressed on, moving as swiftly
through the trees as she could manage.

D AMN IT!" TOM Preston shouted. He looked at the
ground, found their tracks. One going one way,
one going the other. "Leroy, you take that one. I'll
head this one off."

"Got it," Leroy said.

"They can't get too far in this cold, not with their
wrists bound. Should've bound their damn ankles, too."

"Could have hog-tied those girls but you wouldn't
have it," Leroy said.

"What, hog-tie 'em and cut off their circulation?
Ain't no one gonna buy girls missing arms and legs,
you fool. Now get!"

Tom set off, jogging through the trees. Slipping in
the freshly fallen snow and the frosted exposed roots
of the trees but managing to keep from falling over. He

skidded down an embankment, watching for tracks, finding them, markings left by the girl's boots in the fresh snow that had fallen between the trees and settled in a crunchy thin layer.

It was near dark, however, and though his eyes were now adjusted to the dingy light of the woodland, he still couldn't see too far ahead. When you sat near a fire too long and stared into its dancing flames hoping for enlightenment, it dulled your ability to see in the dark. His night eyes were notoriously keen, but not tonight—the fire had seen to that. Now he squinted as he moved, trying to see farther ahead, trying to catch a glimpse of the girl who'd run this way. The tracks were getting muddied now. The snow here had turned to slush where it'd hit wet ground, but he could still tell the imprint of the girl's boots.

Her cadence indicated she was running for her life. There were big spaces between footfalls. Unlike Tom, the girl was not taking care with how she went. She was in flight, taking a chance that she wouldn't slip and hurt herself.

In the winter, it was all too easy to fall and hit your head or break your back. When you were out on your own in the cold, you shouldn't risk any kind of injury at all that could lead to frostbite or freezing to death altogether.

But she was young and scared. She had every right to be.

Once they reached their buyer, she'd be sold off to the highest bidder, into a life of servitude. Tom almost felt pity for the women they'd sold, and the women they were going to sell, but he did not regret what he'd done, and what he was going to do, because everyone had to get by in their own way, and this was his. A man had to change with the times. Find something where there was a demand and try his damnedest to meet it. Capturing and selling young women had proven to be like printing his own money. Another couple of runs, maybe six more women after these, and he'd probably have enough to stop. Buy some land somewhere, set down roots.

But of course, it was a pipe dream. Something he told himself sometimes in order to feel like everyone else. He knew that settling anywhere would drive him nuts. He was not the kind to set down roots anywhere. Tom Preston was a dandelion seed, most comfortable riding the winds, seeing where they took him. It'd always been that way. It'd be that way until he bit the dust and got buried in an unmarked grave somewhere.

He ran out of the woods, a long stretch of prairie before him and the girl running at speed. She was a little colorful figurine against a white background. Tom had no way of catching up with her—she was too far ahead. She was younger, quicker. The girl would just run and run until she tired and had to quit. So he did the only thing he could think of. He pulled his pistol from its holster and fired it into the air.

The girl skidded to a stop as the gunshot echoed around her. She cowered from it, spinning about to look at him. She made to carry on running.

Tom fired again, then aimed the gun at her. "You run and the next shot goes in your back, right between the shoulder blades!"

The girl stopped. She looked at him and he wondered what was going through her head in that moment. If she was anything like him, she'd have been weighing up her options. Wondering if he could make the shot from that far off (he could) and if she could get out of sight before he could pull the trigger (she could not).

"Why don't you just let me go?" she called back to him.

"Not an option," Tom said. "Now come back here and let's be civilized about this. I don't wanna shoot you, girl, but I *will*. Believe me, I will. I've done worse. Far, far, far worse."

She shook her head. "You're gonna kill us eventually anyway."

"No, I ain't," Tom said, laughing. "You ain't worth squat to us dead. Don't you get it?"

The girl was smarter than he took her for. "Then you're not gonna shoot me in the back after all, are you?"

With that, she set off running again.

He grimaced. "The hell with this," he growled, aiming just to the right of her. Close enough she would feel the bullet tear through the air and come to the realization he wasn't messing around.

Tom fired.

The girl shrieked and finally stopped running. She turned to look at him, and this time Tom beckoned to her to walk toward him.

"Told you I'm not messing. You're thinking I won't shoot you. That is incorrect. I will shoot you and just go get myself another girl. It's what I'm gonna do anyways. Get another girl, and another, and another until I'm done and move on to something else. I won't mark you in a way that's gonna jeopardize a sale. But I'd rather shoot you full of holes than carry on with this damned charade. Now either come along and behave yourself, or Leroy and I will go get us a couple of new girls to sell. It's your choice."

She stood stock-still, face flushed from running. Her breath clouded on the cold air.

"What's it gonna be?" Tom demanded.

Knowing she had no choice but to comply, the girl trudged back to him.

"Good girl. You sure are a pretty young thing," he

said, reaching out to touch her face with one grimy hand.

The girl slapped his hand away with her bound hands. "I hate you!"

"I'll say this only once, so listen good." He gripped Annie's face with his dirty hand, his rough, stubby fingers biting into her cheeks. This time she could not fight him off. When she hit at his arm with her bound hands, he refused to budge. "Next time you run, I'll strip you of your clothes and leave you out here to freeze to death, if that's what y'all want. Trust me, I've done it to people before. That what you want, sweetie? To die out here?"

She looked him in the eyes. He saw more anger in that girl's gaze than he'd seen in anyone for a long, long time. It burned inside of her. She was pretty, yeah—and dangerous. He'd be glad to be rid of her. Something about her unsettled him.

"No," she said.

Tom grinned, showing ragged yellow teeth that were rotten through and through. "That's more like it. Time we started walkin' back now, little girl. You go on ahead and know that I'm right behind you, ready to shoot you in the back, you so much as think about runnin' again."

They returned to the woods and headed back to camp.

Ahead of him, the girl said, "When my uncle hears what you done, he's gonna track you down and make you pay."

"Your uncle some kind of badman?" Tom asked, laughing to himself and shaking his head at the audacity of the girl. She had spirit; he had to give her that.

"Used to be."

"So a *has-been*, then."

"Boy, are you wrong about that," Annie said.

"Well, if he ever catches up with us, I'll be sure to oblige him," Tom told her. "Now walk on, little girl."

WHEN THEY REACHED camp, Leroy had Joan in his grip, clutching her arms from behind to hold her still. He had a set of raw red claw marks down his face and was snarling through the pain.

"Damn, Leroy, what the hell happened to you?"

"This thing near clawed my eye out!" Leroy said, shoving Joan forward.

She fell onto the damp earth, and without her hands free to save herself, she hit the ground hard.

Tom dashed forward to help her up. "You fool. If you mark her up, she ain't gonna be worth squat! What're you thinking?"

Leroy exploded. "Ain't you listening? She nearly tore out my *eye*!"

"I heard you. That's your own stupid fault for letting her do it."

Leroy tore away, kicked their gear in frustration and walked off, shouting obscenities.

Tom pushed Joan toward Annie. "You two girls, stay put," he said, and went after Leroy to calm him down.

"Are you okay?" Annie asked. "You got him real good."

"I tried," Joan said. "We almost got away, didn't we?"

"We did. Don't worry. There'll be another chance. We just got to time it right, is all."

Joan shook her head. "I don't think I want to."

"How can you say that?"

Joan said, "Maybe it's better to be sold than dead."

Annie felt her heart sink. "Joan, listen to me. Being sold like we're cattle is as good as dead anyway. Whoever buys us, they'll do what they want to us. You know what I'm talkin' about, don't you? I don't need to spell it out."

"I know what you're talking about," Joan said bitterly. She moved away from Annie.

Annie stood with her back to the tree they'd been tied to. She looked past the fire, to where Tom was calming Leroy down. Eventually he allowed Tom to examine the damage Joan had done to his face. As she looked on, Tom got Leroy to kneel next to the fire as he washed out the wounds, then doused them with booze. Leroy screamed in agony, and it took all of Annie's self-control not to burst out laughing.

She looked to see if Joan found it as funny as she, but Joan was sitting on the ground with her back to her.

Annie decided not to push it. Let Joan manage her own anger and disappointment at getting caught and dragged back to camp.

Eventually Tom approached with one of the cooked rabbits. "Either of you hungry?"

"I'd rather starve. Thank you very much," Annie said.

"Suit yourself," Tom told her. He walked over to Joan. "How 'bout you? Hungry?"

To Annie's surprise, Joan reached out and snatched the rabbit from him and began eating immediately.

Smirking, Tom looked at Annie. "You might want to take a leaf from her book. At least now I know which of you is the intelligent one."

He walked off.

Annie waited until he was gone, then turned to Joan. "What are you doing?" she whispered harshly.

Joan looked over her shoulder as she swallowed. "I ain't following your lead no more."

"You're playing into his hands," Annie said.

Joan tore off a piece of roasted rabbit with her teeth. "Say that tomorrow when you're starving," she said bitterly. She turned away completely and continued eating.

Annie slid down to sit on the ground and looked toward the fire. She watched the two men drinking from a flask they passed between them. She listened to the sound of Joan eating. She smelled the rabbit and her stomach gurgled with hunger, but she tried to ignore it.

It would be easy to give in. To accept what their captors offered. But she was not going to make it easy. Joan had already broken. And though Annie remained firm in her convictions, secretly she wondered how long *she* could remain strong. How long until she, too, faltered and accepted her fate?

Annie hugged her knees and closed her eyes, thinking of home. She wondered if her mother knew that she'd been kidnapped. She wondered if her mother had gone to her uncle Sherman for help. From the stories her father had told Annie about Sherman in his younger days, Tom and Leroy had a lot to be fearful of. If Sherman ever caught up with them, that was. In the privacy of her own thoughts, Annie prayed that Sherman found her soon, before she gave up the fight . . . and let her captors win.

CHAPTER TEN

Titus nosed at the ground. He turned in a circle,
breathing in and following the otherwise invisible
movements of someone or something. Sherman watched
the dog at work, then studied the ground from the vantage point of his saddle. He clung onto the horn with
his one hand to lean over, narrowing his eyes as he
studied the impressions in the frosted grass.

"We're not the only ones out on this prairie," he said.

"What do you mean?" Bobby asked. "I don't see
anything."

"That's just inexperience," Sherman said. He looked
up at his protégé. "A truth, not a criticism."

"Understood," Bobby said. "So what're we looking at?"

"Four riders."

"Four?"

Sherman scanned the horizon. "We're gonna have
to keep our eyes peeled. All three of us."

Titus looked up.

"Yep, you, too, pal," Sherman said. He reached into his saddlebag and tossed Titus a length of jerky. The dog caught it in his jaws and immediately chowed down. "There ya go. You've earned that."

Hattie settled her horse, patting its neck. "Do you anticipate trouble, Sherman?" she asked.

"Not particularly. But you never can tell. Fellas will do as they please, especially when they're out in the middle of nowhere. Seen plenty of that in my time. Lots of men thinkin' they can do what they like to whoever they like. Women, too. Not just men."

Hattie swallowed. "Should I be worried?"

"No, but like I said, we all need to stay alert."

Bobby's hand instinctively fell to his holster and came to rest there, as if he were conscious of carrying it for the first time since they'd left the cabin. "Okay," he said.

T HEY RODE UNTIL dusk. They were out in the open, but with a hill at their backs, shielding them from the worst of the wind. Sherman considered it a good enough spot to make camp for the night. If the rain or snow came, well, there wasn't much he could do about that. There was no such thing as shelter when you were out in the wide-open prairie. If the weather came, it came—not a whole lot man or beast could do but take it.

"We're stopping already?" Hattie asked as Sherman got down from his horse. Bobby followed suit and immediately began setting up their camp. It was interesting to Sherman the things Bobby would do because he'd been shown and what he'd do instinctively. He guessed it depended upon what the kid knew or didn't know from his life before winding up a drunk in Elam Hollow.

"It's dark, Hattie. The horses are beat. *I'm* beat. I know for a fact Titus is beat, coming all this way," Sherman told her. Regardless of whether he'd seen fit to give Titus a break along the way, the mutt was still diminished. "Annie needs us at our best, don't you think?"

"It just feels wrong," Hattie said, looking bereft.

"I know it does." Sherman offered Hattie his hand to help her down from her horse. She accepted and with his help swung down from the saddle with ease. "But you can bet those bandits are stopping, too. When you look at it like that, we're on an even footing."

"I guess you're right. But surely if we keep going . . ."

"Hattie, we're stopping here. I know what I'm doing. Trust me," Sherman said. "Can't track in the pitch-black of night."

His sister-in-law sighed deeply. "I'm just so worried about her."

"I know you are. I am, too."

"What if she's cold or hurt? What if they've done something to her?" Hattie said, her voice cracking. "You know what I'm talking about."

"I do," Sherman said.

He did not add that because the women had been taken in order to be sold, they were unlikely to be molested. In order to demand a higher asking price, the kidnappers probably kept their prey well-fed and free of beatings that would mark them. The thought of Annie being interfered with in any way had crossed Sherman's mind already, but he'd dismissed it. The women had ceased to be human beings as much as a highly sought-after product. The thought was enough to make you sick to your stomach. And yet . . . Sherman thought of the poor souls stolen from their homelands, packed like sardines into boats and sailed across the world to serve a life of enslavement at the hands of cruel plantation owners. Men had been enslaving their own kind for a long, long time.

"How could they do this?" Hattie said.

"It's in our natures to be cruel," Sherman said, his mind still on the Africans and other peoples who'd faced the plunder and destruction of their cultures at the hands of white men. Was it really any different, what Tom Preston and Leroy Jenkins were doing? He did not think so. Taking a life and selling it to the highest bidder for profit. The definition of repugnant.

"I'll get a fire going," Bobby said, wanting to steer clear of their conversation.

Sherman appreciated that. "Good job, kid," he said.

Hattie wiped at her eyes. She wasn't crying—not that Sherman could see—but there was *something* there. "Here, let me help you."

"Thanks. That'd be good."

Titus sat looking on, then busied himself nosing through the hair covering his hindquarters, sniffing so much, it seemed he might inhale something back there. Sherman knew the dog was really just picking up the scent of something he'd run through earlier. Titus would not wander, not in the dark. That was at least one constant with that dog—he could be relied upon to be petrified of the darkness, big as he was. Just as Elmore's dog, Sid, had been. After all, they were from the same blood. It made sense that Titus had not only inherited Sid's sensitive nose, but his nyctophobia, too.

"Where did you come up with the name Titus anyway?" Hattie asked.

"Shakespeare."

"Shakespeare? *Really?*" Hattie said.

Sherman cocked an eyebrow. "Oh, I get it. Because I've slung a bullet a time or two, I can't have no culture at all."

"Okay, satisfy my curiosity some, then."

"What, with the hows and whys?"

She nodded.

Sherman looked at Bobby, who was visibly eager to hear the story. "Well, I was passing through this town. Burnham's Rest, it was called. Kinda like Elam Hollow, to tell the truth. Same layout, just bigger. Anyway, I was there for a few days, and this traveling man was in town with his big wagon. Kinda thing that opens up, and it's a little stage in there. You know, for traveling theatricals."

"I know the type," Hattie said.

"Well, I don't usually pay that kind of thing much mind. But this one night as I happened by, a young woman was up on the tiny stage, performing. I found myself stopping right there and listening to the whole damn thing. Can't say I understood every word of it, but it still made sense, you know?"

"I think so," Hattie said.

"Anyway, I hung back at the end to talk to her, but she'd run off somewhere. However, the guy who drove the wagon from one town to the other, he was the boss, and he explained that she'd been performing part of a play called *Titus Andronicus*. It's all about the last days of the Roman Empire and tells the story of Titus, a general in the Roman army who's stuck in a cycle of revenge with Tamora, an evil queen. I don't think my version of the story does it justice but you get the gist, right?"

"Sure," Hattie said.

"I appreciated the character Titus. Bloodthirsty, vengeful and impulsive. Just how I'd been, way back, before I came to my senses. So, when I finally wound up with a pup on my hands, the name just had to be Titus."

Once the fire was going, Bobby cooked them a meal of beans and corn bread.

As Hattie tucked in, she said, "Hey, Bobby, these beans are really good. Where did you learn to cook?"

"It's one of Sherman's recipes," Bobby said.

"No kidding?" Hattie said, looking at Sherman in disbelief. "Who'd have thought it . . . ?"

"You didn't think I could cook, either? I'm starting to feel insulted," said Sherman.

"Well, I just never thought about it, to be honest. But these are probably the best beans I've ever had. Tasty, not too spicy."

Bobby rolled his eyes. "Please don't make the man more conceited than he already is."

Sherman licked the back of his spoon. "I have a lotta know-how when it comes to cooking. Like I taught the kid, it's important to be restrained. *Too much spice ain't too nice.*"

"Oh, heavens, you've turned it into a nursery rhyme," Hattie said. She turned back to Bobby. "Had you cooked before?"

"No," Bobby said. "Where I grew up, everything was kinda . . . cooked for us." He spoke tentatively, as if it would land him in some kind of trouble—that or he'd lose their respect for being born into privilege. But if he had encouraged either reaction, neither Hattie nor Sherman let it show.

"I see," Hattie said.

Sherman offered around his bag of red-and-white candy. "Care for some?"

"What is it?" Hattie asked. She took a piece from the bag and sniffed. "Peppermint?"

"You got a good nose," Sherman told her.

Bobby took some candy and popped it into his mouth. "Sherman's sweet tooth, this is called."

"You be quiet," Sherman said, grinning as he took a piece of candy for himself, then pushed the bag back into his belongings. "Every man got his vice."

"Better than some, I guess," Bobby said.

"Y'know, when I was riding with all those unsavory types, I got a pretty good education in bein' on the road," Sherman explained. He got up, rescued the coffeepot from the heat. Steam billowed from the neck. Sherman poured three cups of the hot dark brew. "Setting up camp. Cooking. Cleaning. Tending the horses. All of that. You learn real fast to get good at that stuff or face the wrath of the fellas you're riding with."

Hattie accepted her coffee from him. "Thanks. You know, I find it hard to imagine you as a young man, getting kicked in the rear end by cowboys while your brother was at home working the farm."

Sherman handed Bobby his coffee. "It sure was different, I can tell you."

"How old were you?" Bobby asked.

"Nineteen when I first set out," he said, setting the coffeepot down on the grass and sitting back around the fire with the other two. A gust blew in from the side, making the fire dance. The three of them shrank into their clothes until it passed. "Saw a lot of cold winters, I can tell ya."

Hattie sipped her coffee. "Ever think about quitting?"

"Never. I missed Jed, though. Missed him a lot." Sherman looked into the fire, into the shifting amber light, and felt something lift inside of him. He realized he'd never admitted to himself how much he'd missed his brother, let alone to anyone else. It was a lot different saying it aloud. "Especially later, when I rode on my own, huntin' people down and the like. Some of those nights were awfully long and, let me tell ya, awfully lonely. I don't feel any shame in admitting that. Not that I ever imagined I would."

"What, admit it?"

He smiled. "Don't know if you've noticed, Hattie, but it's not often a man says what he really means."

"Believe me, I've noticed," Hattie said. "Men either say one thing and mean another, or they don't say nothin' at all."

Titus wandered over, settled down with his head in Bobby's lap. "Guess he's picked his spot," Bobby said, rubbing the dog's head.

"He likes you, kid."

"Well, I suppose I like him, too. What was he like?" Sherman frowned at him. "Who?"

"Jed."

Again, Sherman found himself turning to the fire. Looking into the heat, the light, the power to destroy and create. He had no idea what fire was or how it had come to be. He understood it only enough to know its dangers and uses. Having respect for something did not mean he had to understand every facet of it. But in the fire he found something he was trying to put into words, and it was the answer he gave Bobby. The only one he could think to give.

Sherman looked at his sister-in-law. Hattie nodded slowly, letting him know wordlessly that she knew how he felt in that moment. She too had the same scar inside, next to her heart—marked by the same loss.

"He was my brother," Sherman said. "And he was a better man than I."

THEY SETTLED DOWN for the night. Bobby checked on the horses, then put himself to bed amid a pile of furs and blankets. It didn't take long for Titus to work his way in with him, taking advantage of Bobby's body heat.

"I guess I'll turn in, too," Hattie said.

Sherman smiled at the sight of Bobby and Titus. "Look at him. You wouldn't believe what he was like, Hattie. Drunk. Living on the street. Looked like a stiff wind would bowl him right over."

"But he's so young," Hattie said, shaking her head. "How do you fellas end up in that state?"

Sherman shrugged. "Life deals them a bad hand. They get themselves caught up in ways they can't break the habit of keeping. I don't know. . . . All I know is, he turned out good in the end."

"*You* done him good." Hattie looked at him. "You know, you're probably as close to a father as he's got."

Sherman waved his hand at her, dispelling the notion.

"No, I'm serious. If he's got nobody, Sherman, don't you think he looks at you like that? You stepped up for him. Otherwise he would've died. Am I right?"

Sherman looked at the kid. "I guess you're right. . . ."

"I know I am." Hattie fed some kindling into the fire to keep it burning into the night. She tossed in one more piece, then turned to look at him. "You weren't wrong, you know."

"How do you mean?"

"When you said that Jed was a better man than you."

Sherman met her gaze. "I know."

"Losing him has been hard."

"I know it has," Sherman said. "Do you know when I was most proud?"

Hattie pulled up a blanket and wrapped it around herself, on top of her furs. "Go on."

"It was teaching Jed how to shoot. You know when we set off, and I made sure you and the kid could shoot proper? And you said you were taught by the best? It made me feel so proud to know that Jed appreciated it. That he remembered the lessons. Just about the only thing I ever taught him, apart from how to fend for yourself when your only sibling runs away from home and leaves you with all the responsibility."

"Do you feel guilty about that?" Hattie asked.

"I do. Some. Yeah."

"You know you've gotta let that go, Sherman. I was married to the man, and I can tell you with all certainty, he didn't hold a grudge about it. Never so much as spoke about it, really. Only in the beginning. Later he was just thankful to have you back in his life."

After she had turned in and Sherman followed suit, he lay for a long time listening to the moan of the wind. He listened to the horses stir. He listened to the fire crackle. He closed his eyes and he thought of that day, teaching Jed to shoot, and how he could hear the gunshots ricochet around them in the emptiness.

By the time the job with Tom Preston came about, Sherman was done with killing. The only reason he took the job at all was that there was to be no violence. That was the idea. A simple robbery. No bloodshed. No more innocents caught in the cross fire of man's murderous desires. That was before Tom Preston committed needless violence; before he left Sherman to freeze to death; before Elmore had to amputate Sherman's hand and several of his toes; before Sherman gave up the ways of the gun and learned how to be a houndsman and a trapper.

But Annie's kidnapping had awakened something in him he'd not felt for a long time. Sherman knew what he would do when they caught up with Tom Preston and his compatriot. For killing innocent people. For nearly killing him. For stealing his niece away from a new life in a new town. For causing Hattie further heartbreak when she'd endured so much already.

Sherman would make him pay, and he would enjoy doing it. He opened his eyes and looked up at the black sky. No stars. Just empty darkness.

*   *   *

B OBBY TURNED OVER in his sleep, lost to a dream, to a memory. The past encircled him like vines, and he could not fight it, could not free himself of its grip.

There wasn't anyone watching as Bobby climbed down off his horse and approached the sheriff's office. His back still smarted from the rough night's sleep he'd had in the cell. But the night had taught him something. It taught him he did not want that life. He wanted to be free of his father once and for all.

He removed a note from his pocket and used the butt of a revolver he'd stolen to nail it to the door. At some point, the deputy would return and find it. And then he'd know all that Bobby knew. The great evil committed by his father and those in his employ—and Bobby's attempt at making good. Hopefully it would lead to his father's arrest and trial.

On his way out of town, he passed the bordello for the final time. Bobby stopped outside and looked up at the windows. Light shone behind Rosa's curtains. She must have heard him riding by, because she appeared in the window and looked down at him, her face lighting at the sight of him there. She lifted her hand and Bobby waved back.

Then Rosa closed the curtains and left him to ride away from Amity Creek for good. He felt the cool air in his face, and for a moment rode with his eyes closed and arms outstretched, catching the breeze, feeling like he was floating. As if he were flying . . .

Bobby opened his eyes. The dream dissipated. It took a moment for his vision to clear, to fully make out the dark outline of Sherman hovering over him. It was just before dawn.

"Come on, kid. Time to get up."

"It's not even light," Bobby groaned.

"Not yet, but it will be. I wanna be riding inside the hour," Sherman said, patting Bobby's upper arm through the fur and blankets. "Come on."

"All right, all right," Bobby said, irritated.

After the day's ride they'd had, sleep had found him easily. His exhausted mind had taken him back to Amity Creek, to the bordello at the edge of town, to Rosa. He'd wanted her to run away with him but even as naive as he'd been back then, he'd known it was just a pipe dream. When he left town for the last time, for forever, he made the bordello the last thing he rode past. He'd said goodbye to it all, but on occasion he found Rosa in his dreams and slipped beneath the smooth, cool sheets with her.

Eventually he had lost everything he left town with. His horse. His hat. The stolen pistol. Every scrap of his mother's jewelry. In the end, after drifting from one town to the next, Bobby had ended up with just the threadbare clothes on his back and a thirst for booze he couldn't kick. He'd had to lose himself before he found himself.

But why?

He'd asked himself the question over and over. All he could think was that once his eyes opened to the truth about his father, drinking dulled the pain, the hurt and the feeling that he did not belong anywhere — that he had no right to be in any one place, because his past was so thoroughly corrupt.

His father had been a bad man. The *worst*. And he'd tried to make Bobby just like him. Almost succeeded, too, before he realized for himself just who and what his father was.

Sherman woke Hattie and left her to get up, then returned to Bobby, who was rolling up his bed. "Sleep okay, kid?"

"So-so," Bobby said.

Hattie joined them, adjusting her clothing. "Morning."

"How 'bout you? How'd you sleep?"

"Surprisingly, with everything on my mind, I slept like a baby."

Sherman smiled. "That's good to hear."

"You're smiling. Do I amuse you in some way?"

"No, no," Sherman said, lighting his pipe.

Hattie stood, arms folded, waiting for an explanation. "Come on. Out with it."

"Just something Jed told me once. It's nothing. Doesn't matter."

"That's unfair," Hattie said.

Bobby joined in. "Can't do that to someone. You gotta come out with it now."

"All right, all right," Sherman said with a roll of his eyes. "Jed said if the house fell down on top of you, they'd find you snoring under the rubble. There, I said it."

"Really? He said that?"

Sherman nodded. "He said you sounded like a locomotive."

"Well, it's a good job he's dead, Sherman, or I'd give him a piece of my mind," Hattie said sternly. "It's the one time a man's been saved by being six foot under, let me tell you!"

The three of them broke out in laughter at that. Sherman wiped at his eyes. "Damn, Hattie. That's the worst, and the *funniest*, thing I've heard in a while!"

She finished up laughing and wiped at her own eyes. "I know. . . . So are you both quite done?"

"I think so," Sherman said, still chuckling to himself. Then he thought of Annie, and his fear for her was enough to sober him, any desire for further laughter extinguished. He inhaled deeply, and the mirth left his features as if he had shed a disguise. "Okay. Now I *am* done. Let's get this all packed up and head out. We've got ground to cover."

A S THEY RODE, the sun broke over the frosted landscape, pushing through the blue shadows. It rose, lifting the veil of dawn and spilling its warmth, giving light and dimension to the prairie. Bobby looked at the sunrise and closed his eyes for a moment, just to feel the fortune of its kiss on his skin. It wouldn't have taken much for him to imagine he was back on his horse fleeing Amity Creek with his arms outstretched, as close to flight as he'd ever get.

Sherman rode up ahead, Titus trotting along next to him. Hattie sat astride her horse next to Bobby's.

"Quite something, isn't it?" she remarked.

Bobby opened his eyes. It had been only seconds, but seconds were enough. There were moments he felt particularly glad Sherman had rescued him from the gutter, and this was one of them.

Hattie nodded toward Sherman. "Glad he has a good sense of direction. I have no clue where we are."

"Me neither."

"Really? You're his protégé, aren't you?"

Bobby tried to explain. "Well, it's not like I couldn't find us a way back or anything, but if you asked me where we are on a map, couldn't tell you. Not the way Sherman can."

"Our leader. Riding so bold and confident at the front. Leading the charge," Hattie said, smiling affectionately. "D'you know, when he turned up on our threshold all those years ago, missing a hand, he was so different from the Sherman we'd always known."

"Really?"

"I mean, he was the same, but . . . *not*. Like a porcelain figure that had been smashed, then glued back together. You know? It looks whole, but it's not. That's what Sherman was like: as if he got glued back together. Fixed but never the same."

"Sounds like it was a good thing," Bobby said. "You know, the way it turned out in the end."

"Can't disagree on that."

Bobby thought about the way Sherman had glued *him* back together and wondered if he could be considered a better man for it. On that score, he reckoned only time would tell.

CHAPTER ELEVEN

SHERMAN RAISED HIS right arm, the one with the hook, to tell Hattie and Bobby to stop where they were. "Hang back a second. Let me check this out," he said, going ahead.

"What is it?" Bobby asked.

Sherman pointed at the ground where mud and grass had clearly been disturbed. The ground had frozen, which meant the evidence of what had taken place was rock-solid. There'd been a light dusting of snow out here, a prelude to what was coming. But not enough to cover what needed to be seen.

Sherman peered up at the sky. "It'll open up before long."

"Better make this fast," Hattie said. "Before we lose their tracks."

Sherman shot her a look. "I know what's at stake."

He turned his attention back to the ground. As he looked on, Titus walked through it all with his nose to the ground. Sherman brought up his horse and climbed down. He walked beside the tracks.

"They stopped here. Correction, they were *forced* to stop here when they skidded in wet mud. Now it's frozen solid, which is good news for us. It means all the evidence is here. We've just gotta figure which direction they went next."

Titus bent his head low, snorting with his big leathery nose. There were times Sherman envied the mutt for his ability to track by scent alone. It was a marvel.

"A lot of activity around here," Sherman said, pointing to the section of ground in front of him. "Two smaller boot sizes. Women's. They got onto horses."

"Where did they go?" Hattie asked, her voice desperate.

Sherman followed the hoofprints. "They went that way," he said, pointing. He beckoned Titus to him and encouraged the dog to smell the horse's tracks. Smell the girls on them. Smell the two men who'd taken them, Tom Preston and Leroy Jenkins.

He'd not thought about Tom for a long time. But since he'd left Elam Hollow to rescue Annie, exacting revenge was all Sherman could think about. He thought he'd moved past it. Clearly, he had not. His hatred for Tom Preston had merely been in hibernation all these years. Now here it was, fully risen from its slumber and ready to go to work. He felt it in his flesh, in his blood.

What were the chances that the man who'd left him to die had kidnapped his niece? Sherman had never believed in fate, not really. But now he had to admit to himself that there was something fateful about everything. With Jed gone, Hattie and Annie were all that remained of his family. He couldn't afford to stay out of things any longer. He'd spent a long time forgetting the man he used to be—but now he realized he had some remembering to do. Because the man who was going to get them through this was a mixture of the Sherman he had been and the Sherman he was now. Both the dark and the light.

Titus had the scent now and began following their trail.

"Good boy," Sherman said. He quickly got back up on his horse and beckoned Hattie and Bobby to follow. "Come on. We gotta keep up with him."

Bobby rode on ahead, right behind Titus. Hattie hung back a moment, seemingly wiping tears from her eyes.

"Hey," Sherman said to her gently.

She sniffed. "I know, I know. I know what you're going to say. I can't behave like this. I have to be strong."

Sherman reached out between their horses for her hand. When she gave it to him, he squeezed her hand reassuringly. "We're gonna get her back."

Hattie squeezed his hand back, accepting what he said.

T HE SNOW CAME in drifts and the wind picked up, screeching like a banshee in their ears. After following the bandits' trail for two hours, the dark finally spooked Titus. He grew less inclined to press on ahead and follow the scent of the bandits' passage with their quarry. He hung back, uncertain. Sherman got down from his horse and walked next to the dog to give him encouragement. But even so, Titus soon lost the scent—he nosed at the ground where the snow was collecting, and walked around in circles, trying to reacquire it.

"What's wrong with him?" Bobby asked. "He's lost it?"

"He's lost it," Sherman confirmed, kneeling to pat Titus. "You done well, though, boy. You got us this far. We're gonna find it again."

"Is that even possible in this snow?" Bobby asked.

Sherman looked from the kid to Hattie, wanting to be direct and truthful but knowing there was a fine line to be walked here. "It *is* possible," he said.

Bobby shivered inside his furs. "Temperature's dropping fast now there's no sun."

"I know," Sherman said.

He turned around, trying to figure out the countryside they were venturing through. His eyes had adjusted to the dark—he'd insisted on no lamps or man-made illumination of any kind. At least, not for the minute. There was a hill up ahead. Tom Preston and Leroy Jenkins might have simply ridden on in a straight line, in which case Sherman would find something promising just over the rise. To the left was flat, empty prairie washed out by moonlight, the same to the right.

"I say we press on a bit. See where that takes us. But we might have to stop for the night. Set out again just before dawn."

"We can't stop again!" Hattie said. "We can't give up on them."

"Nobody is giving up," said Sherman. "But we can't do Annie any good if we don't get some shut-eye tonight. You can bet Tom Preston will be doing the exact same thing."

"It feels wrong," Hattie said.

"I know it does. But it is what it is. I'm askin' you to trust me," Sherman said. "Do you trust me?"

Hattie closed her eyes, bit her bottom lip. She nodded once. "Yes," she said, opening her eyes again and looking straight at him, into him, to his very core. A worried mother desperate to know what was happening to her child. "I do trust you. Both of you."

Sherman climbed back up onto his horse, rescuing the reins from Bobby. "Then that's fair enough," he said.

With Titus keeping up alongside them, Sherman led them up the hill and to the ridge. The snow had gathered there several inches thick now, blanketing the ground. To some extent, when the wind relented now and then, it afforded them more visibility because the ground became a good reflector of the moonlight. The world before them was darkness accented by blue-white land, trees, distant hills.

Bobby drew up next to him. "Any idea where the hell we are?"

"I know this country. Not been this way for a long time, mind, but it's comin' back to me," Sherman said. He pointed to a stream glittering in the moonlight. "See where that comes out? There's a rocky outcropping there we can use for shelter for the night. It's not a lot, but it'll shield us enough we can get a fire going, at least."

"You've stayed there before?"

"Once, a long time ago. It's frequented by a few folk, I believe, when they pass through here and find themselves caught short for the night. We should be fine."

"Sure sounds good, gettin' out of this wind for a bit."

"I know what you mean. We could do with some dinner, too," Sherman said. He looked to the right. "See in the distance there, the woodland?"

Bobby followed Sherman's gaze. "I see it."

"I reckon they went in there."

"You do?"

Sherman nodded. "Can't risk it in the dark, though."

"Why don't we head that way instead? Try to get the jump on 'em."

"There ain't no sneaking up on anybody in the woods, kid. Believe me, I've made that mistake myself, thinking I could creep on somebody. The woods always have a way of betraying you. Gotta know where you're walkin'. Best to cut through there in the light, see if Titus can pick something up. The snow won't lay in there, either. Tracks should be undisturbed."

"Makes sense," Bobby agreed.

"Come on, then," Sherman said, leading them down the hill, across the white flat and toward the stream.

T HE OUTCROPPING WAS as Sherman last remembered it. The stone was ice-cold to the touch, but it didn't matter—the main thing was getting out of the wind and being able to light a fire, which they were able to. Titus dozed at the very rear of the overhanging rock, in the shadows. The dog had a way of lying on his side, head at an angle, rear legs wide open and his saggy fruits on full display.

It didn't take long for Hattie to rustle up some bacon and grits for a quick warming meal. Neither man had asked Hattie to cook dinner. She had taken over of her own accord. Probably, Sherman mused, to keep herself busy. The busier you were, the less time you had to think about what was going on.

"I wish we had some of the sheriff's brandy to hand," Hattie said, staring into the fire. "It really hit the spot, that did."

"Neither of us touches the stuff," Sherman said.

"How come?"

Before Sherman could answer, Bobby spoke up.

"On account of me. A little while ago I had a major problem with the stuff."

"I'm sorry. Sherman told me earlier about your drinking. Hope you don't mind me knowing."

Sherman said, "Hattie, it's fine. Bobby's not embarrassed, are you, kid?"

"Not in the slightest. I had a problem and Sherman helped me through it."

"Did he?" Hattie asked.

Bobby ran his spoon around the edge of his tin, scooping out the last remnants of the dinner. The salty, smoky bacon fat had run into the grits, and the result was heavenly. "I was about to drink myself to death. Not that I realized. Sherman took me off the street and saved me."

"You exaggerate a bit there, kid," Sherman said dismissively.

"Don't you listen to him, Hattie. It's all true."

"Ever think about trying it again?" Hattie asked Bobby.

"Occasionally I get a thirst for it."

Hattie nodded slowly. "Must be hard being addicted to something."

"It is," Bobby said. He wiped at his mouth. "The hardest."

Sherman reclined back on his fur. "He's done real well. You know, back in the day, I helped a couple of men fight off the booze. The demon in the bottle, they called it. I thought it was a good description, to tell the truth—y'know, after what I seen 'em go through."

"Did they stay off it?" Hattie asked. "Once they'd kicked the habit, did they ever try the stuff again?"

Sherman looked from Hattie to Bobby. Then he looked away, unable to hold the kid's gaze. "Eventually. To varying degrees."

Bobby set his tin aside and lay back on his own fur, looking up at the top of the outcropping. The firelight made the shadows dance, casting what was overhead in strange shifting shapes.

Sherman got up. Went back there. "Hey. Sit up so I can talk to you."

Reluctantly, Bobby sat up and looked at Sherman.

"I don't think you'll go back to the booze, kid. It's just what happened to those guys. They fought it on and off the whole time I rode with 'em. All the time you're workin' with me, you won't find a drop of the stuff at the cabin. That's a guarantee. But I can't watch over you everywhere you go. And you know . . . I ain't gonna be around forever."

"I know that."

"Keeping clear of that stuff . . . that's on you. Listening to you say I saved you, I keep thinking how wrong you are."

Bobby frowned at him. "How d'you figure?"

"I didn't save you. You saved yourself. Only *you* could stop, and that's what you did. Don't you ever get to telling yourself that it was me stopped your drinking. It was you and only you. One day when you're tempted to take a drink, it won't be me holding you back. It'll be you, kid."

"Sherman . . . ," Hattie said, her voice tight with fear.

Sherman turned around.

Four shapes appeared beyond the reach of the firelight. They seemed to form out of the darkness as they drew near and at first Sherman thought his eyes were playing tricks on him. But then he realized what those shapes were.

Four men.

The fire lit their features from beneath so that each of them looked devilish and mean. Bobby made to spring up, but Sherman told him to stay where he was.

Hattie cried out.

"Well, look what we got here," one of the men said. He had an eye patch and a short gray beard. All four men wore hats and thick furs. They were covered in snow, head to toe. Sherman heard horses stamping their hooves not far away—probably their own rides, which they'd hidden under a second outcropping farther down the stream. It provided less shelter than the one they'd set up camp in, but it was enough for the horses.

The other three men were equally sinister in appearance. One was bigger than the others, his round face split by an eager grin. One had been slashed across the face at some point in his life—a scar ran from one ear to the other in a thick jagged line across his cheeks and nose. The fourth man had covered the lower half of his face with a red-and-white bandanna. Each of them held their weapons at the ready.

Eye Patch sniffed the air. "*Mmmm*. It appears we just missed supper, boys."

"We don't want no trouble," Hattie said, her voice trembling as she took several steps back.

Bandanna laughed. "Hear that? The woman don't want no trouble!"

Sherman strained his ears to listen for their horses. He hoped to God that they hadn't cut them loose or done something to them. Without horses, they were truly without hope. They could not make the journey on foot. It was impossible.

"What do you fellas want?" he demanded, his hand already hovering over his pistol. He glanced back at Bobby sitting on his fur. The kid's hand drifted to his own gun belt.

Round Face said, "Whatever you got."

"Nothing worth having."

Scar licked his lips as he looked at Hattie. "Well, you got one thing I can think of."

Sherman grimaced. "Over my dead body."

"That'll be the general idea," Eye Patch said.

They stepped around the fire. Two closing in from one side, two the other.

"Now, we can do this the easy way," Eye Patch continued, "or we can do it the hard way. Give us your gear and the woman, we might just let you boys live. Do the opposite, well . . . I don't think I need to spell it out."

"You can't just sneak up on folk and take what you want," Hattie said.

Eye Patch lifted a finger, grinning. "Excuse me, miss, but I think we can."

"I won't let you," Hattie said.

"If you think you're gonna have time to pull those shooters, you're wrong. You'll be dead before you fire off a single shot. So don't even try it. There's four of us and three of you."

A growl rose from the shadows at the rear of the outcropping. The growl became an angry snarl.

Eye Patch's one good eye twitched toward the sound. "What is that?"

"That's Titus," Sherman said, stepping to the side. He stuffed his fingers into his mouth and blew, producing a shrill, piercing whistle. Titus leapt out of the dark, teeth bared, and lunged at the man with the eye patch. The man with the scar turned toward him in shock as the dog knocked Eye Patch to the ground.

Bobby rose up behind Hattie, aimed at Round Face and fired. He hit the man square between the eyes, leaving a big hole. As Bobby watched, the fat man slid to the ground like a sack of wet meat.

Meanwhile, Eye Patch fought to get out from under Titus, screaming as the dog sank his teeth into his neck. He pushed the snarling dog away and scrambled to his feet. "Get away! Leave me alone!" He ran off, clutching at his throat, his own blood running through his fingers to fall on the cold stone.

Dragging his eyes away from Eye Patch, Scar turned his gun on Sherman.

Beating him by a fraction of a second, Sherman pulled the trigger of his own shooter in rapid succession, plugging Scar twice in the chest. The man staggered back, over the lip of the cave, falling into the dark beyond the fire's light.

Hattie pulled her gun free and fired at Bandanna. The man ducked away just in time, her shot blowing the hat clean off his head. He scarpered away, leaving his hat where it fell. Hattie went to follow after him, but Sherman's hook came down to push her gun toward the ground.

"Not you. We'll go."

Hattie nodded reluctantly.

Without hesitation Titus went after the men, gone in a flash. Sherman turned to Bobby. "Come with me, kid." Sherman jumped down from the outcropping, the landing jarring his old bones, Bobby close behind. Scar was off to the side, at the edge of the stream, bleeding out and trying to crawl away without success.

Making better progress in escaping, Eye Patch scrambled up the embankment after Bandanna, one hand holding the torn flesh of his throat as he climbed. He got to the top, Titus right behind him.

"Titus, leave!" Sherman yelled.

The dog immediately turned on his heel and ran back to him.

"Check our horses," called Sherman.

"On it," Bobby replied.

Sherman pointed at Titus. "Stay." The dog whined his disapproval. "I mean it."

He climbed the embankment, short of breath by the time he reached the very top.

The two bandits were about to escape. They were on horseback and each one held the reins of a fallen man's ride.

"Come on! Let's get out of here!" Bandanna yelled as he glanced behind him and saw Sherman, gun at the ready.

Eye Patch slammed his heels into the sides of his own horse. "Yah!" he cried to get the beast going.

Sherman surged forward, aimed at the man's back and fired. The bullet punched through, right between Eye Patch's shoulder blades. As his horse took off, he slumped forward in the saddle like a rag doll. Several yards away, he slid lifeless off the horse altogether.

Bandanna spurred his own horse on. Sherman shot at him but somehow he missed and the bandit made it away. He took aim, then decided against firing again; at that distance, with the adrenaline coursing through him and the lack of light, the shot was far from sure, and Sherman didn't want to waste another bullet intended for Tom Preston.

B ET YOU COULD do with that brandy now, huh?" Sherman asked Hattie when he returned with Titus.

"That c-came out of nowhere," she said, her hands shaking.

Sherman took her hands in his to still them. "Hey, hey. It's over now. This is how it happens. When you least expect it."

"It was s-so quick."

"It always is," Sherman told her.

Bobby returned, red in the face. "Horses are fine."

"The body of the fat one is down by the water. The other fella is still alive, by the looks of it," Sherman said.

"What shall we do about him?" Bobby asked.

"I'll deal with him."

"What're you gonna do?" Hattie asked.

Sherman checked his gun. "What's gotta be done."

"Do you mean . . . ?"

"I mean, I'm gonna end him, Hattie," Sherman said. "Kid, drag the fat one up over the bank and leave him somewhere out of sight. I'm not burying 'em. We'll leave these desperadoes for the wolves."

With that, Sherman stepped down off the ledge of the outcropping and walked to where the man with the facial scar lay breathing raggedly, blood bubbling from his nostrils. He looked at Sherman fearfully.

Just like the old days, Sherman thought. He kicked the man's gun away, then holstered his own weapon.

The man swallowed. "What're you gonna do?"

"Help you," Sherman said, hooking his arms under the man's armpits. Scar did not resist. He couldn't; he was too far gone. Sherman dragged him away, around the corner and up a shallow embankment to a narrow flat area behind a cluster of rocks several feet high. He pulled him past that, through the snow, far from the stream and the outcropping, to where a gathering of hardened bushes stood covered in a thick blanket of snow. He laid the man there.

Scar coughed. Blood spilled from his mouth. "Don't," he gurgled.

"No choice."

Sherman pulled his gun and aimed it at the man's ruined face.

"Please . . ."

Sherman spared him one last look. "It's already done," he said, and pulled the trigger.

B OBBY PULLED THE fat one's body away, out of sight, then checked the man's pockets for anything that might be of use. He found some money, some ammunition. He took the fella's gun; it might come in handy. It felt wrong to be taking the property of a dead man and yet he thought he would be a fool not to.

Somewhere nearby he heard low voices, and then the sharp report of a single gunshot snapped through the air.

In the man's inner pocket, he found a dented metal flask. Bobby opened the top, took a sniff. It was filled with whiskey. He went to toss it away, then thought better of it. Checking there wasn't anybody around, Bobby hesitated, then hurriedly pushed the flask into his pocket.

What am I doing? he asked himself. *Why am I taking it?*

But he knew the answer—knew why he couldn't just walk away without it. He had a sickness. Had a taste for the stuff and couldn't leave it be. Not when he was being given the chance to quench his thirst.

Sherman appeared out of nowhere. "Hey."

Bobby stood and showed his mentor the gun. "He had some money and ammo, too."

"Good. Might come in handy."

"That's what I thought."

Bobby went to walk off. Sherman reached out. "Hey. Wait a second."

Oh, no, Bobby thought. *He saw me take the flask....*

"Are you all right?" Sherman asked.

"Yeah."

"Sure?"

Bobby nodded. "I mean, I just killed a man, but other than that, I'm right as rain. Why d'you ask?"

"Just checking," Sherman said. "It's a big deal, killing someone."

Both men looked down at the fat man with the big round face. He hadn't been nearly as heavy as he looked or Bobby had expected him to be. The big hole in the man's forehead seemed improbable and yet there it was. Red, fresh, with a stream of blood oozing from it. The man himself seemed to be looking up at the snow. It was disconcerting.

"How about Hattie?"

"She's in shock but she'll be fine," Sherman told him. "I finished the one with the big scar across his face."

Bobby nodded slowly. "I heard. What happened to the other two. Did *they* get away?"

"No, they did not," he said simply. He could tell by Bobby's expression that the younger man understood his meaning. "Come on, kid, let's get back to the fire."

As they walked, Bobby asked, "What about Titus? He really ripped that guy's throat out, didn't he?"

"That mutt's fine. I bet he's lying next to the fire, licking his lips."

Sure enough, when they got back to Hattie, they found Titus sprawled out before the fire, doing just that. Licking the blood from his lips.

CHAPTER TWELVE

SHERMAN FOUND IT impossible to fall asleep. He was on edge still. Worried the man with the bandanna would return, seeking vengeance for his fallen comrades. And another thought had crossed Sherman's mind: those four men could've belonged to a larger gang. Who was to say that Bandanna wasn't on his way back with more men?

Such thoughts kept him from relaxing fully. When he woke around three in the morning, after finally dozing off for a moment, he found Hattie snoring, dead to the world. Bobby was lying on his fur with his eyes wide open.

"Hey," Sherman whispered.

Bobby sat up.

"What're you doing?"

"Same as you," Bobby said.

Sherman accepted that. "Fair enough. Try to get some sleep, kid."

"I keep thinking—"

"I know what you're about to say," Sherman interrupted. "I don't think that dude is coming back this way anytime soon."

"Can you be sure?"

"No . . . I cannot."

Bobby lay back down to continue staring up at nothing. Sherman followed suit. He shifted onto his side to look out into the darkness. The fire had died now, but he could still see the smoldering remnants glowing red-hot within the gray ash. As such there was still some heat emanating from it. He burrowed down within his fur and closed his eyes, hoping that sleep would find him and it did, eventually, washing over him like warm water. He was back in Elmore's cabin all those years ago. Skinning martens while Elmore chatted away, saying a lot and saying nothing at the same time. Sherman's hands were working away at the fur, attempting to remove it from the carcass in one go. Of course, it was a dream, so he had both hands but it was a surprise. He marveled at it and thought, *It's grown back!* But when he looked away and then back, it had disappeared, leaving a bloodied stump where Elmore had hacked his hand clean off.

Sherman looked up. Elmore still had the knife in his hand, its blade coated with blood. As Sherman watched, Elmore lifted the blade and ran his tongue along the broad side, licking the blood off. As he retreated into the shadows of his cabin, his eyes flashed metallic green like those of a mountain lion.

When Sherman woke a couple of hours later, the first thing he did was reattach his hook to his forearm. He examined the curving metal, to be sure it had all really happened. Then he noticed that Hattie was gone.

"Relax," Bobby said as Sherman shot up. "I just watched her leave with her canteen in hand. She won't go far."

Sherman flopped back, holding his chest. "That scared me half to death."

"I could tell," Bobby said with a smirk. "You were crying out in your sleep."

"Was I?"

Bobby nodded. "You kept saying something about your hand."

Sherman got up. "No surprise, is it?"

"Guess not," Bobby said.

"Let's get most of this packed up, eh? Then we can get some coffee in us before we go. I got a feelin' we're gonna need it, kid."

IN THE AURORA of dawn, Hattie Knowles watched the rose light break upon the horizon, rising into the pale canvas of the sky with promise. The day before she had harbored only despair and fear in her heart. But this morning, with the air so clear and crisp, Hattie had woken with the warmth of hope in her breast. She wondered if Annie was seeing the same sky, the same color bleeding into the world. And she wondered if her daughter had a moment to appreciate it. After the violence of the night before, it felt transformative to find the world so renewed.

She bent to the gurgling stream and filled her canteen, holding it under until no more bubbles burst from the neck of the vessel, then securing the cap to prevent it from spilling. She looked to the spot where the man with the scar had lain bleeding. There was a frozen puddle of blood there, and a trail of red from when Sherman had dragged him away. Hattie had heard the shot and was almost ashamed to admit to herself that it had not scared her, had not left her horrified. She had, instead, felt the way she did when a cow or a pig was put down because of ill health or injury. That it was something that just had to be done. Better to end a creature's suffering than allow it to linger, when the inevitable was going to happen whether they liked it or not.

If anything, the sudden violence of the night before had let Hattie find something inside of herself she had never known was there. And whereas she'd been doubting whether she could ever stand up to the men who'd taken Annie, she knew now that she could. Where she'd felt weakness, there was strength.

Hattie walked back through the rocks and mud to their camp. "You boys got up and got busy, I see," she said, gathering her things together.

"No time to waste," Sherman told her. He worked on filling his pipe and peered up at the sky as he pressed the tobacco in with his thumb. "Beautiful morning."

Hattie didn't say anything. She wanted to keep her appreciation of it to herself, that secret inner communion she had held at the water's edge moments before.

"How about those fellas last night, huh?" Bobby said, stretching. "I thought they was sure to come back. I hardly slept."

"Me neither," Hattie said, sounding exhausted.

Bobby set about getting the coffee going, and before long, they were drinking it, their breath turning to clouds as they talked. Hattie stamped her feet to keep them warm.

As Sherman drank, he thought about standing over the man with the scar and telling him, *It's already done.* He thought about his lack of feeling in that moment and how he'd pulled the trigger and silenced the man forever. After so long it should've made him feel sick to his stomach, but the truth was . . . he felt the old icy hardness in his heart. Like an old friend coming home. He examined the contents of his cup, swirled it

about and drank a mouthful. Then he tossed the rest
of the coffee to one side. It hit the ground and within
seconds was a frozen brown slick on the hard stone.

"Time to saddle up," he said.

A T THE EDGE of the woods, Sherman told Bobby
and Hattie to dismount; they'd have to head inside on foot, because there wasn't enough clearance
for them to ride on horseback. While he said this, Titus
seemed to pick up on something, nose low to the
ground.

"He's got the trail, I think," Sherman said.

They walked their horses in by the reins. There was
a definite path of worn ground through the woods
made by travelers over the years, a bare corridor
through the trees. Flints and roots protruded through
the packed soil, so they had to watch their footing.
Many years before, Sherman had seen a man trip on an
upturned root and crack his head open on the way
down. When you were out in the middle of nowhere,
there was no excuse for being complacent with your
safety. A small risk became a big one when you realized you were miles from help.

The woods were silent, and even picking their way
forward as quietly as they could, Sherman was conscious
of the noise three people, three horses and a dog made
when they weren't trying to make any at all. Suddenly
Titus ran off ahead of them. He had the scent now, and
nothing Sherman could do or say would deter him.

"He's getting it strong now, huh?" Hattie asked.

"You bet," Sherman said. "When he gets like that,
he can go miles ahead. I lost him completely once.
Didn't find him for two days. You ever been on a locomotive when it shoots through a tunnel and all you see
is the light at the very end?"

"I have."

"It's like that. The course of the rails is the scent, and all Titus sees is the station at the end, away in the distance. I swear, dogs like him, huntin' dogs, they'd run themselves to death if you let 'em."

Hattie shook her head. "One-track mind."

"Definitely."

"You know, Jed could be like that," Hattie said with a chuckle. Her gaze became distant, and a smile appeared on her face. "So single-minded when he wanted to get something done."

"Don't surprise me none," Sherman said. "Jed was like that when we was no higher than saplings."

Silence fell between them then, both lost in their own memories, their own sadness. Sherman had thought about his brother on and off since leaving Broken Bow and heading back home. But seeing Bobby right had kept him occupied. Now he realized that because of Bobby he hadn't had time to grieve Jed's loss. Either the kid had deprived him of his grief or saved him from it.

"I miss him, Sherman. He'd be here now with us, trying to find her, if he were still alive."

"I know he would. I miss him, too. When I spoke to him last, he told me he was scared not knowin' what would become of you and Annie."

"He did?"

Sherman nodded. "I told him I'd look after you both. I told him the way it is, that you and Jed were my compass when I needed one."

Hattie smiled but her eyes shone with tears. "He was proud of you, Sherman."

"He was the man I always wanted to be. I was ashamed of myself for heading the other way, for doing what I did. I sure wish I had told him."

"Important thing is, you came right in the end,

Sherman. Jed knew you would eventually. He never lost the faith."

"Is that the truth?"

"He knew for everything you did with your guns, you were still a good man. I think you proved to him that you are. That he was right about you."

Sherman looked ahead. Without the path to guide them, they'd have been lost in the woods. He had only a vague notion of where the sun was, of what direction they'd come already. He guessed it had always been this way, him lost and wandering so long he eventually ended up finding his way.

B OBBY ALLOWED HIMSELF to fall back somewhat as Hattie and Sherman talked. He held the horse's reins in one hand and with the other he patted the flask in his pocket. *Why did I take it?* he asked himself over and over. *Why haven't I tossed it already?*

Bobby thought about reaching inside his clothes, removing the flask and throwing it away. But something in him refused. It would not let him reach in for the flask, let alone throw it away. His mouth salivated at the thought of its contents. He could almost taste the whiskey on his tongue. Feel its burn as it slid down his throat, trickling down into his stomach, a hot vein of fiery nectar that would enrich his soul if he just let it.

But Bobby knew it wouldn't stop at the contents of the flask. He'd need another drink, and *another*. The thirst could never be quenched. It was there and always would be.

So the best thing is to get rid of it. Right now, before Sherman or Hattie spot it. Right now, before it becomes a problem.

And yet his hand remained on his clothes, feeling the outline of the flask. He patted it again, assuring himself that there would be a grand reacquaintance before too long.

He just had to pick his moment.

T HEY CAUGHT UP with Titus in what remained of a camp. Sherman told Bobby and Hattie to hang back so as not to confuse the tracks and markings. He took in the ashen remnants of a fire, some twigs that had been used as skewers to roast meat. Sherman lifted one of the skewered carcasses and sniffed what scant meat was left on its bones.

Rabbit.

He tossed it aside. Saw the spot where both men had sat, the indentations of their rear ends in the dirt visible to the naked eye. He saw where they'd slept, too, on opposite sides of the fire. Sherman circled out, studying the ground, eventually finding himself at the two trees where the women had been tied. He knelt, touched the cold dirt. *So close*, he thought. Titus fell in next to him and Sherman showed the mutt some attention, rewarding him for getting them this far and hoping the dog would get them farther.

"What do you smell, boy?"

Titus looked at him, head cocked to one side.

"Do you smell 'em?"

Titus barked.

Sherman stood. "Come on boy! Get 'em!"

Turning in a circle three times, tail wagging, Titus could have been a pup again. Sherman wound him up, then let him loose. The hound tore off through the woods, and Sherman returned to his horse.

He turned to Hattie and Bobby. "Guess we press on. He's got their scent all right. They weren't here too long ago. Half a day at most."

"She's close?" Hattie asked.

Sherman nodded. "Real close."

Hattie threw her arms around him. "Oh, Sherman. We really gonna get her back?"

"I promised you that we would. Now let's get moving before that damn dog gets to them before we do."

PART FOUR

—— ◇ ——

NINE YEARS AGO

CHAPTER THIRTEEN

ONE DAY ELMORE left with Sid and never came back. Sherman was not worried. He was not Elmore's keeper, after all. Often, they would set off in different directions to check on their traps and be gone all day. It was hard work. If you didn't know how to set the trap correctly, it could go off unexpectedly and take your hand with it—and Sherman couldn't afford to lose another. As it was, he found operating the tough iron contraptions difficult with one hand and a hook, but he adapted and discovered his own way of doing things, just as Elmore told him he would.

"Life's different for you now, Sherman. Gotta adapt with the times," Elmore told him one morning. "Once you master it, that hook's no less of a hand than you had before."

Sherman found it hard to agree with his mentor on that score. He struggled mightily with the hook, mostly with remembering that it was there. How many times had he gone to catch something before it fell, only to find he was knocking it away with his hook? More than he could count now that he had only five fingers to do it on.

So it was not unusual for Elmore to head off and stay out until dark. Sherman set off himself to check on the beaver traps down by the lake, and while it took most of an afternoon, when he returned there was no sign of Elmore. He removed the beaver meat, prepared the skin and waited. Night fell and Sherman stood outside, watching for any sign of Elmore returning to his cabin. Laden with furs and traps, as he so often was. Sid running ahead of him on his long legs.

But no one came.

When it reached midnight and Elmore still hadn't returned, Sherman was struck with the sense that something bad had happened. Desperate as he was to go look for his friend, he knew it was futile to do so in the dark, on his own, not knowing where to look. To find Elmore, Sherman would have to rely on everything he'd learned from the old man. That meant reading the signs, finding a trail and following it. Elmore was a big man, so it wouldn't be too hard to find his tracks. But for that, he needed light, so it made sense to start at daybreak.

Sherman opened the cabin door as the pink dawn broke behind the trees. He did not spare the time to make coffee or breakfast. Sherman simply donned his boots and got going, a single pistol at his hip. They'd tried different ways of getting a bow and arrow to work, but with the hook protruding from his wrist, it proved impossible.

Elmore had conceded that Sherman would be best served using his pistols. "Well, either one you want to carry. Obviously, it don't make too much sense carrying both no more, if you take my meaning," he'd told Sherman.

After Sherman had practiced his aim and gotten back into the way of things, Elmore remarked upon how good a shot Sherman had proven himself to be.

"What're you, some kind of gunslinger?" Elmore asked.

Sherman holstered his piece. "Something like that. Not no more, though."

"Glad to hear it," Elmore said, patting him on the shoulder. "Hopefully, you don't even have to draw that thing."

"Maybe I can get by without carrying anything at all," Sherman suggested.

Elmore had laughed at that suggestion. "Peaceful as it is out here, Sherman, you never know what's coming. Not really. Always best to carry something, just in case. You might never need it . . . but you can't be sure, you know?"

A COOL MIST MOVED through the pines. Sherman looked up, at their tops so improbably high. A bird flew overhead here and there, but otherwise all was quiet. He could see the allure of a life like this. A man could live out here on his own and never have to worry about the motives of the neighbors living around him. You were alone with nature. It felt as if it were the way it was always meant to be. In truth, Sherman had never minded riding on his own and spending a few weeks with only himself for company. He'd always been at peace with himself in the silence because in the silence you knew you had nothing to fear from others. It was people he didn't trust, and for good reason, too.

Now he quickly picked up Elmore's tracks and followed them. Elmore's movements were clearly defined by his boot markings through the dirt and mud, in the broken young branches that had bent as he brushed past them. Sherman also came across Sid's scat—no mistaking the leavings of a dog big as Sid, especially when there were no wolves in this stretch of woods.

Presently he found himself at one of Elmore's traps. It'd been reset with fresh bait. His mentor liked to use aged strips of elk if he could get it. Elk were notoriously hard to find and to bring down, but Elmore had killed his fair share of them. He'd described to Sherman how he cut some of the skin into strips and aged them in a container for months so that they turned rancid and stank of decay. The critters Elmore caught went nuts for the stuff. Not only could they pick up the scent a mile away; they couldn't resist it, either.

Sherman found the smell hard to stomach and preferred to stick to less repugnant bait for his own traps. He breezed past the trap and continued deeper into the woods, to where it grew shaded and dark and the air got close enough to stick to your skin. He must have walked that way for hours, not that he had much sense of the time anymore. He arrived at a spot where the ground sloped down, and Sherman had to fling what he'd brought with him down to the bottom, then slide down holding on to protruding tree roots and shrubbery to slow his descent. He could see where Elmore's boots had dug in, scoring the mud all the way down. At the bottom he gathered his things and looked for the tracks to tell him which direction to go, but they were confused by water that had gathered there, forming a wide, boggy puddle. Sherman stepped over it, casting about for anything that might indicate Elmore's passage through this section of woodland, but he found none.

He was sure that something was wrong and that Elmore was waiting for Sherman to come find him, help him out of a tight spot. Elmore was a good man. For all he knew, Sherman might've been a murderous maniac, but he'd pulled him from the snow anyway, saving him from certain death, and had now taught him a trade from which he could make a living. Sherman had to find him. There was no other option.

"Come on . . . ," Sherman mumbled, feeling desperation wash over him. He pictured Elmore lying dead at the bottom of a ravine. He pictured him being held hostage by a gang of bandits. Finally, by a tree trunk not fifteen feet away, he saw a frenzy of paw prints and the half-formed impression of a boot. Now Sherman pictured Elmore running from something. "I'm coming," he said.

E LMORE LAY FACEDOWN in a clearing. He was not moving, and as Sherman drew near, he saw the claw marks all the way across the big man's back. Like he'd been sliced open by giant knives. Sherman knelt by his side and turned Elmore over. To his surprise and relief, Elmore was still alive. Sherman felt the man's neck for a pulse. It was weak and irregular, but it was there.

"Elmore!" Sherman said urgently. He looked around for any sign of whatever or whoever had attacked him, but the woods were still and peaceful. There were just the trees and the whisper of their branches in the breeze.

Elmore blinked up at the daylight, eyes pale. "Didn't see it, didn't hear it coming."

"What was it?"

"A bear. Got Sid, too," he said, swallowing. "Do you see him, Sherman? Is my dog there?"

Sherman tried to spot the dog, but there was only a puddle of blood several yards to his right. He figured that it was probably Sid's blood and that the dog had been carried away by the bear that attacked them both.

"No . . . ," Sherman said. "I'm sorry."

Elmore closed his eyes, squeezing them shut in pain. Tears rolled from both, down his temples, skirting the topography of his ears. It was hard to see such a strong, resourceful man reduced to tears by the death of his companion. Then he grabbed Sherman, his grip uncompromising, and stared hard, eyes burning. "Don't rest your face here. It'll be back."

"No, I'm going to move you. I can take you with me."

"I'm done for."

"Don't say that," Sherman admonished. "I can fix those wounds."

He knew, deep down, that he could not. Whether he treated Elmore there or back at the cabin, Elmore was going to die and soon. Sherman also knew that Elmore was right—the bear would be back.

"You know what you need to do," Elmore told him, sagging back, overcome with weakness. He looked off to the side, to where the ground was dark and wet with Sid's blood. "What has to be done."

Sherman shook his head. "I can't. I don't want to do that no more."

"Just finish me, damn you," Elmore snarled. He looked at Sherman—he'd now turned a pallid shade. "For once in your life, have mercy on your fellow man. Finish me, Sherman. It's the least you can do."

Sherman got up. Pulled his pistol free and thumbed back the hammer. He stood, arm stretching down, gun pointed at Elmore's forehead. He should have been trembling. Any other man, emotions would've gotten the better of his nerves and rendered the shot impossible to take. But Sherman had learned long ago that this was when he was at his best. In the face of death, he was calm, collected. Dispassionate. Right there, in the stillness of the woodland, about to deliver a mercy killing, Sherman knew precisely why he had to be done with his old ways, because it was too simple, and it was too easy, to extinguish life with just a pinch of his fingers.

"Do something for me, Sherman," Elmore said.

"Anything," Sherman told him. "Tell me."

"There's a box in the cabin. Inside you'll find a locket and a letter in an envelope sealed with wax. Take them to my daughter. She lives in Helmstone. Goes by the name of Winona Watson these days. You won't miss the similarity between us."

"I'll see that it's done. Don't you worry about that. Anything else?"

"Just some money tucked away in the cabin. It's yours. That and the mares. That's about it. All I have in the world to say I was ever here. Now don't you get designs on burying me. Just leave me out in the open, right here. Seems a good spot. Good as any I suppose. Let me pass into the earth the way it's meant to be done. Don't much care for the idea of bein' left down there in the dark. Better to see the moon pass."

"Whatever you want."

"Thank you."

"You've been good to me, friend," Sherman said, the tender words sounding odd in his mouth; he wasn't used to speaking in such a way.

"Nice of you to say." Elmore smiled through his pain. "Go on, then. Get it done."

Sherman said, "I'll make sure it was all worth it."

The woods seemed to hold their breath in anticipation. Elmore closed his eyes. Sherman flexed his finger on the trigger.

Suddenly a great crashing sound broke the silence and Sherman had just enough time to look up. A bear came bounding out of the trees, growling ferociously, its gigantic teeth on display. It reared up on its back

legs to give Sherman a full display of its physical potential, of how futile it would have been to run from it. He
could see the blood on its lips just as its mouth opened,
and the roar that exploded made the blood in Sherman's veins turn to ice.

He aimed the gun at the bear. Right between the
beast's eyes. It snarled and braced to charge, and for an
awful moment, it just stayed that way, glaring at him,
huge muscles poised. Then suddenly it surged forward,
all fur, muscle, teeth and claws coming directly for him.

Sherman fired. Once. Twice. Three times. The shots
rang out, loud and crisp and echoing through the trees.
The bear groaned and took several steps forward before stumbling over its own feet and crashing to the
ground. Blood pumped from the center of its head. It
shifted a couple of times, then with a final sigh lay
completely still. Sherman kept his gun trained on the
big brute for a full minute before slowly lowering it.
Each shot had ripped into the bear's skull, to his relief.
If he'd hit its body, it would have still come for him.

His heart hammered in his chest and he had to take
a moment to breathe again. "Damn, did you see that?"
Sherman gasped, looking at Elmore.

The man was gone. His eyes were closed, his skin
already turning gray. He looked at peace. Sherman
wondered if Elmore had seen him take down the bear
that had mortally wounded him. Whatever the case,
Elmore looked as if he were resting. Sherman sat upon
the ground, unable to move or do anything for the
minute. Nesting birds fluttered up into the sky. Sherman looked up to watch them fly away and wondered
if Elmore happened to be flying with them.

E LMORE HAD TOLD Sherman to leave him out in the
open, but as much as Sherman wanted to abide by

the big man's wishes, he couldn't stand to leave him that way. He tried to think of an appropriate way to cover his body; then his gaze fell on the downed bear. He did a hasty job of stripping the fur from the bear's back—not the way Elmore would have approved of if he'd been alive to see it, but one man could not turn a bear over by himself to do the job properly. It was not a fur that could be sold, but it would do for this purpose well enough. The resultant piece of bear hide, four feet wide and seven feet long, smelled awful as he laid it over Elmore's body, but it was a symbol of the life Elmore had led as a houndsman, not to mention it seemed fitting to cover him with the fur of the beast that had been his downfall. He was still respecting Elmore's wishes, just giving him some dignity. Sherman stood over Elmore's body in the dimming light and tried to think of something to say. He was suddenly aware of being entirely alone in the middle of nowhere. Even Sid was gone.

"Don't know how long I'll last living out here by myself," he said. "I'll get by long as I can. It'll be hard, though, with you and Sid gone. I'll see to it your daughter gets what you want her to have. And thanks for the money. . . . It won't get wasted. Not much else to say, I suppose. Hope you like what I did. Thought you might appreciate it, you know. Keep the chill out a while. I know you had no love of the cold."

Sherman walked back the way he'd come and glanced back just the once to see Elmore's form beneath the bearskin. He already knew he would never come this way again; he would avoid it at all costs. This was as good as hallowed ground to him now. Sherman liked the idea of flying away when he died; it sure beat the hell out of being left in the open.

When he reached the cabin, he hesitated at the threshold. Somehow it didn't feel right, like he was trespassing somehow. But then Sherman stepped over the sill and walked inside, aware that the cabin was his now. He got a fire going and sat before it deep in thought. *What am I gonna do now?* he asked himself. He was not immune to the aching of the human heart, and he mourned Elmore's passing just as any man would have mourned the passing of a friend or brother. But he did not allow himself to fester in loss. So the next morning Sherman went out trapping, just as Elmore had taught him.

CHAPTER FOURTEEN

SOME WEEKS LATER, Sherman made the decision to leave the cabin. The cold weather was setting in, and he missed the company of Elmore and Sid. The warmth of the fire was all the cooler without a friend to share it with. He regretted the lack of conversation and the friendly nuzzle of Sid's big wet nose against his palm. He thought often of Elmore dying and couldn't be sure why it seemed to bother him so much. But Sherman didn't have to ponder too far for the answer. Deep down, he knew the reason why—because he'd been about to deliver a mercy kill. Shoot Elmore to end his suffering. It troubled him far more than any killing ever had. Maybe because he'd liked Elmore. Maybe because he was changed and didn't have the stomach for it anymore.

Or both.

So he packed up what was there, finally locating the small box Elmore had told him about and opening it up. Inside, he found some letters, including the one that was sealed with red wax, intended for Elmore's daughter, Winona. The locket was at the bottom of the box. Sherman opened it up. There was a picture of a baby on one side, and a faded photograph of a woman on the other. Sherman assumed the baby was Winona, and the woman her mother.

Sherman found the money Elmore had told him about. There was enough there to last him six months if he was frugal. There were furs to sell, too. All in all he could wander freely for over a year if he chose to. There wasn't a whole lot else to take from the cabin, apart from his own clothes, what few there were, and his shooters. For a crazed moment, Sherman considered just leaving them behind. Letting somebody else continue their story. But in the end, he took them along, knowing he might need them. After all there were always other bears.

SHERMAN RODE THE laden wagon, led by Elmore's two mares, across open countryside falling under autumn's spell. The air had a decided nip to it, and by the time he reached the town of Little Chester, he was pulling his jacket about him to keep warm. He sold the furs to a trader there Elmore had had dealings with over the years, and while the price he got wasn't the best, it would do. Sherman was aware that he was still very much a wanted man. The chances of anyone putting a name to a face were slim, especially given the beard he'd grown since living with Elmore. That and the missing hand, of course. No one would think he was Sherman Knowles . . . unless they managed to spot his pistols. Sherman had taken extra care to hide them away, just in case.

He bought supplies and a warm winter coat, gloves, everything he would need for spending time out on the road.

"Goin' somewhere, son?" the tailor asked as Sherman looked at himself in the full-length mirror. He barely recognized himself.

"Maybe I am," he said simply.

H E'D LEFT THE boy at the general store loading his supplies into the back of the wagon, and tipped the kid for his efforts. Inside he purchased tobacco from the owner of the general store, a man named Mead. He'd just finished describing how Elmore had met his end. Sherman and Mead were not friends, exactly, but the two could stand and chew the fat awhile, which sometimes was just as good as friendship.

"That bear got Sid, too?"

Sherman nodded as he accepted the tobacco from Mead and tucked it away into his pouch. "Sure did. A cryin' shame if you ask me."

"It really is. Both of 'em," Mead said, momentarily lost in thought. He looked at Sherman. "I remember selling Elmore that dog."

"He got Sid from you?"

"Yessir. One of Barney's offspring. Barney's gone, too, now," Mead said, voice tinged with regret at the dog's loss. "Mind, Sid didn't go before siring another litter with our bitch."

That stopped Sherman in his tracks. "Really?"

"Yessir. Last run Elmore made, last time I seen him. You didn't come with."

"There was too much to do."

"That's what Elmore said," Mead agreed. "Anyway, he let Sid mate with our bitch, and low and behold, she got pregnant."

"Are they for sale?"

"Sure. Wanna come see 'em?"

Mead led him out the back where Sherman found

the mother, a well-tempered mixed breed, with puppies crawling about her that were no bigger than Sherman's fist. He saw one that looked a lot like Sid. And there was another, dark gray in color, that looked spookily like a dog he'd had as a child. Sherman lifted the puppy out and examined it.

"How much?" he asked.

Mead scratched at the stubble on his jaw. "For you? In honor of Elmore, this one's on the house."

"No, no."

But Mead was insistent. "Honestly, no charge."

"Are you sure?"

Mead insisted he take the pup with him. "The litter's too big anyway. I'm not sure I can even find homes for 'em all."

Sherman held the puppy in front of him. It looked back with its big dark eyes and Sherman thought it just might have been the greatest gift he'd ever received. "Thank you," he said simply.

"No bother." Mead offered a smile. "Hope he's as good for you as Sid was for Elmore. Now, you be sure to come back this way someday."

"I will," Sherman said.

He never did.

O N THE WAY out of Little Chester, Sherman considered buying a bottle of whiskey but thought better of it. Drinking on the trail was an old habit coming back to him and he knew that he'd do well to ignore its impulses. When you were out on your own, you needed your wits about you. Sherman couldn't count on both hands the number of times he'd been set upon while traveling; the only difference between him ending up destitute or dead was the pistols at his hips—that and his speed.

"Not this time," he told himself, and the wind picked up as if in answer, Sherman realizing the big warm coat wasn't so good at keeping the cold out after all.

He had the pup tucked inside the coat and peeked in at it. The puppy yawned, its jaws lined with tiny needlelike teeth.

Sherman grinned at the sight and knew that, if Elmore were still around, he would have, too.

In the evening Sherman happened upon the lights of a farmhouse and asked the farmer's permission to make a camp on his land. He was secretly hoping the man would invite him into the house for the night but was not so fortunate. The farmer directed him to a fallow field up from the house, and said he'd get no trouble from passersby up there.

"Shot a fella trespassing on my land just last summer," the farmer told him, proud of himself. "Don' worry about no trouble here."

Sherman made a modest fire and cooked some sausage he'd purchased back in Little Chester. He ate first, then sat feeding the puppy cooled pieces of the sausage until it was full and could manage no more. When that was done, he lay back and watched the fire with the puppy working its way inside his coverings to keep warm.

"You cold?" Sherman asked.

He'd known eventually he'd get himself a dog to train as Elmore had done with Sid, but coming across a litter from the same dog that had fathered Sid had to be destiny, didn't it? There was no way he could pass that up.

Sherman let the puppy share his body heat and lay back. The night sky was surprisingly clear, and he could see every star there was available in the firmament, like diamonds on black velvet. Whenever the world took something away from you, it gave something back to balance the scales. And sometimes, what it had given you since the beginning, you only began to see when the time was right—when you took a moment to gaze up at what hung over your head.

T HREE DAYS OF travel later, he arrived in Helmstone, a town he'd never heard of, let alone been to. It was a small place, with a sorry excuse for a main drag consisting of about six stores. No sign of a sheriff's office or jail. No bank, though that was not to say there wasn't an office hidden away somewhere. Sherman left the puppy in a crate in the back of the wagon and covered it over with a thick blanket. He headed to the saloon, where four sorry patrons sat.

"Help you, friend?" the bartender asked.

"Sure. I'm lookin' for Winona Watson. That name ring any bells with you? I didn't see no law office out there. Otherwise I'd have checked in with the sheriff first."

"If you're after the sheriff, you're out of luck," the bartender said, nodding in the direction of an old man slumped in the corner. He was fast asleep, the snore issuing from him worse than anything Sherman had heard in his life. "He's been out of it since yesterday suppertime."

"This a regular thing?" Sherman asked.

The bartender rolled his eyes. "Afraid so."

"No point bothering with the sheriff, then," Sherman said, shaking his head.

"Afraid not. We're not the kinda place sees any trouble, tell the truth."

"Fortunate, I'd say," Sherman scoffed.

"Be that as it may, I *can* help you. Winona lives at the doctor's place, opposite the church. You can't miss it."

"That so? I appreciate the help."

The bartender frowned at him. "You, uh, family, are ya?"

"Friend of the family," Sherman said. He reached across the bar to shake the man's hand. "Thanks for your help."

"You're welcome."

Sherman left the saloon and looked up the street. The steeple of the church jutted up into the dull gray sky; across the road from it he saw a whitewashed timber building with "Dr. Watson" written on the front in dark blue paint.

Sherman checked on the mares, made sure they weren't going anywhere and headed up the street toward the doctor's office. It was a strange little town, a "blink and you'd miss it" kind of place. There wasn't much to offer folk to seek it out and live there, not unless you were looking to get off the map in more ways than one. Sherman knocked hard and waited for an answer. None came. He tried to peer through the windows, but couldn't see any illumination within and no sign of movement. It was dark inside.

"If you're looking for the doctor, he's up at the Crouch farm, delivering their fifth child," a woman's voice said behind him.

Sherman turned to see someone who bore a striking resemblance to Elmore. The same big cheekbones and flinty eyes. "Howdy, miss."

"How do you do?" she asked uncertainly. "As I said, the doctor is liable to be several hours yet. Not one of the Crouch children ever came easy. Is it an emergency?"

"No, no, nothing like that," Sherman said. "As it happens, I've not come to see the doctor. I've come to see you."

The woman backed up a step. "You have? I don't mean any offense, sir, but I'd much rather have this conversation in the presence of my husband. I've never met you before, and—"

He cut her off. "It's nothing like that," Sherman said, offering Winona the box. "I don't mean any harm. Don't be alarmed. . . . I have something to give you."

She frowned quizzically at the box. "I don't understand."

"You *are* Winona Watson, aren't you?"

"Yes."

"Then this is yours."

"What is it?" she asked, accepting the box.

"Just some things your father wanted you to have," Sherman told her, and he looked on as Winona opened the box.

When she looked up, her eyes shone with tears. "How is it this is in your possession, sir?"

Sherman removed his hat. "I think we'd better talk inside," he said.

WINONA SAT ACROSS from Sherman as he explained how he had come to be in the company of Elmore. He gave her his impression of the man, his kindness, the calm, easy way he had about himself. Sherman told Winona how Elmore had taught him how to track, and hunt, and trap. How to survive out there in the middle of nowhere, living at the mercy of Mother Nature. Then he told her how Elmore had died.

"A bear?" Winona gasped, her hand to her chest.

Sherman explained how he'd felled the beast and left Elmore there in the clearing, as he'd wanted. He was selective in what he shared with Winona—not duplicitously so, but there was no need to give her all the grisly details. Her father had died, and that was awful enough.

As he looked on, Winona opened the box again. She

reached inside, pushed around at the contents to see what was there and withdrew the locket. "Oh," she said.

"I saw the pictures inside. Reckoned one must be you as a babe."

"Yes," Winona said, smiling fondly. "I haven't seen this since childhood. My mother took me away. Dad went to the woods. We came here."

"I see. Is she still around, your mother?"

Winona looked up. "She died two years ago."

"Sorry to hear that."

She shut the locket. Enclosed her hand around it. "Thank you so much for bringing this to me. He wanted me to have this?"

"It was his dying wish."

"Can I offer you coffee or something to eat?"

"No, no," Sherman said, shaking his head. He pushed his chair back and stood. "I must be heading out. I promised your father I'd deliver that box to you. So now I guess he can rest easy, knowing you got that."

"And he's in a clearing? I'm not sure how I feel about him not getting a proper burial and all."

"It's the way he wanted it. He said he deplored the thought of being underground. I can't say I blame him. At least now he'll be under the sun and under the stars. I like that thought, unconventional as it is. Being left out there, he'll nourish the woodland and live on in some way, I guess."

"When you put it like that, it isn't so bad," Winona admitted.

Sherman picked his hat up off the table. "Can I ask you something before I go?"

"Anything."

"What was he like when you were young?"

Winona put the locket back into the box and closed the lid. A shadow passed over her features and she adopted an aggrieved expression. "He was not the man you described to me. We left because my mother feared his cruel heart. That's the way she explained it to me. Of course, she is not here to elaborate. And he is not here to defend himself. That's the way I look at it."

"Did he ever hurt you or your mother?"

"Not that I know of. But I think it was more that he had the capacity for inflicting hurt that scared her," Winona said, smiling thinly. "Unlike you. I can see just looking at you that you have a good heart. You couldn't hurt anybody."

H E SAT WITH the puppy in his lap and took the wagon out of Helmstone. On his way he passed the doctor's office and Winona was on the threshold, waving him off. Sherman smiled at her and waved back, but the moment he was clear, the smile was gone. He thought on what she'd said: *We left because my mother feared his cruel heart.*

Was that what people would say about him when they tallied up the sum of his actions? The number of men he'd brought to justice righteously and those he had not? There was a reason he had chosen not to become a bounty hunter but a hired gun. One operated within the boundaries of the law. The other did not.

You couldn't hurt anybody, she'd said. In Winona's innocence she believed him to be a good man while Sherman knew that, given a reason, he was anything but. His own capacity for inflicting hurt was beyond what Elmore's daughter could possibly imagine.

Sherman turned in his seat to look back at Helmstone as it receded behind him. Then he faced the road ahead once again. She'd talked of cruelty, but Winona had no idea she'd been in the presence of a badman, right there in the sanctity of her own kitchen.

CHAPTER FIFTEEN

W HEN SHERMAN REACHED Broken Bow, he made a detour to see the Mountain Fork River, which ran almost a hundred miles, or so he'd heard tell. The river was bordered by thick pine forests, and Sherman thought he'd never breathed air so clear. He looked at the deep green water, its banks home to bald cypress trees shedding their golden leaves in the breeze, and just knew he had to fish the Mountain Fork before he left. He wasn't even sure where he would go from here. His only thought had been to visit Jedediah, his wife, Hattie, and their young daughter, Annie. Beyond that, he had no clue. Seeing his brother seemed the right thing to do, however.

He arrived in town before midday and oriented himself toward Jed's farm, asking at the general store for directions. Before leaving, he used some of the money Elmore had given him to purchase gifts—candy for the girl, fine chocolate for Hattie and a box of cigars for Jed. It'd been a while but he assumed his brother still enjoyed a cigar now and then.

Sherman tried to think about the time that had passed since he'd visited Jed last. Not since Annie was just a baby. How long ago had that been?

It dawned on him that he had no clue. He remembered Jed telling him that they were moving to Broken Bow. He remembered reuniting at the old house when their mother died, Jed talking about his farm in Broken Bow, how well it was going.

Still, Sherman had not visited.

He began to feel a knot tighten inside his stomach as he drew near to his brother's farm, unsure about showing his face after however long it had been. He contemplated just stopping the wagon and turning around. Perhaps they were better off not knowing him at all. He could leave town now and they'd never know. But he did not give in to his fears, deciding to do what he'd always done and ride them out instead. Follow the road before him, wherever it might lead.

T HEY WERE OUTSIDE before he arrived, the sound of his approaching wagon announcing his visit before they saw any sign of him. Sherman saw Jed do a double take at his appearance, perhaps finding it hard to believe that the rugged bearded man before him was his brother.

"Sherman? Is that you?" Hattie asked, one hand on her hip, the other shielding her eyes from the sun.

He brought the wagon to a stop and raised his hand in greeting. "Afraid to say it is," Sherman said, climbing down. He bounded forward and Hattie drew him in with a hug.

"It's been a long time," she said.

"I know."

They parted, and Sherman turned to his brother. Jed was staring at the hook where his right hand had been. "Sherman . . ."

"Don't I get a hug, Jed?"

"Of course . . . ," Jed said, doing as Hattie had done. Sherman was certain they were sharing looks with each other, wondering what in the hell was going on.

Sherman stepped back. He felt emotional in a way he never had before. *How could I have entertained the notion of just turning around and not bothering? How could I have thought I'd be any better off for it?* "The, uh, mares could do with feed and water if you're able."

"Of course. Barn's over yonder," Jed said, tipping his head in the direction of a low-slung barn away from the house. "We'll meet you inside when you're done. I'm guessing you'll be eager for food and water, too."

"My appetite's much the same as it always was," Sherman admitted. He looked around. "This is one helluva place you've got here, you two."

Jed made a humble face as he hooked his arm around Hattie's shoulders. "It's been good for us."

"I'll reckon it has," Sherman said with a smile. "Let me release these mares and get them set."

"See you in a minute," Hattie told him.

He moved the wagon and positioned it behind the house, out of sight—conscious of the fact he was still very much a wanted man in certain circles. He then unbridled the mares one at a time and led them to the barn, where he stabled them and provided feed and water. It was warm inside and lined with fresh hay. They'd get a good rest there. There were two horses in there, a big chestnut and a smaller light gray horse. Before leaving the barn, Sherman made sure to say hello to both, rubbing their broad noses and running his hand down their necks. They were good horses and must have cost Jedediah a princely sum.

Sherman stepped outside and closed the barn door
behind him. Jed and Hattie had done well for themselves. After years of hard work, Jed deserved to the
see the fruits of his labors. He hadn't lived fast and
squandered things like Sherman had.

Sherman fetched the puppy from the back of the
wagon and carried it into the house with him.

"What's that?" Hattie asked.

"A pup I got given. I'm gonna train it up."

Hattie took the little bundle of fur from him and
looked at it adoringly. "Oh, look at you," she said,
glancing at Sherman. "What's his name?"

"Don't know yet."

"You mean you haven't even got a name for the
poor creature?"

"Afraid not."

"Is that a puppy?" a small voice asked. Sherman
turned to see young Annie in the front doorway, staring first at the puppy, then at Sherman. "Who are you?"

"Annie, don't be rude," Jed said.

Sherman knelt to look into her eyes. "You're full of
questions, aren't you, little one?"

The girl bit her lip.

Jed came to stand next to Sherman. "Annie, this is
your uncle."

Sherman offered Annie his hand. He cradled the
puppy in the nook of his right arm, hook on show. Annie shrank back. "What's that?"

"That?" Sherman said, regarding the hook, as if
seeing it the first time. "I lost my hand."

"How?"

"It fell off. So a man made me a hook for it. Do you
know what they call something like this?"

Annie shook her head.

"A prosthetic. My other hand is real, though.
Nothin' wrong with it at all," Sherman said. "If you

shake my hand, maybe I'll let you look after my puppy for a spell. How does that sound, huh?"

Annie weighed up her options. Unsure about shaking the hand of the stranger who'd appeared in her home, but enamored with the puppy trying to wriggle out from Sherman's grasp, Annie shook her uncle's hand.

Sherman smiled. "See? Not so scary after all. Now can you take care of this little rascal for me? Just for now—I need him back after. But he probably needs a friend right now. Can you be his friend, Annie?"

Annie nodded and took the puppy.

"You take good care of him for Uncle Sherman," Hattie warned her.

"I will."

Sherman stood. Reached out and touched the top of Annie's head as she fawned over the puppy. "You know, when I saw you last, you were but a baby," Sherman said. "Now look at you."

"I'm a big girl now," Annie said, stroking the puppy.

"You sure are. How tall are you anyway?"

Annie didn't miss a beat. She was straight there with an answer. "I'm four feet tall. Look, it's here on the doorframe," she said, leading Sherman over to the door that led to a bedroom. Sure enough, measurements of her height were carved into the frame in notches. They marked how she'd grown over the years, some measurements farther apart than others. It was interesting to Sherman to see the growth spurts. Not so dissimilar to the rings in a tree trunk, each marker of its life impacted by different factors.

"That reminds me," Sherman said, producing the candy. "I got this for you."

"Thanks!" Annie said, accepting the candy.

"Go take that puppy to your room," said Hattie. "See if he wants to play."

"Okay," Annie said, walking off.

Sherman watched her go. "She's wonderful."

"She really is," Jed agreed. "Glad you got to see her before she got too old, brother."

That stung. Sherman fetched the presents he'd bought for Jed and Hattie. "Got you both something, too. Chocolate for you, Hattie. Cigars for you, Jed. Just a little somethin' from me."

"Much appreciated," Jed said, admiring the box of cigars.

Hattie deposited the chocolate into the front pocket of her pinny. "Thank you very much. I'll be sure to partake of this when Annie isn't around."

"Be sure you do. She's got her own," Sherman said.

"Oh, don't worry. I will."

Jed removed one of the cigars and ran it under his nose.

Sherman cleared his throat. "Uh, Jed, listen . . . ," he said awkwardly, trying to choose his words, pick around at what he wanted to say.

But his brother held up both hands. "No need to go over old ground, huh? Come on. Take a seat at the table and tell us how you ended up here. You in trouble?"

"No more than usual," Sherman said with a twinkle in his eye.

Hattie poured coffee into mugs and tutted. "Still blowin' through life like a breeze, I take it."

Sherman sat down. "Not so much." Hattie set the coffee down for him. "Thank you."

"Food will be a bit longer," Hattie said.

Jed sat at the head of the table and warmed his hands on his cup of coffee, studying Sherman from across the tabletop. "Am I gonna have the law at my door, Sherman?"

"No."

"Your word on that?"

Sherman nodded once. "My word."

"All right, then. So tell us what you gotta tell us," Jed said.

Sherman looked first at Hattie, then at his brother. He opened his mouth and it all just unspooled from him: the thread of the years falling around his feet, and his life open for his brother and sister-in-law to see. No bluster, no lies. No making what was ugly more palatable. Nothing but the truth. His story, his life, the way it had happened.

When he was done, Jed sat back in his chair, deep in thought. Hattie got up, collected the coffee mugs and set about finishing the meal. Sherman tried to think of what to say next, but found he'd expended himself. Words failed him.

To his relief he didn't have to say a thing.

"So you've turned over a new leaf," Jed said finally. "About time, too."

"Yes, I agree."

Jed looked at him. "You fish, you say?"

"Elmore taught me."

"I seem to recall our father taking us to fish," Jed said.

Sherman smiled. "No, that was just you. He never took me."

"Sure?"

"Pretty sure," Sherman said.

"Bet you noticed the Mountain Fork on your journey here, didn't you?"

Sherman grinned. "Sure did."

"Well, how's about you spend the night here. No need to rush off. Don't seem like you have anywhere particular to go."

"True."

Jed ran a hand over his chin. "Spend the night, and tomorrow morning, we'll head up there to the river. Fish it together."

"I'd like that," Sherman said.

"Seems to me we never done that," Jed said.

Sherman thought about it. "I think you're right."

"High time we did, then."

"Warn you now, I'm a mean fisherman, Jed."

His brother pulled a face. "I ain't so bad myself, you know."

THAT NIGHT SHERMAN lay on the floor, on a makeshift bed Hattie had assembled for him near the fire. He listened to the house creak slightly in the breeze. It was warm inside and snug, and he could hear his brother's and sister-in-law's soft snoring coming from their bedroom. The puppy was sleeping with Annie. Sherman considered gifting her the dog, but he'd grown fond of it himself. Not to mention that it came from good stock. It'd make a fine hound if he trained it right.

He decided he'd get her a puppy in town if he could find one.

The house didn't feel like the cabin he and Elmore had shared. It felt like a home. A place where memories were made and folks made something their own.

Jed and Hattie had welcomed him in with acceptance and understanding. They'd shown him empathy when he of all people least deserved that empathy.

Sherman closed his eyes, drifted off to sleep. He dreamed of Elmore, out under the stars, and the bearskin covering his body rising and falling as he breathed. Every time he inhaled, the stars paled. When he exhaled, they bloomed in the night sky, filling it with light.

The bearskin slipped, revealing Elmore's face. He sucked in a deep breath. The darkness closed in. Breathed out, they flared brightly. In again, even deeper than before, and the sky went completely dark. Elmore stopped breathing and the darkness remained. And in the black, Sherman could make out only one thing moving through the darkness—a single white bird flying up and up until he could no longer see it.

T HEY TOOK JEDEDIAH's horses out to the river in the predawn, because Jed said he had to return to the farm before midday. "Hattie will take care of things for the morning, but there's a lot of work, and it don't wait for me to fish," Jed told him on the ride out. "That's one of the things I like about a farm. Ain't a single day of rest."

Sherman thought that notion summed up his brother entirely. He had to be kept busy. Perhaps left to his own devices, Jed might've ended up more like Sherman than either of them wanted to admit. Idle hands had led to Sherman being a hired gun, and at the other end of the scale, it had led to his brother finding solace in hard work and routine.

"Bet it ain't been that way for you, has it?" Jed asked as they negotiated a steep rise, taking it at a crisscross to avoid the horses' hooves slipping in the mud.

"I've worked hard over the years," Sherman said. "You wouldn't understand."

"Probably not. Your idea of hard work ain't mine, brother. You know that."

"Well, I will concede there've been times when I found rest and took time for myself," Sherman said.

Jed snorted. "Did it help you any?"

"No," Sherman admitted. "I never found solace anywhere or doing any one thing. Only time I ever did was after I lost this." He raised his hook.

Jed nodded. He understood completely. After all,

Sherman had found peace in nature much the same as he had.

"I'm happy being out of that. Roaming around from one place to the other, never settling anywhere."

"I always thought I'd read you'd been killed somewhere in a gunfight," Jed said. "That's why I've bought the paper all these years."

"I came close to it, I can tell you," Sherman said. "In a way, when I lost my hand, I sort of died out there on the prairie. It's like . . . I died so I could live. Like someone up there decided to give me a second chance. Does that make sense?"

"Kinda, yeah," Jed said. "Sure sounds like you might outlive that reputation of yours."

They rode over the shingle and mud at the shore of the river where it narrowed, the green water slowing but running deep. Sherman and Jedediah hitched their horses to a few of the cypress trees there. Jed passed out the fishing equipment, and both men made short work of assembling their lures.

Jed watched Sherman at work and nodded appreciatively. "So you do know what you're doing."

"Told you I did."

"One thing hearin' it, another seein' it with your own eyes. Let's see if you can cast, though," Jed said with a wink.

Sherman shook his head, laughing. Both men waded out into the river, up to their knees, and cast out into the water in the early-morning light. A mist rolled out of the pines on the opposite bank, cascading over the edge of the water there. The sky adopted a deep blue color, the sun barely risen. Sherman reeled in his line and cast again, then watched Jed do the same.

How much he had missed over the years. How many memories he had missed out on.

No more, he told himself. *No more.*

Jed got a bite, and Sherman stood close by, watching as Jed wrestled the fish in to land.

"That's a fair size for a bass," Sherman said.

"It's a brown trout," Jed corrected him. He carried it to the shore and used the blunt end of a knife handle to smack the fish in the head, killing it instantly. As Sherman looked on, Jed gutted it right there on the riverbank, then wrapped it in paper and put it in his saddlebag. He washed his hands in the river. "That's supper sorted."

"Nothing like that feeling, is there?" Sherman remarked, casting out again into the green water. Now everything was lit pink, the sun lifting. The mist across the river began to dissipate as the light caught it.

Jed began disassembling his fishing gear. "You come out here with nothing, and you leave with your supper. Something so simple as a hook, line and lure. And if you only take what you need, there's enough for everybody. There's always enough for everybody."

"You sound philosophical."

"I reckon I've got that way, yeah," Jed said.

Sherman felt the tug of something at the end of his line and slowly reeled it in, careful not to let whatever it was slip off the end.

"Easy," Jed said.

Sherman pulled his rod to the right, then reeled, then pulled to the left and reeled again. "I got it," he said, the fish visible now. Sherman lifted it out of the water by the line. "Another brown trout?"

"Sure is," Jed said.

Sherman carried it to shore and Jed handed him his knife to use. He made short work of preparing the fish and handed Jed back the knife. "Have any more of that paper?"

Jed handed him some and Sherman wrapped the fish up into a parcel. He stood and handed it to his brother.

"You caught it. What're you givin' it to me for?" Jed asked, accepting the trout from him. "I already caught us supper."

Sherman swished his hands around in the water at the river's edge. "What are we going to eat tomorrow night?" he said.

CHAPTER SIXTEEN

A LL TOLD, SHERMAN stayed with his brother and sister-in-law in Broken Bow for the better part of a week. He'd never felt so well rested by the time he decided it was time to make a move. But there was one thing to take care of before he left. He headed into town and did some asking around at the market. Eventually a young boy directed him to the butcher's wife, who was burdened with finding homes for three puppies. Sherman picked the one he liked the most and returned to the farmhouse.

"Another puppy?" Annie asked excitedly.

"Yeah, little one, but this is yours."

Hattie shook her head. "I wish you'd asked us first."

"I was going to," Sherman said. "But then I thought, what the hell? I'd just do it and see."

Hattie watched Annie scoop the puppy into her arms and fawn over it. "Now, you know I can't very well refuse her," she said, glaring at Sherman.

"I know." He grinned.

"A dirty, rotten trick, Sherman Knowles."

"Guess I ain't that reformed after all."

S HERMAN CUT A deal with his brother—Elmore's wagon and mares for either one of Jed's horses.

"You know you're worse off from this deal, right?" Jed asked.

"I know. On paper. But I'd get where I'm goin' a helluva lot quicker without having to pull that damn wagon."

"True," Jed said, lighting a smoke. He sighed contentedly. "If that ain't a fine cigar, Sherman . . . Well, if you want one of the horses, it's yours. Way I see it, you're coming out worse than me."

"Appreciate it."

"Where're you heading to anyway?"

Sherman shrugged. "Not sure. Any suggestions?"

Hattie appeared on the porch, wiping her hands on a rag. "What're we discussing out here?"

"Where Sherman's gonna go next," Jed said.

"A big decision to make, for sure," Sherman told her. "What d'you think?"

"About you leaving? I say it couldn't come soon enough, especially since you got Annie a puppy to care for. . . ."

Jed chuckled. "Oh, leave off, Hattie girl. Did you see her face?"

"I did."

"She was so upset, knowing you were gonna be leaving and taking that thing with you. I think getting Annie her own was a good move."

"See, I have his approval," Sherman said.

Hattie rolled her eyes. "He's easily persuaded," she said. Jed broke out in laughter, and Sherman laughed, too. Eventually, after keeping a serious face, Hattie had to laugh, too. "Oh, hell. Sherman, take this one, will you?"

"Only room for one, I'm afraid," Sherman said.

Jed spat to the side. "There's a place. Elam Hollow. I can show you on a map. It's several days' ride. Quite a jaunt. But it's small, out-of-the-way. Kinda place a man could go, make a fresh start if he keeps his head down and sticks to his own affairs."

"Elam Hollow? Never heard of it."

"Like I said, I'll show you," Jed told him. He turned to Hattie. "Remember that salesman fella stopping by here, telling us all about it."

"Oh, *him*," Hattie groaned. "Couldn't get rid of that character until we had no choice but to be rude and tell him to peddle his wares elsewhere."

Sherman rubbed at his temple. "Sounds like it might be what I'm lookin' for, to be honest. I need to go somewhere I can disappear. I don't need nobody connecting the dots if they see my face on a wanted poster."

"I think that's come and gone if I'm honest," Jed said, looking at him. "Besides, you don't look like you used to. I don't think anyone would recognize you off a drawing on a poster. But I guess you can't be too careful. You got that money still to start over with?"

"I got enough," Sherman said.

"Then I foresee no issue," Jed said. "What d'you think, Hattie?"

"Sounds good to me. Someplace no one will know you. Somewhere you can be left alone and see whatever is coming your way."

Sherman took out his pipe. "I think I'm sold," he said.

HATTIE HAD MADE Sherman a makeshift carrier to hold the puppy in front of him. When Sherman

was all set to leave, he climbed up into the saddle and
Jed called for Annie to bring the puppy.

"Come along now. Your uncle's gotta leave," Jed
said.

Annie held both puppies in her arms. She stood still
so that Hattie could take Sherman's puppy and pass it
up to him.

"Thanks," he said, situating the puppy in the carrier. "Hey, it works pretty well, don't it?"

"Glad to see that," Hattie said.

Annie peered up at him.

Sherman said, "You take care, little Miss Annie.
Look after that puppy."

"I will," Annie said. "I'm going to call him Cob."

"Cob?"

Jed chuckled to himself. "You've never seen this girl
attack an ear of corn, brother. It's her favorite thing in
the world."

"Lots of butter," Annie reminded him.

"Oh, sure, lots of butter. See what I mean?"

"Cob it is, then," Sherman said, pleased.

Hattie said, "You need to name your own pup."

"It just so happens I thought of a name the other
night. Titus."

"Titus? What kinda name is that?" Hattie asked.

"He was a Roman general back in ancient times,"
Sherman explained. "Don't ever come by that name,
which is why I like it. Matter of fact, not many folk
walkin' around got the name Cob, either."

"Now, that is true," Hattie admitted.

Sherman looked ahead. The sun was reaching its ze-
nith. If he was going to make some headway before dark,
he had to leave there and then. "I guess I have to go."

Jed reached up, shook Sherman's only hand. "Nice
seein' you again, brother. Don't be a stranger around
here. Drop by."

"I'll write when I can, and I'll be sure to come down here now and then, see how you're all getting on," Sherman promised his brother.

Hattie patted the puppy's head. "Titus . . . what a name," she said with a chuckle.

"Hattie, Annie, I'll be seeing you," Sherman said. "Thanks for everything."

"Anytime," Hattie told him.

Sherman pressed his heels and spurred his horse forward, walking through the farm until he reached the road in and out. He looked back, saw that Jedediah, Hattie and Annie were still watching him. He waved, then got the horse moving at a trot. Next time he looked back, there was only the road.

E LAM HOLLOW WAS exactly what he'd had in mind for himself. Small. Out-of-the-way. Completely unimportant. It made him think of Helmstone and the feeling he'd gotten when he walked through the town there. Wondering why anyone would want to live in a place like that. And here he was, in a similar town, with a mind to setting down roots there.

He asked a local for directions to a livery and paid a man there to care for his horse while he checked out the place.

"What kind of town is this?" Sherman asked him.

"Whatever you want it to be," the man told him. "I guess Elam Hollow ain't one thing or the other."

"Right," Sherman said, none the wiser. "Can I leave this in your care, too?"

The blacksmith eyed the puppy. "I got a crate you can use."

"That'll do," Sherman said.

He headed out onto the main street to get the lay of the place. There was a saloon. He wanted to avoid that entirely. He'd seen too many men come to trouble with booze, and he hadn't touched the stuff since Tom Preston's betrayal. Tempting as it was, he thought of meeting Tom that night in the saloon. Perhaps if he hadn't been drinking, he'd never have cut a deal with him. Might have suspected what Tom had had in mind.

But that was yesterday. That was how he looked at it.

Sherman headed into the general store and waited for the man behind the counter to finish serving someone before approaching. Then he removed his hat and ambled over.

"Howdy."

"How're you doing?" the man said. "Not seen you before. You new to town?"

"Just arrived. D'you own this store?"

"Sure do. Mac's the name." He offered his right hand to shake.

"That's gonna be difficult," Sherman said, showing him the prosthetic.

Mac looked abashed. "Oh."

Sherman offered him his left hand. "Better?"

The two men shook. "First time I've seen a man with a hook before," Mac told him.

"Must be some sheltered life up here, is all I can say."

"I suppose," Mac said. "So what can I do you for, sir?"

"Directions, really. Who runs this place?"

Mac shrugged. "Nobody, really. There's a town council, and we got ourselves a mayor, but he don't do nothin' apart from deliver lectures now and then."

"Got a lawman?"

Mac nodded. "Sheriff's office is down the road. Why, you in trouble?"

"No, no, nothing like that. I was thinking of settling

down this way. Wanted to see if there'd be any objection to it."

"What kind of trade you in?"

"Houndsman."

"Houndsman? Really? I've heard of 'em, you know, from the papers. But I ain't never seen one of those around here," Mac said, leaning against the counter. "You know, they say to find your niche. That's the way to get rich. That's what I read anyway. Like them guys selling booze up in the hills where them crazy fools are digging for gold. They're making more dough than the miners because every time they find gold, they sell it to buy more booze. Actually, I heard they started accepting gold for the booze and cutting out the middleman. Crazy times we're living in. Crazy times."

"Sure are," Sherman agreed, not entirely sure what Mac was wittering on about. "What kind of man is the sheriff?"

"Fair. One of the best we've had, to tell the truth. You'll like him. I can see you got that easy way about you, too, even if you do look like you wandered down from a mountain. No offense."

"None taken," Sherman said, thinking he looked like he'd wandered down from a mountain because that was literally what he had done.

He thanked Mac for his time and headed for the sheriff's office. He walked in, removed his hat and addressed the man who was leaning back in a chair, boots up on his desk and hat pulled down over his eyes. He seemed to be steadfast asleep.

Sherman cleared his throat.

The sheriff did not so much as stir.

"Excuse me," Sherman said.

The sheriff threw himself forward, startled, the chair legs slamming down hard against the floorboards. The hat fell off his head and he just managed to catch it in his hands. "Hello? Who . . . uh . . . who are you?" he asked, flustered.

"Someone who knows you."

"Huh?"

"Your face. It's familiar to me."

The sheriff frowned. "Can't be, sir, since we've just met."

"No, no, I'm pretty certain," Sherman said, folding his arms. "I was in Broken Bow not a week ago. I seen your face on a poster there."

The sheriff's face turned red. "Who are you?" he demanded.

"Name's Sherman Knowles."

"Knowles? You're a wanted man!"

"So are you, Sheriff."

"That's it!" the lawman stood. Pointed to the door. "Get out!"

"Listen, I didn't come here to start trouble. Matter of fact, I came here to leave trouble behind," Sherman said, pulling up a chair but not sitting in it. Not yet.

The sheriff said, "I don't know who you think I am, but I assure you that you are mistaken."

"Don't think I am. The man I heard tell of was called Delbert Crothers. Seems he got himself in trouble for cheating at cards. Working his way from one town to the other, cheating at every game he played. Lot of folk on the lookout for Crothers. I suppose if he were settled in a backwater town like this, he might go by a different name now."

"You're insinuating that I am this man?"

Sherman produced the poster in question. After deciding to come to Elam Hollow, he'd swiped one of the wanted posters on his ride through. Now he unfolded it from where it'd been resting in his back pocket and deposited it on the desk. "No, sir. I am stating without doubt that you are Delbert Crothers."

The sheriff looked at the sketch on the wanted poster and his face turned from the red of embarrassment to the white of fear. He looked up at Sherman. "What do you want?"

"First, I ain't after no trouble. You're a wanted man. Well, so am I. We got that in common. Both of us are here looking to escape, so how about we help each other out, huh? If not, I'll be on my way. I won't say a word about who or where you are. And I know, being in the precarious position you are, you won't want to report me to nobody, either."

"Is this blackmail? I'm finding you hard to follow," Sheriff Freehan said.

"I used to be a hired gun. That's why they're after me. Or they used to be. Anyway, you're a wanted man, too. At least you were until you came here to Elam Hollow."

"Hold on a second," Freehan said. He leaned forward. "I don't get it. It's like you knew I'd be here."

"Ah," Sherman said. He rummaged around in his pocket for another piece of folded paper. "You see, my brother down in Broken Bow, he reads all these newspapers. Ya know, always lookin' for news I'd been shot or what have you. He had them lying around the place and last week I got to reading a few of those old papers. Well, there was a picture of you in there apprehending a fugitive when he came through here a few months ago."

Freehan slumped back into his chair, defeated. "Oh. *That*."

"Recognized you from the wanted poster straightaway. I'm surprised nobody else made the connection, to be honest. I bet that exposure really played on your nerves, huh?"

"Like you wouldn't believe," Freehan said. "So what's the deal?"

"I want to live here, and I want to work. That's it. Once I'm set somewhere, I won't be coming into town all that often if I can help it. I've kinda got used to my own company if I'm honest."

"Not the Sherman Knowles I read about," Freehan said. "The Sherman Knowles I read about was right up there with Ashford Sinclair."

"Yeah, well, that Sherman Knowles died a cold death out on the prairie one winter. Before you sits a reformed character if ever there was one. My hell-raising days are well and truly over, Sheriff."

"I guess I'll have to take your word on that. Anyway, how do I know you're not gonna turn on me one day, shoot me in the back?"

"Well, for that matter, how do I know *you* won't?"

The sheriff had to concede that Sherman had made a good point. "Fair enough."

"I won't say a word about you so long as you let me be in peace here, just as you are. Seems only fair us old criminals stick together. Agreed?" Sherman said, offering his hand across the desk.

Freehan hesitated. "You ain't here to start any trouble, you say?"

"You have my word."

"All right, then," Freehan said, accepting Sherman's hand.

The sheriff took the wanted poster and the newspaper clipping and balled them up in his hands.

Sherman said, "Two crooks together."

"Please don't ever say that aloud again . . . ," the sheriff said with disdain. "The people of Elam Hollow consider me a decent, lawful man and I intend on maintaining that image. As you saw when you walked in, I got it pretty sweet here. There's very little I have to deal with. The occasional drunk, that kind of thing. The odd vagrant I have to move along when they eventually—*inevitably*—make a nuisance of them-selves. There're no gangs in Elam Hollow, sir, no deadly killers or any of that nonsense."

"Sounds nice."

"It is."

Sherman sat slowly forward. "So are there any va-cant properties here? Not in town, but just outside of it."

"Come to think of it, there is a cabin at the outskirts of town. It's not much to look at, but I'm sure you could do it up or pay one of the local boys to do it up for you. The owner recently died and it's just sitting out there."

"Who owns it?"

"The man's son lives in town. I could make the in-troductions. I think Jimmy will be more than happy for a quick sale. Get it off his hands. He ain't done nothin' to it yet, and his father's been in the ground three months. I'll try to convince him that it might be in his best interests to let you have it at a fair price."

"You'd do that?"

"We've got to look out for each other, haven't we?"

E LAM HOLLOW WAS surrounded by prairie land, some rivers and in the distance hills and mountains. A man could sit astride his horse at the town's edge, as Sherman was doing, and see for miles all around. As Hattie had said, see what was coming his way.

The cabin was modest but perfectly suitable. There was a small barn, too. He could work with it, make it how he wanted it. The sheriff had been correct in his assumption that Jimmy, the son of the owner, would want a quick sale. The man hadn't even haggled over the price Sherman offered. He just took the money and signed the deed under Freehan's watchful eye.

Sherman still wasn't entirely sure Freehan wouldn't

ride out in the dead of night and kill him in his sleep, but he guessed it would take time to completely trust each other's intentions. He hoped that nothing like that ever happened—he liked the place. Had a good feeling about it since the moment he'd arrived. A town where old criminals like him and Freehan could begin again. Living new lives as good men.

Now he sat on his horse looking at his cabin, his new home, the puppy in the crook of his right arm, the horn of his saddle in his left. "Titus, the Roman general. Big and fearsome," he said, smiling as he studied the dog. Then he looked up, filled his lungs with the fresh, clean air. "You and me, we're gonna do just fine."

PART FIVE

◇

THE HOUNDSMAN

CHAPTER SEVENTEEN

IT WAS DUSK when Sherman and the others found the bandits.

They'd pursued their tracks through the woods until they reached the other side, to a jagged gorge with a river running through it. It was passable at its narrowest point, and on the other side of the river, the bandits' tracks were visible in the hardened mud. The snow came in intermittent drifts now, rendering their visibility poor as they worked their way to the top of the gorge and on through uneven terrain. Eventually Sherman lost their tracks. He had a general sense of their direction of travel, but the snow was smothering the markings they'd left on the now wide-open prairie.

Luckily they had Titus. Through some miracle, or a combination of God-given senses and Sherman's training, the dog was able to pick up the bandits' scent, however faint it might have been. They were following the thinnest of threads now, Sherman knew, with little room for error.

The wind beat at their faces, burning their skin and snatching their breath. It was hard going, with every part of them feeling frozen solid, but they pressed on.

"I can't see where we're going!" Bobby yelled over the roar of the wind.

"Just gotta trust Titus," Sherman told him. "He'll see us true."

"Maybe we should stop," Bobby suggested.

The three of them drew closer together so that they didn't have to shout to be heard.

"We can't," Hattie said from her horse. "Can't stop now."

Sherman agreed. "No shelter. Gotta keep goin' now. We can count on Tom Preston and Leroy Jenkins to stop, because they'll be eager to get out of the wind. That's how we'll catch up."

"Unless they know they're being followed," Bobby said.

Sherman considered that. "Good point. But I think if they did, we'd be dead already. Sometimes you can see what's behind ya better than you can see what's afore."

For a long time, they blindly followed Titus into the white wall of the blizzard, not knowing what they might come across or what the dog would lead them to. But gradually the subtle glow of firelight up ahead, like a false dawn behind the faint skeletal forms of trees, became visible through the white haze. Sherman called Titus back to them and dismounted. The others did the same.

"Is that them?" Hattie asked.

"Could be. I think we should find some shelter for the horses, maybe in the trees to the right here. Then we should take a look on foot. We'll make less noise."

They led their horses to the right, as Sherman suggested. There was a scant stand of trees barely fifty feet across—just enough tall, thin trunks to offer partial shelter from the storm.

"We'll leave the horses here, in your care," Sherman told Hattie.

She looked at him in disbelief. "You're not serious! I'm coming, too."

"No, I can't allow it. Me and Bobby should take care of this part."

Hattie stepped forward so they were almost nose to nose. "You don't get to dictate to me, Sherman. I'm coming." She pointed in the direction of the firelight. "That's my Annie out there. I'm not going to wait hiding in the trees when my daughter's so close. We've almost got her back."

"Hattie, I need to protect you. I swore to Jed I'd look after you both. I can't do that if you're puttin' yourself in harm's way."

"The risk is mine to take," Hattie insisted. "Jed would understand."

Sherman closed his eyes and winced as if pained. He opened his eyes and met the fierceness and intensity of her gaze. "Okay," he said. He checked his weapon, emptying the chamber and reloading it to be sure, then pockcted extra ammo, too. Bobby and Hattie followed his lead. "We'll have a recon of their camp, but best to be prepared, in case we're caught unawares."

"Won't he bark when we leave and give us away?" Hattie asked. "Cob always went nuts whenever we'd leave him at home."

"Titus knows better than to do that. Don't you, boy?" Sherman said, rubbing the dog's head. "We'll be back soon."

He set to work fixing Titus's lead to one of the trees, then said, "Sit. Stay."

The light was fading fast, the sun already resting

beneath the lip of the world. In the thick of a storm, it just got dimmer. There was no sunset. But Sherman had been out in those conditions enough times to be able to tell what time of day it was without the aid of falling light or lengthening shadows.

They walked back the way they'd come to orient themselves. The glow of firelight in the distance was even more prominent as the day turned to a darker gray.

"Quiet does it," Sherman told Bobby and Hattie. "You never can tell how sound is gonna carry on the wind. Right now it's blowing *at* us, which works in our favor. No tellin' if it's gonna change tack, though."

They pushed into the wind, the snow up to their shins. It would have been easier and quicker on horseback but Sherman wanted discretion. He wanted to sneak up on their quarry. They could have gone in guns blazing straightaway, but that could have resulted in Annie and the other girl getting hurt. And there was always the slim chance it wasn't Tom Preston and Leroy Jenkins's firelight they were investigating. As they'd learned from the attack the night before, they weren't the only ones out on the prairie. . . .

There was a scant line of trees, stripped bare by the winter, just black trunks and black branches in stark relief to the flat gray sky. Sherman told Hattie and Bobby to spread out and watch where they were walking—even something so small as a twig broken underfoot could be enough to give them away and announce their approach. The three of them instinctively ducked down to lower their profile. They pushed in, slowly, hesitantly. The glow of the fire grew in intensity the closer they got. Sherman signaled for Bobby and Hattie to hold where they were, and he pressed on alone, across an open area blanketed with inches of thick snow. To his surprise, he reached a point where the ground began to slope down steeply. He got onto his stomach and crawled to the edge. If he went off to his left, he'd find himself following a shale path down an incline to an enclosed space of gray stone. It concealed the entrance to a narrow slot canyon, barely six feet wide. The fire had been set two strides in front of the slot canyon, its glow visible to them from above due to the gradient of the ground. Across the way was a straight twenty-foot-high wall. There was no other way in or out.

Preston and Jenkins were busy with their horses, getting them set for the night, stowing their saddles and gear. Tom Preston looked the same as he had years ago, just a little older. Leroy Jenkins had a set of angry red claw marks down one side of his face. Sherman guessed one of the girls must've tried to fight her way free of him. *Good for her,* he thought. He saw that the abducted girls were tied together beside the fire. Their feet were bound, and there was a loop of rope around their waists, pinning them next to each other, but their hands were free. He knew that because they were holding their palms out to the fire, trying to warm the numbness from their fingers.

He studied the area. The fight would be tough. The bandits had the upper hand; even though Sherman and the other two had the drop on them, Preston and Jenkins had the slot canyon to retreat into and use for cover. Once inside, they'd be practically untouchable until their ammo ran out. There'd be no way of going in after them, not without a good line of sight. *Tom's not the idiot I took him for,* thought Sherman.

He worked his way back on his belly, easing away from the edge before standing to be sure he wouldn't be visible from down below. He hurried back to Bobby and Hattie, signaling for them to retreat with him.

"Did you see her?" Hattie demanded in a hushed but strained voice. "Did you see my Annie?"

"Let's get back to the horses and I'll tell you," Sherman assured her.

A NNIE LOOKED AT Joan, who'd not spoken to her since their escape attempt. They were roped together to prevent any further inclination to take off again. Joan was rubbing the feeling back into her hands, and Annie followed suit.

"Are you still ignoring me?" she asked.

Joan didn't answer.

"Well, I know for a fact you're not deaf. So you can hear me even if you don't wanna answer. To be honest, that's fine by me. I don't want to converse with somebody ain't gonna converse back. It's just rude," Annie said.

"I'm not being rude," Joan said through gritted teeth. "I am angry as *hell* that I listened to you."

"You're angry as hell why? Because I wanted us to *escape*?"

Joan was red in the face. "Yes! You've made this whole situation worse."

"How d'you figure?"

Tom Preston looked over at them. "What're you two talkin' about?"

"Nothing," Annie said.

The bandit frowned in her direction. "Best not be."

Annie lowered her voice. "Joan, we gotta stick together. Don't you see it? All we got is each other right now."

"Yeah, and sticking together done a whole lotta good last time, didn't it?" Joan said sarcastically, raising her voice. "I couldn't be tied to a worse person."

"Same to you!" Annie snapped.

Tom approached, riding gear tossed over his shoulder. "I told you, if you can't be civil, don't talk at all. And if you can't stop talkin', I'll gladly gag the pair of you. So what'll it be?"

"We'll get along," Annie said reluctantly.

Tom nudged Joan with the toe of his boot. "And you?"

Joan glared up at him. "Whatever you say."

For a moment, nothing happened. Tom looked at Joan, and Joan looked right back at him—captor and captive silently communicating their contempt for each other. Nothing happened, and then Tom expressed his contempt physically. He slapped Joan across the face, the sound dry and sharp. The force of the strike knocked Joan's face to the side and her eyes instantly filled with tears, her face turning a bright shade of pink. She bit her lip to stop it trembling and Annie could see that all Joan wanted to do was scream. Tom had left a dirty red handprint across her cheek.

"You'd best pray that mark fades by the time we get to the auction," he told Joan. "Only one thing happens to inventory that don't sell. We bury it. Ain't that right, Leroy?"

"That's right for sure," Leroy said in his far-from-dulcet tones.

"We bury it," Tom repeated. He jabbed a finger in Annie's direction. "As for you, behave or you'll get the same."

Annie swallowed hard. She did not relish the thought of receiving what Joan just had. But she held his gaze, though it took all she had to prevent her lip from quivering like Joan's. "You don't scare me," she said.

Tom smiled slyly, his mouth thin and tight. "Maybe you ain't as smart as I reckoned."

*   *   *

H E'D BEEN THINKING about Fred Nilson on and off for two days. Nilson with his hands up, trembling with fear.

Please, mister. I surrender. . . . Don't shoot me.

Sherman thought about pulling the trigger and watching the bullet rip through Fred Nilson's throat. The man clamping his hands there as blood pumped through the cracks between his fingers. Gasping for air.

I am not an innocent, he thought, *but Annie is. I have to save her.*

It seemed that when Tom Preston had left him to die on a frozen prairie all those many years ago, their paths had diverged like tributaries breaking away from the flow of a mighty river. A confluence of coincidence and fate had conspired to see that the tributaries were now rejoined, their two destinies combining once and for all.

Sherman squatted down to pet Titus, his thoughts on Annie and the other girl, prisoners through no fault of their own. Taken simply because they were women and because they were young and innocent. For those monsters inclined toward conquest, there was nothing so alluring as the purity of virginity.

"Good boy," Sherman said, giving Titus plenty of attention, even as his emotions roiled inside of him. How many women had Tom taken and sold off to the highest bidder? How many lives had he destroyed? Sherman wondered how such a man could live with himself. But then he considered the lives he himself had taken and wondered what line could be drawn between himself and Tom. It did not serve to lift his mood—that was for sure.

"So?" Hattie said, her patience running short.

Sherman stood. "She was there. Another girl, too."

"Were they all right?"

"They seemed to be. They were warming their hands by the fire while the men settled the horses. They've picked a decent spot. It'll be hard to attack it without getting the girls hurt or, worse, killed in the cross fire."

Bobby tipped his chin. "What do you suggest?"

"I have a plan. But it's . . . risky."

"Tell us," Hattie insisted.

Sherman laid it out for them. "The element of surprise is one of only two advantages we have. We'll have precious few seconds to make it worth it."

"So . . . what's our *other* advantage?" Bobby asked.

Sherman could feel the pull of what was to come. In saving his niece, he might see the end of Tom Preston.

Or he might find his *own* end.

Whichever was the case, Sherman was resigned to it. Destiny would have things its own way, and no one could change that.

"Most important advantage we got," he said, unholstering his pistol, "there's three of us and two of them. When the shooting starts, that's all that'll matter."

CHAPTER EIGHTEEN

Leroy Jenkins looked up at the sound of approaching horses. "Hey," he said, whacking Tom Preston on the arm to get his attention. *"Hey!"*

Tom swiped at him in irritation. "What is it?"

Leroy held a finger to his lips. "Ssshhh. Listen."

Tom angled his head. For a moment he didn't hear a thing. Could be Leroy was imagining things. Or it could be his own hearing was so shot from years of gunfire and loud explosions that he really was deaf as a drum and just didn't know it.

But then Tom heard it, too.

"Horses. Could be two or three of 'em," Leroy said, ear cocked. "Heading this way."

Tom stood. "Remember we camped here not three months ago?"

"Sure do."

"Might just be folk lookin' to camp here, too," Tom said.

"Can't have that, can we?" Leroy asked.

Tom pulled his pistol. "Naw, we can't. Let's get the girls to the mouth of the canyon so they're out of sight. Then we can see 'em off, whoever they are."

"If they don't wanna go?"

Tom shrugged. "Then we see 'em off the other way."

His partner grinned. It was not a pretty sight. His jagged teeth resembled rotted corn kernels.

Together they ushered the two girls beneath the opening of the canyon. Tom pressed them back into the shadows. "Don't either of you move, or I'll come back here and finish you. D'you hear? Not a sound, either. Act like you don't exist. Be good little girls," he said, gripping Joan by the face and squeezing hard. She shook her head to get out from his grip and Tom sneered. "There it is," he said, admiring her spirit.

He stepped back out, stood next to Leroy and watched for movement from above. The sound of the horses drew nearer and nearer, the clip-clop of their hooves more defined with each passing second, accompanied by the jingle of the riders' gear.

"Sounds like a pair," Tom said.

Leroy said, "Well, I said two or three. Hard to tell sometimes."

Tom watched the ridge. The wind up there moaned and sighed, the storm bearing down. Down by the mouth of the slot canyon, they were relatively sheltered, save for the whistle of wind coursing down the length of it from the prairie on the other side. Even so it did not compare with the folly of making camp where the storm could hit them full force. It was one of the few places they could have a fire going, and whoever was approaching no doubt thought the exact same thing.

"Tom . . . ," Leroy whispered.

Two riders were bringing their horses carefully down the slope, navigating it with caution. The first rider, a woman, led the other horse by its reins. Tom could see why: the second rider, a young man, sat slumped forward, bobbing this way and that on the back of his horse. He didn't even look conscious. The woman looked at Tom and Leroy with relief more than anything. In need of help and glad to see another face.

Damn if she ain't mistaken on that score, Tom thought.

Leroy stepped forward. "Wait up there, miss. You can't just intrude here. We already got a camp set up."

"Please, don't turn me away. I don't know what else to do. He's injured. He needs help."

"Turn around, head back up there and go someplace else."

But she was insistent. "Oh, please now. There isn't anywhere to go!"

Tom took in the woman, then the boy. It didn't seem to be an act. The kid looked to be out for the count, and the woman was clearly distraught. He studied her features, deciding she was too old to take captive and sell at auction. She wouldn't be worth the bother. Besides, older women tended to have more fight in them, more spirit.

"We can't help you," Tom told her sternly.

The woman wiped at her eyes. "Please, have mercy on us," she pleaded. "He took a bullet to the stomach and I couldn't stop the bleeding. Now he's unconscious. Do either of you know what to do?"

"I ain't no surgeon," Leroy said.

"Naw, me neither," Tom said, his face tight with tension. "Get outta here before we do you a favor and put him out of his misery."

SHERMAN LISTENED TO the voices carrying from down below. They were almost amplified by the ancient stone surrounding them, as if they were reciting the lines of a play in an amphitheater. He thought back to watching the performance of *Titus Andronicus*. *I tell my sorrows to the stones*. It was a line he'd remembered when he was in a fever after Elmore rescued him. That was his way. He'd always kept his sorrows to himself, where they couldn't hurt anybody.

Now more lines from the play came back to him.

> *Vengeance is in my heart, death in my hand,*
> *Blood and revenge are hammering in my head.*

"'Vengeance is in my heart . . . ,'" he whispered to himself, edging forward.

"Please, have mercy on us," he heard Hattie plead. "Do either of you know what to do?"

"I ain't no surgeon," an amused voice told her.

"Naw, me neither," another voice said. That was Tom. Sherman could tell right away. "Get outta here before we do you a favor and put him out of his misery."

Even the sound of his voice made Sherman's blood boil. He edged ever closer, careful not to be seen from down below or the game would be up entirely.

"Please . . . ," Hattie began to beg, just as they'd planned.

Tom pulled his pistol. Aimed it at her. "You heard me. We ain't interested in anythin' else you gotta say. Let the kid die someplace else. We ain't lookin' to get saddled with your problems."

So callous. So cold-blooded. That Sherman recognized himself in Tom's words made it all the worse.

The time had come. Sherman drew a breath, strode to the edge of the cliff and made his presence known. "Your days are ended, Tom Preston!" he bellowed at the top of his voice.

Both Tom and Leroy spun about at the sound of his voice: Tom in shock, Leroy frowning in utter confusion. For a second, nothing happened. The bandits stared up at Sherman. The wind whooped as it tore down the slot canyon. Recognition flashed in Tom's eyes, seeing past the years and the beard to the man he'd left to die on a frozen prairie so long ago that he'd almost forgotten.

In one smooth movement, Bobby shook the blanket from his shoulders and raised his gun, which he'd been holding by his stomach. He took aim at Leroy.

Tom saw the movement out of the corner of his eye and glanced in Bobby's direction. "Leroy!" he yelled, diving to the left. He hit the ground, turned his gun on Sherman and fired.

Sherman danced back from the edge, the shot ricocheting off the hard stone inches from where he'd been standing.

In the same instant, Bobby fired. His shot caught Leroy in the cheek, lancing through bone, the unexceptional contents of Leroy's head bursting through the other side in an explosion of watermelon red. Leroy sagged, his right arm flailing out, his trigger finger contracting reflexively. His gun went off and the bullet struck Bobby in the chest, punching him clean off his saddle.

"No!" Hattie cried.

Tom Preston looked from Leroy, to Bobby, to her.

Still atop her horse, Hattie took aim at Tom and fired, but he rolled quickly out of the way. Before she could fire again, he was up and moving, surprisingly swift, making a dash for the dark opening of the slot canyon. He turned and fired off a shot, causing Hattie to duck and turn her horse to the left. It was skittish from the noise, and she struggled to keep the beast in check and under her control.

Sherman came running down the gravel slope, boots skidding on the icy stones.

He brushed past Hattie climbing down from her horse, and felt the familiar rush of adrenaline. There was something strangely thrilling about potential death—the not knowing if this would be your last stand. The knowledge that everything was on the line. One wrong move, you ended up like Leroy Jenkins.

"Don't come no closer!" Tom shouted, and marched the two girls out, one arm around their necks, the other pressing his pistol into Annie's side.

Her eyes grew wide at the sight of her uncle; then her gaze shifted to her mother directly behind him. Her expression was a mixture of relief and abject horror. The girl next to her was similarly terrified and caught in the grip of shock.

"Annie!" Hattie screamed. "My Annie!"

Sherman didn't move. "Hattie, check on Bobby. Make sure he's all right."

"But—"

"Do as I say!" Sherman snapped.

To her credit, Hattie ran straight to Bobby's side. Sherman knew how hard it was for her. But they couldn't allow themselves to be derailed now after they'd come so far.

"Been a long time," Tom said.

Sherman glared at him. "This ain't got nothin' to do with anyone else but me and you."

"I thought you were dead."

"Seems you thought wrong."

"Clearly," Tom said. "I knew I should've shot you full of holes the moment I turned my back on you. It was a mistake to leave it to chance. You're one lucky son of a gun, Sherman Knowles. That much is for certain."

"I should never have trusted you," Sherman said.

"Because you didn't have the guts to pull the trigger?"

Sherman shook his head. "I never killed in cold blood, unlike you," he said. But in his mind, he saw

Fred Nilson with his hands up. *Please, mister. I surrender.*

"So, hired you to find these girls, did she?" Tom asked. "I'm assuming that's the mother hen over there tried shootin' me dead a second ago."

"Let them go."

Tom cocked his head to one side as he weighed it up. "Or . . . perhaps you're related to one of them?"

Sherman flexed his hand on his gun.

Tom's eyes moved from the gun and fixed on Sherman's hook. "Say, did I cause that? I sure hope not."

"Frostbite's a helluva thing," Sherman said bitterly.

"I've heard."

"Let them go, Tom. Cut them loose and I might show you mercy."

Tom shifted his stance, weighing up his options. He removed his arm from around their necks, and for a fleeting moment, Sherman wondered if his foe had turned reasonable. But Tom reached inside his clothes and produced a knife.

Tom held it up for Sherman to see.

"Sherman!" cried Hattie, who was kneeling at Bobby's side.

"I swear, if you hurt so much as one hair on their heads . . ."

"Like this?" As Sherman looked on, Tom sliced through the rope holding the girls together. Then he passed the knife to Joan. "Cut your feet clear. Don't try nothing. Remember I got a gun here. So much as flinch and I'll shoot you both through the side so you bleed out nice and slow."

Joan nodded obediently. With shaking hands she bent down, cut through her bonds, then Annie's.

"I'll send 'em to you one at a time," Tom said, taking the knife back.

"Don't play games with me," Sherman warned.

Preston smiled. "No games," he said, and instructed Joan to walk forward. When she was less than three feet away, Tom abruptly kicked her in the back. She flew forward, staggering awkwardly over her own feet until she fell over. Instinctively, Sherman rushed forward to help her—and Tom used the distraction to aim his gun and fire. The bullet tore into Sherman's shoulder, knocking him back.

"That's the difference between you and me, old man. I'd have let her fall."

Hattie took aim at Tom but did not fire. He'd already ducked behind her daughter to use her as a human shield.

"Good call, mother hen," Tom said, pulling Annie over to Bobby's horse. "Don't want to hit the princess."

"Ma!" Annie screamed. "Ma, help me!"

"Annie!" Hattie cried, her gun hand trembling as Tom forced Annie up into the saddle. Using the horse itself for cover, he swung himself up into the saddle behind her, his gun in the small of Annie's back.

"In there," he ordered, indicating the narrow, dark fissure of the slot canyon.

Annie shook her head.

Tom grabbed a handful of Annie's dark hair and pulled tight. "Get!"

Annie screamed, but she spurred the horse on anyway. They headed into the canyon and were lost to the darkness within seconds. Sherman got to his feet, then helped Joan up. He scowled into the shadows but there was no movement. Tom was gone and he'd taken Annie with him. "Are you all right?" he asked Joan.

She nodded. "I think so."

"I think he's bleeding out . . . ," Hattie said.

Sherman ran to Bobby and knelt by his side. A dark patch had spread through his clothing, saturating him.

"Oh, no," Sherman muttered. "No, no, no."

Hattie stood. She paced to the entrance of the canyon, then back again. "They're getting away, Sherman, they're getting away."

"I know," he said, panic in his voice. He tapped at Bobby's face. "Come on, kid. Open your eyes. Say something."

Bobby stirred.

"Come on . . . ," Sherman urged desperately. "Say something. *Anything.* Damn it, I didn't go to all that effort for nothing. Come on now. Give me a sign."

"Owww," Bobby groaned.

Sherman frowned. A distinct smell rose from the kid. Not the smell of death but something else. He pulled Bobby's jacket open and the smell got stronger. Sherman patted his fingertips to the dark wet stain and pressed them to his tongue.

"What the . . . ?" He checked Bobby's clothes to see where the bullet had hit; then he reached inside Bobby's breast pocket and retrieved a dented hip flask with a bullet embedded in it.

"What is that?" Hattie asked.

"Booze."

"Booze?"

Bobby opened his eyes. "He got me, didn't he?"

"He got something all right," Sherman said, holding up the hip flask. "Did you get this off those bandits we shot?"

Bobby nodded slowly. "I did."

"Why?" Sherman asked. "What in the hell for?"

"I think I . . . planned on drinking it," Bobby told him.

"But you didn't."

"No," Bobby said.

"Well, however it came about, the damn hip flask saved your life."

Sherman tossed it away and helped Bobby up.

Bobby noticed the blood running down Sherman's front and said, "Hey, you've been shot."

"I'll live," Sherman said.

"Grab Titus. Hurry." He'd left Titus tied to a tree.

Hattie made for the cave and Sherman grabbed her arm. "No, you need to stay with the girl. She can't be left on her own, Hattie."

"But Annie—"

"Will be back with you soon enough," Sherman said. "Let me handle it. Besides, I'm gonna need your horse."

Hattie threw her arms around him. Sherman winced from the pain in his shoulder. But that was forgotten about when he felt Hattie's hot breath in his ear. "Bring her back to me."

"I will," he promised firmly. Bobby returned with Titus running ahead of him. Sherman bent down, pulled the hide free from Titus's jaws. "Let's go, boy," he said.

Hattie led her horse over to Sherman and he climbed up into the saddle. He reloaded his pistol and snapped it shut, peering into the dark slot canyon with distrust. A damp smell came from within, the cold breath of a tomb, and Sherman shivered. Titus whined at the entrance, eager to get going.

"I know, I know," Sherman said.

"Wait," Bobby said. "Let me come with you."

"No, this is on me now."

"Sorry I deceived you."

"Don't apologize, kid. I'm mighty proud of you."

"No one has ever told me that."

Sherman smiled. "Maybe they should have," he said. Then he took the horse into the canyon, followed by Titus, and was lost to the shadows.

CHAPTER NINETEEN

THE WIND MOANED through the cave, icy air hitting Sherman's face. A cold hard knot formed in his gut at the realization that Tom might have already killed Annie just for the purpose of hurting him more, because the man was bad through and through, right to the core. There were too many men like Tom in the world . . . and too few who sought a better calling, as Sherman had done.

The canyon ran up at an angle now. It took him up, the cold increasing, the wind whistling down the long, dark, rocky corridor.

He saw a cool glow up ahead lighting his way. The storm had abated, and the sky had cleared momentarily, showing him the moon, in all its pale glory, and the deep blue-black of the night sky.

"Nearly there," Sherman told himself.

He reached the top of the canyon and was faced with a steep downward slope dotted with trees. Sherman could clearly see tracks in the snow. In one spot it looked like Tom had dismounted and mounted again, presumably to take Annie's place at the front of the saddle. Titus sniffed at the heavy indents of the horse's hooves in the snow, his keen sense of smell hard at work. Sherman's gaze followed the tracks down through the sparse woodland and out onto long open fields at the bottom. If it weren't for the sudden clear sky and the moonlight to guide their way, he wouldn't have been able to see more than a foot in front of his face.

As Sherman was weighing up how to get down there without killing himself and the horse in the process, Titus locked onto the scent and took off downhill, bounding through the deep drifts of snow.

"To hell with it," Sherman growled, digging his heels into the sides of the horse. It burst forth, thundering down the steep gradient of the hill, barely dodging the trees and the thin, razor-sharp branches that whipped past Sherman's face with inches to spare. He felt the horse's fear, on a par with his own. But despite that, and the pain of the gunshot wound in his shoulder, Sherman grinned from ear to ear. He was old, but he felt renewed by his own reckless abandon. He clattered to the bottom, the horse breathing hard, pushed past the last of the trees and tore out across the endless prairie, white expanses of flat land stretching as far as he could see.

That was when he spotted them moving against the white. Tom rode with Annie's arms around his sides. Just as Sherman had suspected, Tom had changed to the front of the saddle to have control over their ride. Knowing he couldn't leave his fate in the hands of a young girl.

A strong wind rushed in from the right. Sherman glanced at the dark gray storm front heading their way. *And there I was thinkin' it'd blown over,* he thought.

He knew from experience that the heart of a storm could lull you into a false sense of security, because it got to be so quiet, so still. Glancing at the storm clouds, he felt the panic rising in his chest, the all-too-real fear that he would never beat it. The front would sweep in and any chance of saving Annie would be lost.

In a whiteout you lost all sense of direction and could quickly succumb to the wind and the ice. What was headed Sherman's way could prove as deadly as taking a bullet to the head.

Tom Preston looked back, redoubling his efforts to flee with Annie in tow. He pulled his gun and fired a warning shot that zipped wide over Sherman's head. The sound of it echoed, rebounding off the emptiness and the silence.

Sherman looked off to his right just as the clouds rushed in to block the moon entirely, darkness falling in an instant. He had his night vision now, so he could see enough to continue, but could no longer make out Tom and Annie. He tried to close the gap before the worst came. The wind picked up, turning from a steady gust that buffeted him to a howling scream that threatened to lift him off the horse and fling him away into oblivion. The snow came with it, tiny shards of ice grating the exposed skin of his face. Sherman looked for Titus and saw the dog was having a tough time, too. But despite that, Titus kept going, running at an angle against the sweep of the wind. It wasn't so different from the night Tom Preston left Sherman for dead. Lost in a whiteout in the dark. As if it weren't enough to bring Sherman and Tom Preston together for one final confrontation, with Annie's life hanging in the balance, Fate had had to throw a storm into the mix, too.

Sherman thought he saw movement, but he couldn't be sure. He tried to clear his vision, but it was nigh impossible. Visibility dropped to a hundred yards. Then fifty. Then twenty. Soon he could not see any farther than a few yards ahead of him. The tracks Tom and Annie had made through the snow were steadily being blasted out of existence. Smoothed out until they were no longer there, leaving just sparse blades of pale green grass jutting up from the white blanket like whiskers.

Titus's sense of smell failed him in the high winds and the cold. The dog struggled to plow on without a clear direction to follow. Sherman slowed the horse to a stop, knowing the futility of riding blind. The roar of the storm was deafening, as if it were right on top of him and bearing down hard.

"Annie!" Sherman yelled into the wind. He tried to narrow his eyes against the storm to see, but it was impossible. He was lost. Sherman turned the horse in a circle, unsure and disoriented.

As he looked for any sign of Tom Preston's tracks in the thick windbeaten snow, it occurred to Sherman that his adversary might've used the storm to his advantage. He frowned down at the snow. "It's a trap . . . ," he murmured, realizing it all too late. The trap was not only set but sprung, and he was firmly within it. Sherman sat up, peered into the rushing debris and snow and ice, watching for any sign of movement.

A gunshot erupted directly behind him and he felt the bullet rush past him—too close for comfort. Sherman ducked instinctively as Tom Preston and Annie came charging in from behind. Tom had used the storm to circle back and sneak up on Sherman.

The oldest trick in the book and I fell for it, Sherman scolded himself.

Tom shot again, forcing Sherman to push the horse forward at a gallop. Tom and Annie drew up to his left, Tom leaning across to take aim, and Sherman wove

the horse back and forth as he aimed his own pistol at
Tom's horse so there was no danger of hitting Annie.
The horse swerved out of the way.

Sherman had lost sight of Titus, but he saw him now,
running at full force and crossing over to the side.

Good boy.

Preston looked down, startled by the dog aiming to
clamp its jaws around his ankle. He lifted his leg and
Titus sank his teeth into the side of the horse instead,
causing the beast to rear up, wheeling its front hooves
in the air as it bucked both Tom and Annie off into the
snow. Titus dashed back and forth in front of the horse,
barking sharp and loud. Annie scrambled up, dazed,
but with sense enough to know she should get out of
the way.

Sherman got down from his horse. "Take the reins
and get clear!" he told Annie, then charged toward
Tom, gun raised.

Tom got to his feet, lifted his pistol and aimed at
Sherman. They fired at the same time, exchanging hot
lead. Sherman pulled the trigger and the gun clicked
uselessly through empty chambers before firing the
last of his ammunition. His sole bullet was carried by
the wind side and smashed into Tom's hip, sending him
sprawling back onto the ground.

Sherman felt something punch him in the chest. He
staggered forward a step or two, then found himself
unable to continue. His legs sagged beneath him, and
he dropped to his knees. The useless weight of the gun
dropped from his hand.

For a moment, all was quiet, save the roar of the
storm and the sounds of the frightened horses. Sherman breathed, but there was a strange sound coming
out of him. Sherman glanced down, saw the red
spreading across his chest and knew what that sound
meant.

"Uncle Sherman!" Annie cried.

Tom pushed himself up and attempted to take aim at Sherman, his hand wavering as he swayed in the wind.

With great effort, Sherman pressed the first two fingers of his left hand into his mouth and whistled loud and sharp. With that command, Titus lurched forward from Annie's side. He closed the distance in seconds, lunging at the bandit's throat. Tom screamed, trying to fight him off, but it was no use. Titus sank his teeth into the soft flesh of Tom's neck and refused to let go. Tom hit at the dog uselessly before his arm flopped back on the snow and he ceased to move at all.

"Titus, come back here," Sherman commanded. The dog returned and nosed at his face, whining. "I'm all right, boy. You done good."

Then he collapsed back against the snow, his energies spent. His blood seeped out into the snow upon which he lay, bright scarlet on the white prairie. The storm died down, and the sky overhead began to clear as the clouds passed, moving on.

Titus whimpered. Sherman reached up and patted Titus's neck consolingly.

Annie knelt by Sherman's side, her hand on his shoulder. "You saved me."

"I did," he said, and managed to smile.

Annie turned at the sound of a horse approaching from the way they'd come—it was the young man who'd been at her uncle's side earlier. He raced across the prairie, his ride spewing steam from its nostrils as he pushed the horse hard. He reached them in seconds, brought the horse to an abrupt stop and hurried down from the saddle.

Annie looked up at him. "He got hit."

Bobby looked first at Sherman, then at Tom Preston. Drawing his weapon, he stalked over to where

Tom lay. He'd been shot in the hip, and his neck had been torn open. He lay back on the snow, turning gray, his bulging eyes locked in an expression of terror.

"Good," Bobby said. He returned to Sherman and knelt in the snow next to Annie. "Is there something I can do, Sherman?"

Sherman smiled at him. "Look after my dog."

Titus lay with his front paws over his master's body, his head resting on Sherman's legs. Waiting for his master to get back up, quit playing lame.

"Consider it done," Bobby said, softly.

Sherman reached up for Bobby to take his hand. "Remember what I said, kid," he told him. "It was the truth."

The remnants of snow continued to fall around them. Sherman looked up and watched them drift to the ground.

His body became as ice. He felt Annie stroking his shoulder until he could no longer feel. He saw Bobby watching him die until he could no longer see. He heard Titus whine in sadness . . . until he could no longer hear. He breathed in, exhaled slowly, then breathed no more.

Everything melted away. Those around him. The world. All earthly senses, all time, the present moment and the past blending into one. From the stillness he rose into the dark sky, pushing up from the ground, the veil of gray clouds parting to reveal the grandeur of what lay beyond—endless stars floating in an ocean of moonlight. It filled him up, every part of him, and then it was his turn to be the white bird flying through the darkness, the stars bearing him home.

B OBBY AND ANNIE emerged from the mouth of the slot canyon. Neither of them had spoken a single word since watching Sherman pass on the snow, his enemy at rest not far from where he lay. As if it were meant to be.

Annie climbed down from behind Bobby, and mother and daughter ran toward each other to embrace.

"Thank God!" Hattie said. "When Sherman didn't come straight back with you, I thought . . ."

Bobby felt something catch in his throat.

Hattie looked past Annie at the horse Bobby was leading behind his own.

"Ma . . . ," said Annie.

Hattie frowned. "Where's Sherman? Is he coming along?"

Bobby was unsure how to say it, how to break the news.

"Bobby, where is Sherman?"

"He fell," Bobby told her, trying his hardest to fight back what was rising within him, the loss and pain he was feeling, but it was impossible. His eyes filled with tears and he wiped at them to clear his vision. His chest heaved and it took him a moment to say anything further, so racked with grief was he that words momentarily failed him. "I'm going to take him back to Elam Hollow for a proper burial."

Hattie's gaze shifted once again to the horse behind Bobby, now seeing Sherman's body positioned across it, wrapped in a blanket. Out on the prairie Annie had called Titus to her side and made a fuss over the dog while Bobby prepared Sherman for the journey back. He had laid a blanket out on the snow, then rolled Sherman onto it. When he'd stowed Sherman's body on the back of his horse, he helped Annie climb up into the saddle behind him. She wrapped her arms around his waist as they trotted away. Titus was nosing at the reddened snow where Sherman had lain, so Annie called, "Come on, Titus!" and the dog had followed along.

Hattie's eyes filled with tears as it sank in that Sherman was gone. Bobby got down from his saddle and removed his hat, and Hattie enveloped him in her arms, squeezing him tight. No words were necessary in that moment, their mutual sense of loss a language in and of itself. Finally Hattie let go and stood for a moment with her hand against the blanket shrouding Sherman's body. She closed her eyes, and the silence of her grief was prayer enough for all.

CHAPTER TWENTY

T HERE WERE HORSES enough for all of them. Annie
watched Joan struggle at first to hook the toe of
her boot into the stirrup until Hattie helped her along.
She pulled herself up into the saddle, using the horn
for purchase. Then Joan swung up clumsily onto the
back of her own horse.

"You get the hang of it eventually," Annie said.

"I've rode before," Joan told her. "But it's been a
while."

"Okay," Annie said.

Joan sighed. "I'm sorry, you know, about the way I
treated you and everything."

"Don't mention it."

"I'm not like that normally."

Annie reached across their horses, offering her
hand. "Don't mention it, Joan. Agree to leave all that
here?"

"Sure," Joan said, relieved.

They took the horses up the slope to the top side,

and Annie watched Bobby take the reins of Sherman's horse and lead it out through the trees. She didn't know his story, where he'd come from or how he knew Sherman, but he had fought as hard as her uncle to get her back. Although he didn't know her at all, he had put his life on the line to save her. She pushed ahead, past her mother and Joan, and fell in with him. "Hey."

"Hey."

"How are you?" Annie asked.

Bobby looked broken. "Probably 'bout the same as you, I'd imagine."

"Yeah," Annie said, looking ahead. "First time I ever met Uncle Sherman, I was little. Maybe six or seven. Something like that. Anyway, he turned up with this puppy in his arm. He didn't even have a name for it yet, but he ended up calling it Titus. The whole time he was visiting, he gave Titus to me to look after. When he saw how attached I got, he went into town to buy me my own puppy. I had that dog until two years ago. I called him Cob."

Bobby cocked an eyebrow. "Cob?"

"Because I liked corn."

Bobby laughed, despite himself. "That might be the sweetest thing I ever heard."

"Isn't it?" Annie said, laughing, too.

"I'm assumin' you still do?"

"Like corn? Sure, it's my favorite thing in the world."

Bobby led them out of the trees and out onto the prairie. Titus trotted alongside, mouth still stained with drying blood. "You said you had Cob until two years ago. What happened to him?"

"Ran into the road, got hit by a coach full of people."

"I'm sorry," Bobby said.

Annie looked ahead, her gaze not on where they were going, but on what had been, on what she had felt back then, lifting her dog from the road and carrying him home in her arms. "In a way, it prepared me for my father's passing. And now for Uncle Sherman's passing. Loss is one of those things you can't comprehend until it happens to you."

"He told me he was a selfish man once," Bobby said. "That he did bad things. Sure sounded like he had a helluva wild life. But the man I knew, he was good. He was completely selfless. The whole time we were chasin' after you to get you back, he never once thought about his own safety. About what might happen to him. He only cared about saving you."

"How did you come to be workin' together?" Annie asked.

Bobby looked at her. "He saved me," he said, and swallowed. "Just like you."

B OBBY HAD DONE his level best to orient them back toward Elam Hollow.

At nightfall, they made camp and Hattie prepared a meal that Bobby had no appetite for. He wasn't sick. He felt nothing, just the ache of emptiness inside, which could not be satiated by food.

He gave Hattie Sherman's pistol. "I think you should have it. They make a nice pair when they're worn together."

"He meant a lot to you, didn't he?"

"He did" was all Bobby said in reply.

Hattie looked away, toward Annie and Joan, and wiped at an errant tear spilling from her eye. "Are we to head back to town?"

"If I can remember the way."

"Well, I suppose we find out for sure now if Sherman really taught you everything he knew."

In the dark Bobby lay by the fire while the others

slept, but rest did not find him. He kept watching the dark for sign of anyone, or anything, that meant them harm. But nothing stirred. No one came by their camp or imposed on them in any way. No predators of the night attempted to steal away with their gear, their food. The world seemed to be content to leave them alone for now, and Bobby was thankful for that small grace.

In the morning they passed the place where they'd had the shootout with the roaming bandits, and while neither Bobby nor Hattie was eager to relive that night, it did serve as a signpost. Bobby knew they were headed in the right direction.

By that evening he was famished, and he ate what Hattie cooked for him. Titus came and lay next to him, and while Bobby didn't intend to let his guard down and sleep, the lure of a good night's rest was hard to resist with Titus's warmth next to him. In the early hours, he stirred to find the dog gone. He sat on his elbow, and by the dying firelight, he could just make out Titus stretched out beside Sherman's body, sound asleep.

In the morning he woke to hot coffee and grits. As he drank, Bobby looked over at Sherman's body where they'd laid him for the night. Away from the camp, but visible at all times. This would be the last time they loaded him back onto his horse. The next time they lifted him down, they'd be back in Elam Hollow.

"How're you feeling?" Annie asked, plopping down next to him to eat her own bowl of grits.

"Better," Bobby said.

"You've hardly spoken," she said.

Bobby glanced at her. "I know."

"How old are you anyway?"

Bobby cocked an eyebrow at the question. "Twenty-four. Why? How old are you?"

"Eighteen."

"You don't *look* eighteen."

Annie laughed. "Well, to be frank, you don't look *your* age, either."

"Fair enough," Bobby said, smiling.

"There it is. Knew I could get you to smile eventually," Annie said.

Bobby nodded in the direction of Joan, who was helping Hattie pack up the camp. "She seems happier."

"She's all right. She was just angry because she didn't know what to do."

"Did you?"

Annie sighed. "Not really. We tried to run, but they got us back."

"How far did you get?"

"Pretty far."

Bobby nodded along. "Impressive."

"I had no plan beyond that, though. Thinking about it, we both probably would've frozen to death. You don't really weigh these things up properly at the time. Just after."

"It's easy to think about it later on and tell yourself you could have done this or you could have done that."

"True."

"I know you both did the best you could."

"Thank you for saying that," Annie said, and they sat studying each other for a moment, eyes locked, a connection being made. Until Titus came lolloping over and stuck his snout in her grits. "Hey! Get out of it!"

Bobby stood and gave Annie his hand to help her up. "We'd better get going. We've got miles yet before we hit town."

"Sure," Annie said.

Hattie, who'd been standing to the side pretending to fold a blanket, watched the whole thing.

* * *

S HERIFF FREEHAN REMOVED his hat as they pulled up
outside his office. He'd been looking for Sherman,
and when he saw the limp shape on the back of Sherman's horse, he knew what had happened.

"Sheriff," Bobby said.

"Kid," Freehan replied as respectfully as he could
muster. He walked down the line until he stood before
Sherman and rested his hand on the blanket. "Damn
shame . . ."

"He died a hero," Hattie told him.

"Didn't expect nothin' less," Freehan said. He looked
at the two girls. "One of you must be Annie, am I
right?"

Annie offered her hand. "That'll be me."

"Nice to be able to put a name to the face."

"Pleasure to meet you, Sheriff. This is Joan," she
said. "My friend."

Joan smiled.

The sheriff tipped his head. "Nice to meet you, too."

Bobby said, "Excuse us, Sheriff, but we gotta get
Sherman to the undertaker. Is he around?"

"Saw him just this morning sanding down a set of
chairs out front. Just give him a knock. He'll know
what to do. Sherman won't want for a finer casket, rest
assured," Freehan said. His hands caressed the brim of
his hat. "I really was lookin' forward to seeing him
again, I must say."

"I know," Hattie said.

Freehan perked up a bit as he remembered the bandits. "What about Tom Preston and Leroy Jenkins?
You get 'em?"

"Dead," Bobby said flatly. "At great cost."

The sheriff cast his eyes away, unable to hold Bobby's gaze.

"Hattie, how's about you and Annie help Joan give all her details to the sheriff? We can help her get home," Bobby said.

"We should all go—"

"I'd like to do this," Bobby said.

Hattie nodded, understanding his intent. "Okay."

As Bobby led Sherman up the street to the undertaker, the sheriff said, "Let's get you inside, miss, and write down your particulars. We'll have you back with your folks in no time. . . ."

W ITH SHERMAN'S BODY left in the capable hands of the town's carpenter and undertaker, Hattie suggested taking him by wagon to Broken Bow and burying him beside his brother, Jed.

At first, Bobby felt that he should object. Sherman had made his home right here in Elam Hollow. Shouldn't that be where he was laid to rest? But then it dawned on him that nowhere in particular had ever been Sherman's *real* home. Perhaps the closest he had to a home was the love he had felt for his brother.

Bobby said, "I think that'd work out just right. I'll travel back with you if you'd like."

"I'd like that very much," Hattie said.

"Me, too," echoed Annie.

They told Sheriff Freehan of their plans, and he assured them he could arrange to lease Mac's wagon from him. "The same one we used to haul your drunken behind to Sherman's cabin that day," he said.

"I remember it well, thanks," Bobby said sarcastically.

"We'd be most appreciative, Sheriff," Hattie put in.

The next day Sherman's casket was done, and they loaded him into the back of the wagon and set off for Broken Bow. Hattie and Annie waved goodbye to the sheriff, and he stood in the street watching them until they navigated a bend in the road and disappeared out of sight.

Titus rode in the back with his master from the moment they left Elam Hollow right up until they arrived safely in Broken Bow days later.

T HEY HELD A quiet service for the Houndsman, just the way he'd have liked it. When the preacher finished his oratory, Annie asked Bobby to say a few words.

"Sherman told me he used to be a badman. A gun for hire. He said he'd done plenty of things in his life he wasn't proud of. I never saw that side of him. The Sherman I knew took me off the street when I was at my lowest and saved my life. The Sherman I knew gave his life to save his niece, who he cherished dearly. I am proud to have known him. He was a friend and a father to me. I will never forget that he said I made him proud. And I will live my life continuing to make him proud. I owe him everything. We all do."

The preacher took over, blessing Sherman into heaven, then gave the nod to the diggers to begin shoveling the dirt over his coffin. They stood a moment watching the men work, listening to the drum of the dry dirt hitting the coffin lid, then headed back to the house, Titus at their side.

B OBBY WAS PREPARING the wagon to travel back. It seemed odd not to see the casket in there anymore. As if he were returning to Elam Hollow but leaving something behind, which he supposed he was. In a way, he thought that he'd always feel as though a big part of him had been left in Broken Bow.

"What was the name of the lawyer you were heading to Elam Hollow to work for?" he asked Annie, trying to sound casual.

"Clarence Bergamot," she said.

"You reckon that job's still going?"

Annie looked at her mother, then back to Bobby. "More than likely. Can't see why not."

"You thinkin' of letting it go, then?"

"Well, no, I . . . uh . . . hadn't really thought about any of it."

"Because I don't think you should."

Annie frowned at him.

Her mother stepped forward. "What're you working your way around to say, Bobby?"

"I was gonna ask if you wanted to come with," he said awkwardly. He cleared his throat, which had suddenly run dry. "You know, with *me*. Back to Elam Hollow. Take that job. See how you get on."

"And live where?"

Bobby rubbed the back of his neck. He was no good at any of this. "Well . . . you were gonna stay at the cabin till you got settled in town, right?"

"Are you suggesting I live with you at the cabin?"

Bobby shrugged. "Well . . . yeah. I mean, Titus will be there, too."

Annie looked at Hattie. "Mom, what do you think?"

"I think, if Uncle Sherman thought Bobby a good man, then so do I. I've seen his character for myself, Annie. I trust him. No question about it."

Annie beamed with delight. "I guess I'm coming with you, then," she told Bobby, and ran inside to gather her things.

Hattie stepped up to the wagon and laid her hand on Bobby's arm. "You *will* look after her, won't you?"

"Of course. You have my word."

"You don't feel the need to . . . you know, drink . . . ?"

"No," Bobby said. "I don't."

Hattie smiled. "I thought it was really nice, what you said at his service."

"It was the truth," Bobby said simply.

Hattie patted his arm. "Yes, I think it was."

THEY LEFT BROKEN Bow at sunset and headed past the Mountain Fork River, where Sherman had often fished with his brother, Jed—where the passage of time was writ in the smooth stones beneath its surface and in the layers of silt and sediment along its shores.

Men and women had come and gone and would continue to as the years, decades and centuries passed. Men like Sherman and Bobby. Women like Hattie and Annie and Joan. All leaving the mark of their existence in those they cared about and left in their wake. Their passing like the waters of the Mountain Fork, carving their influence into what had been, with love and with truth. Bobby offered Annie his open palm as they rode. Annie did not hesitate in resting her hand in his, and for the first time, Bobby Woodward could say that he felt truly complete.

EPILOGUE

Ten Years Later

ELAM HOLLOW NEVER changed, just the people who
lived there. Mac grew old but was unchanged.
Sheriff Freehan passed away following a bad bout of
pneumonia, and his funeral service was attended by
almost the entire town. Annie went to work for Clarence Bergamot and he never took on another secre-
tary, because she proved so capable and competent.

Bobby was known to all as Sherman's heir when it
came to trapping and hunting and keeping predators
away from the farms. So when they considered who
would make a fine sheriff for their quiet town, there
was only one candidate.

At first Bobby turned them down immediately. But
the townsfolk were insistent; they wanted someone
with grit and honesty to uphold the law, so they continued to press Bobby until he relented.

No one spoke of the time he'd been the town drunk.

In truth, that history had almost been forgotten. But they did talk of Sherman and how he'd handled those three men who attacked Bobby. The story often ended in laughter when they described Sherman stabbing the man in his big belly with his hook. And on occasion, Bobby found himself laughing along with them.

He never took another drink. Not once—even though the thirst did come to him from time to time. Bobby knew that would never change. He'd always want a drink. The trick was not to have one. The closest he'd ever come to drinking again was when he'd taken that hip flask from one of the bandits out on the prairie with the intention of drinking it in secret. He still felt ashamed whenever he remembered it—even if it had saved his life.

He and Annie married and had two children—a boy and a girl. Gertrude Hattie Woodward looked just like her grandmother and seemed to have inherited her fiery spirit as well. David Jedediah Woodward, on the other hand, was the spitting image of Bobby.

When he thought about Sherman, as he often did, Bobby reflected on his own father. Before taking on the name Jack Denton, Bertrand Woodward had been cruel and evil. When he'd adopted a new identity, he had not changed. He'd continued to be just as cruel and malicious. But not so with Sherman. Whatever sins he had committed in his gunslinging days were long behind him by the time he settled down in Elam Hollow. He did not bring the shadows of his past with him and find comfort in them. He lit every corner and kept the shadows at bay. There had been a time Bobby had thought he might follow in his father's footsteps. As if it were inevitable that the sins of the father be bequeathed to the son, an unruly inheritance. But he had run from that fate, and that flight had eventually led him to Elam Hollow.

In Sherman he had found the father he had always sought, and it made him a better person. Now he was sheriff, filling Freehan's shoes as best he could. Sherman had come to town to escape the past, and in many ways, so had Bobby. Now he was respectable. He didn't have much, but he had a wife who loved him, and two children he would lay down his life for without a moment's hesitation.

He was a good man. Somehow, from the chaos of life, he'd reached the shore on the other side. Bobby knew he would have drowned if it hadn't been for Sherman.

T HEY ARRIVED IN Broken Bow in the winter, and Bobby drew the wagon up alongside the old farmhouse, pulling on the reins to bring the ponies to a stop. "Whoa, whoa. That's it," he said, reassuring the beasts. "Good girls."

They'd been back to Annie's childhood home a dozen times since marrying, and Hattie had also traveled out to stay with them on occasion. It was important to Annie to stay close with her mother—it was important to Bobby, too.

Some years before, Hattie had arrived with something for Bobby. He accepted the wooden box from her, curious what might be inside.

"Something I think you should have. I've thought on it, and I think it's only right."

"What is it?"

"How's about you open the box and see?" Hattie told him.

Bobby lifted the lid of the box to find Sherman's twin pistols inside. "These are his . . ."

"Yes," she said. "Now they're yours."

"You don't know what this means to me," Bobby had said, closing the box.

Hattie had just smiled at him. "That's where you're wrong."

Now he opened the back of the wagon and helped David and Gertrude down. Before their feet had hit the frosted ground, Hattie flung the door open in delight. The children ran to her and wrapped their arms around her waist. "Grandma!"

Hattie beamed down at them. She looked much as she always had, but where before her hair had been dark it was now streaked with veins of silver. "Oh, I've missed you."

Annie got down from the wagon. "Mom, you speak as if it's been an age. It's only been three months."

"Three months *too long*. Come here, let me look at you," she said, studying her daughter's face. "Not a line or a wrinkle."

"I should hope so. I'm not yet thirty!"

Hattie laughed. "That's when it all starts going downhill. Ask Bobby there."

"Speak for yourself," he said.

He ushered Lucius from the back of the wagon, where he'd been lying at the children's feet. The dog hopped down and ran to the porch, light gray tail swishing from side to side with happiness.

Hattie saw the children and Lucius into the house, where she continued to make a fuss over them all.

Bobby lifted the back flap of the wagon and bolted it into place.

"Head on in. I'll get the ponies set in the barn. They deserve the rest," he told Annie.

"Sure?"

Bobby kissed her. "Of course."

When the ponies were safely inside the barn, free of their tack and fed and watered, Bobby stood at the threshold of the old house and looked in. Hattie and

Annie sat on the floor before the fireplace, playing with the children.

Annie looked over. "Aren't you coming in?"

"You don't need an invitation, Sheriff," Hattie said with a smirk.

Bobby smiled back. "I know. I was just watching. Thought I might go for a stroll. Pay the old man a visit."

"Give us a moment and we'll come along, too," Annie said, about to get up.

"No, no, it's cold. It's been a long journey. Besides, I think I'd like to go by myself this time," Bobby told her. "Stay here in the warm."

Annie understood. "Okay. Don't be too long, though."

"I won't," he said, patting his thigh to get Lucius's attention. "Come, boy. Let's take a walk."

THE SKY WAS crisp and bright over Broken Bow Cemetery, not a cloud in sight. It had not yet snowed, but there was significant frost covering the ground, so much so that Bobby's footsteps crunched as he made his way among the graves. Lucius ran ahead of him, nose down, picking up whatever had come through recently—foxes and rabbits, most likely. The dog knew the way to the graves, too. He'd been there enough times. Bobby never came to Hattie's without visiting. It was the least he could do.

There was Jedediah's grave. Next to it, Sherman's. And next to Sherman's, unmarked but for a small wooden cross in the ground, was Titus's grave. When the old dog had finally passed, it had seemed only right to make the journey to Broken Bow to finally reunite him with his master. Without him, they never would have tracked across miles and miles of frozen prairie the bandits who'd kidnapped Annie. They'd never have gotten her back.

Bobby got down on one knee. There was no one around, so he spoke freely, as he sometimes did. He talked of Elam Hollow and several minor incidents he'd had to deal with as sheriff. He talked of the hunting he still liked to do and how good Lucius had proven as a hound.

"After all, he has Titus's blood. Anyway, I'm no houndsman. Not by a mile. But I keep it going in my way. Not like there's a whole lot to do as sheriff. I guess when David and Gertrude are of age, I'll teach them how to track and hunt, too. They're both bright as buttons. I'm fairly sure they don't get it from me. . . ." He looked for Lucius, saw him sniffing at something at the bottom edge of the fence and called the dog to his side. He patted the animal, then scratched him under the chin the way the dog liked. "Until next time, then," he said, smiling to himself.

Bobby stood, brushed off his knees and headed out of the cemetery, back the way he'd come. "Come now, Lucius. Come on, boy. Let's go home," he said, and walked down the hill with his hound by his side.

ACKNOWLEDGMENTS

Thanks to my fantastic agent, Sharon Pelletier of Dystel, Goderich & Bourret, for being the best there is. No one fights for their authors harder than Sharon, and you'd better believe she's as tough as they come.

A big thank-you to the lovely Tracy Bernstein, and the rest of the team at Berkley, for letting me sow further discord and chaos through the Wild West.

This novel is dedicated to my nephew, Charlie—I hope that he will read it when he is old enough and find it worthy.

Of inspiration to me in the writing of this novel was "A Cowboy's Prayer" by Badger Clark. In November 2018, I was at my friend Brian's side as he passed away following a long battle with mesothelioma. A few weeks before he died, I introduced him to "A Cowboy's Prayer" and I think he found great solace in its solemn words. The poem certainly holds great meaning to me because of that connection, and I know it always will.

Seeing as this novel is about mentorship, brotherhood, duty and death, I could think of no better metaphor for Sherman's passing than giving him the same freedom Badger Clark describes in his poem: *it was his turn to be the white bird flying through the darkness, the stars bearing him home*.

Until next time, dear readers—happy trails.

Ready to find
your next great read?

Let us help.

Visit prh.com/nextread

Penguin
Random
House